A Town Called Forget

C.P. Hoff

Alice,
Hope you like
my strange little
Book
CP Hoff

FIVE RIVERS PUBLISHING

WWW.FIVERIVERSPUBLISHING.COM

Published by Five Rivers Publishing, 704 Queen Street, P.O. Box 293, Neustadt, ON N0G 2M0, Canada.

www.fiveriverspublishing.com

A Town Called Forget, Copyright © 2016 by C.P. Hoff.

Edited by Lorina Stephens.

Cover Copyright © 2016 by Jeff Minkevics.

Interior design and layout by Éric Desmarais.

Titles set in Segoe Script designed by Carl Crossgrove based on the handwriting of co-designer Brian Allen in 2006 for Microsoft.

Text set in Joanna MT Std designed by by Eric Gill in 1930, based on type originally cut by Granjon. The designer described it as, "a book face free from all fancy business."

Published in Canada

Library and Archives Canada Cataloguing in Publication

Hoff, C. P., author

A town called Forget / C.P. Hoff.

Issued in print and electronic formats.

ISBN 978-1-988274-03-4 (paperback).—ISBN 978-1-988274-04-1 (epub)

I. Title.

PS8615.O358T69 2016   C813'.6   C2016-901088-0

C2016-901089-9

To Alicia whose laughter filled these pages.

Contents

Chapter One

"It's NOT often I meet a young girl travelling alone," the older woman said as she stared hard at the girl sitting across from her. "There must be a good reason."

The girl said nothing. Instead, she frowned, looked past the stranger and tried to catch the conductor's attention. At first she thought a little wave of her hand would do; she had seen her father attract attention that way quite successfully. It didn't work; the girl cleared her throat and raised her arm a little higher. The conductor looked confused and checked his pocket watch. The older woman nattered on and flapped her arms about as she talked about God-knew-what. The girl felt like wadding up her ticket and beaning the conductor in the head; her mother had paid him a generous tip to keep her isolated.

"My daughter is in no mood for polite company or idle chit-chat," her mother had said, a sentiment the girl agreed with whole-heartedly. But the elderly woman with the round build, and hair the girl was sure a pixie had wrapped in frayed gauze and scattered with dandelion fuzz, seemed oblivious to her mood.

"You'll not get his attention that way," the older woman said, tapping the girl on her knee. "Lord knows I've tried.

Ever since I walloped him on the backside, he gives me a wide berth." She furrowed her brow. "Perhaps he'd preferred more of a squeeze. I'll corner him in the dining car later and ask. He won't know what hit him."

The girl sighed and let her ticket drop to the floor.

"Where was I?" asked the older woman. "Oh, yes, I was appraising my overall impression of you. As I was saying, you are rather well-dressed: some might even say handsome, with your dark hair and high cheekbones. These things seem to be in fashion; even your willowy frame might draw attention. I would never say you were handsome though; it can make one vain. A vain young woman is of little use to anyone." She leaned closer. "You're not vain, are you?"

With a deep breath, the girl tried again to get the conductor's attention, but to no avail. He seemed to deliberately turn his back to her. Her only other option, as every seat in the car was taken, was to pretend to be asleep. Unclenching her fists, she closed her eyes, and let her head bob slightly with the sway of the train.

"I'm Harriet Simpson. You may call me Mrs. Simpson if you like. Although, I've never married. I've imagined what it might be like though." Harriet's voice cracked. "He was a real brute, and I was glad to be done with him."

The girl opened her eyes.

"Ah, you can hear. I thought perhaps you were deaf, and that's why you didn't respond, but now I see it's just because you're a mute. How terribly exciting! I've never met a mute before. What's it like?"

The girl's jaw dropped.

"Forgive me, dear, I forgot; mutes don't speak." She paused for a moment and pursed her lips in a most unattractive way. "I bet I can guess what it's like though; I'm awfully good at guessing. Let me see, let me see. You were born under a full moon, and the first thing you saw was a black cat. Am I right so far? Just nod if I am."

"No, you're not right."

"Oh." Harriet seemed more disappointed with her

7

inaccurate guess than amazed at the girl's ability to speak. "If you were born under a full moon and saw a black cat, you would surely have been a mute. I can almost guarantee it."

The train lurched, causing both Harriet and the girl to shift in their seats. They watched each other for a moment before Harriet resumed the conversation. "Travelling by rail is only slightly better than by motorcar. Although I've never travelled by motorcar, but I'm sure of it. Motorcars are quite unpredictable: a little bit of bad weather and you're stranded. Can you imagine! Me and that brute of a husband standing by the side of the road in the pouring rain; what a sight that would be." Harriet dabbed her forehead with a gloved hand. "It would be my undoing." Mrs. Simpson looked out the window and sighed.

The girl thought Mrs. Simpson must be envisioning a marooned motorcar and a furious husband in his duster and goggles. Harriet in a wide brimmed hat and ripped veil. It was the only way the girl could picture Harriet Simpson: thinking herself de rigueur, but in reality being quite passé.

"It's much different on these black devils with their coal fires burning." Harriet grabbed the arm rest and yanked on it as if she were trying to rip it from its foundation. "Dependable as the day is long. From a seat, much like this one, I've spied the wonders of Saskatchewan. From the vast openness of the south, to the mid- and northerly parts where I've watched quivering aspen, birch and poplar transform into spruce and pine." Her fingers spread wide as she moved her hands like the fans of a Japanese geisha. "The soil is so full of life. I've seen places where the dirt is so dark you'd swear it's wet."

The girl wasn't sure how to respond. She too had seen changes. From the bustle of Toronto streets and Union Station to the ever-changing landscape of hills and trees dotted with farms and intermittent pockets of civilization, to the flat barren southern prairies. A place so open there was a naked vulnerability to it. It made her uncomfortable.

She was sure no one could keep a secret in such a place, as there was nowhere to hide.

Mrs. Simpson hadn't been privy to all the girl's impressions, as she was only a recent travelling companion, boarding this train as she had in Saskatoon. The place where the girl and her parents had parted company.

"It doesn't feel like a grand adventure anymore, not since that so-called Great War....." Harriet paused and looked past the girl as if unable to finish her thought. The girl followed the older woman's gaze to a young man sitting two rows down and across the aisle, an empty shirt sleeve pinned to his shoulder.

Nodding, the girl rubbed her arms. There was nothing grand about her adventure either.

"You haven't told me, dear," Harriet reached out and touched the girl's arm, "why are you travelling alone?"

The kind touch brought the girl to tears. Harriet pulled a hanky from her sleeve and slipped it into the girl's hand. "There, there now, it couldn't be that bad."

"Oh, yes it is. My parents abandoned me in Saskatoon."

"They must have had their reasons. No one abandons a perfectly good daughter for no reason. You must have done something."

The girl shook her head.

"How old are you, child?"

"Sixteen."

"And you can't think of anything you've done wrong?"

"No, I've done nothing wrong. My parents and I were taking a trip across the prairies and when we arrived in Saskatoon my luggage and I were transferred to another train and they went on without me."

"Without a word of explanation?"

"They said I'm to stay with my eccentric aunt. We're to get acquainted."

"Eccentric?" Harriet dismissed the comment with the wave of her hand.

"And they gave me a bundle of letters."

"What did the letters say?"

"I'm not supposed to read them yet."

"That doesn't make any sense. Start from the beginning, dear, and let's figure things out." Harriet leaned back in her seat. She looked particularly pleased with herself. "You're in good hands, dear: I'm a splendid listener you know. I nod at the most appropriate time and click my tongue in support. There has been many a weary soul that has commented on my ability. I call it my magnum opus."

Every word Harriet Simpson spoke made the girl wish she were a deaf mute. And although she had her misgivings, she ignored them; she needed to talk to someone.

"My mother has always fussed over me," she found herself saying. "She's never abrasive or demanding. All my friends envy me; they think I'm indulged. With my parents, I've been almost everywhere in Toronto that's considered fashionable. Before the war, we were supposed to go on a European tour. Have you ever been to Europe?"

"No. Saskatchewan trains don't travel that far." There was a hint of bitterness in her voice.

"When my mother packed our things she said we were going to catch a train in an hour. I was excited, but my parents weren't. They boarded the train as if it were a great misfortune. Mother feigned a headache for most of the trip, excusing herself to go lay down in the sleeping car whenever I pressed her. Father hardly looked up from the newspaper he had brought with him. He must have read it at least a half dozen times."

Harriet clicked her tongue and winked at the girl.

The girl ignored her and continued. "When I asked them where we were going, they said to Forget. 'To forget what?' I asked. My father told me that Forget was a place, and that was where I was going, not them."

Harriet sat up straight in her seat. "You are a lucky girl. I'm from Forget and it's far better than Europe. I've never been to Europe, but I'm sure it's just dreadful and expensive. It sounds expensive."

The girl shrugged and blew her nose.

"You'll love Forget; everyone does. Our slogan is, *Forget is a place you won't forget*. Very ingenious, don't you think?" Harriet didn't pause long enough for the girl to answer. "Forget is full of picaresque souls. I read that word in a book once. Didn't know what it meant until I looked it up in a dictionary. It describes our town so precisely, beguiling rogues to the core. Picaresque." Harriet's voice lowered and became almost grave. "Remember what I am telling you dear, and don't believe a word of what some townsfolk might say. We are not all related." And as if to prove the point she added, "We have a class three railway station."

The train slowed, and the girl looked out the window.

"That's our sign." Harriet pointed to a signpost flanked with pussy willows at the edge of the tracks.

"That's not how you spell *Forget*."

"Yes it is. It's the French spelling. Forgetta. Makes us sound a bit more exotic."

"That's not how the French spell *forget*."

"Oh, it is now. The town had a vote. Keep it under your hat. We haven't told the French yet. They are so persnickety." Harriet smiled, and her eyes almost pinched together. "*Persnickety.* I read that word in a book as well."

Although she tried not to, the girl furrowed her brow in frustration. "But what about your slogan, *Forget is a place you won't forget?*"

"Silly girl. Our slogan isn't French."

Chapter Two

AS THE train approached Forget, Harriet pinched her cheeks, straightened her hat and reinserted her hatpin. "Where will you be staying, my dear?"

"At my aunt's. I only found out this morning. Until then, I didn't know I had an aunt."

"What's your aunt's name?"

"Lily, just like—"

"You must have misunderstood. There's only one Lily in town, and surely you wouldn't be staying with her."

The girl opened her pocketbook, pulled out a slip of paper and handed it to Harriet. The older woman examined it and bit her lip. "Your parents have made a mistake. Most certainly they have. No one would send a dog to such a horrid place."

"It's no mistake." The girl's hand trembled as Harriet returned the slip. "Besides the letters, it's the only information they gave me."

The girl watched Harriet Simpson as she pulled another hanky from her sleeve and twisted it around her fingers. Harriet blanched.

"Are you all right?"

"Don't fuss child, you'll need all your strength. You haven't met your Aunt Lily have you?"

The girl shook her head.

"Even though she claims she's sick, even dying, I doubt it's true. God doesn't want that woman. Death will be her only kindness."

"No one can be that dreadful."

"Yes they can."

"There must be something good about her."

Harriet paused, then: "She has chickens." She leaned over and patted the girl's hand. "Forget has its faults as most towns do. There's gossip, and of course, unspeakable rumours which are spoken of often. It's all quite lovely. But then there's your aunt; her name should be synonymous with Lucifer himself. Ask anyone in Forget, they'll say the same. She's a woman with no soul."

The girl began sobbing again. "I can't go to such a terrible place. What do I do?"

"Only one thing I can think of. It won't change things, but it will make us both feel a lot better."

"Really?"

"Really."

The older woman closed her eyes, and when she reopened them, they were crossed. Her nostrils flared, and her nimble fingers flitted through the air. Although the girl couldn't make out most of what she was saying, she did understand enough to get the gist of it. Harriet Simpson had placed a pox on her parents and their cats.

"My parents don't have cats."

"Don't worry, poxes are poxes. With or without cats, I'm sure your parents are thoroughly cursed." And as if to add a bit of cheer she said, "they'll probably be dead by Christmas."

Harriet's apocalyptic words whirled around in the girl's mind. Picking up speed they made her question everything she had thought was sound. Her parents not only abandoned her but were now cursed. Her aunt was some kind of devil. It was more than she could bear. She doubled over and wept as if her life were being torn from her. Harriet stroked her hair, "There there, dear," she said in an attempt to sooth through her own cries of anguish. "We all have to meet our end sooner or later."

Their wailing intertwined into one woeful chorus. The girl was sure the other passengers were staring—she could feel it—and not just at Harriet, they were staring at her as well. How could they not; she had become part of the spectacle known as Harriet Simpson. She knew her parents would disapprove. The girl tried to compose herself, but it was difficult the way Harriet Simpson was carrying on. The woman looked like she was in her death throes. And just to horrify the girl a little more, Harriet tilted her head back and howled, "My magnum opus has forsaken me!"

When the train finally screeched and ground to a stop, the older woman, with hair of frayed gauze, was so overwrought she had to be carried off.

Chapter Three

THE GIRL stayed with Harriet until she recovered. "Thank you," said Harriet, placing her hand on the girl's cheek, sympathy brimming in her eyes. "It's as if many plagues have been placed on your slender young shoulders. Boils are probably festering under your skin as we speak."

"I don't think so."

Harriet pulled her hand away and wiped it on her skirt. "But you're not certain?"

The girl frowned and shook her head.

"The only kind thing I can do for you, besides putting you out of your misery, is to advise you to run away."

"I have no place to go."

"Go to the woods. You can eat insects and make shoes out of bark."

"I don't imagine I could do that." The girl dropped her gaze and picked at the hem on her sleeve. "Why don't I stay with you?"

Harriet gasped and brought her hand to her throat. "And bring all your pestilence with you? How utterly thoughtless!"

The girl said nothing. She took a deep breath before she turned and trudged towards the third class railway station,

leaving Harriet behind. The two story wooden structure was
how she had imagined it, almost. Painted white with red
trim, it stood parallel to the tracks, with a wooden walkway
that ensured long-suffering passengers would not soil their
feet upon disembarking. There was nothing grand about it;
the station was almost a carbon copy of so many others.
The facades of the office, freight shed and waiting room
were indicated with a script like etchings that were nearly
impossible to read. The sign that hung from the awning
was no different. *Forgetta*. The girl made out the markings
after squinting her eyes. It was as if the town only wanted
clearly motivated passengers to step off the train.

Her only comfort was the smell of lilacs that hung in the
air. If she closed her eyes she could imagine she was at
home: their springtime freshness would waft through her
bedroom window. The scent was strongest where the bushes
hugged the edges of the station, leaving only enough space
for a dirt road to curve around the building's edge. The
trees that towered behind the lilacs were so dense they gave
no indication of what lay past them. Even when the girl was
still on the train, she saw nothing beyond their crowns. It
was as if she had been dumped into the wilderness.

All the girl could think of was to get away, but that was
impossible. She was penniless. Her father said it was better
for her to travel that way; she wouldn't be tempted to do
anything rash. She rubbed her head with the palm of her
hand. The day had been too much. When she had arrived
at Saskatoon that morning, she hadn't anticipated such
changes in her life. From somewhere deep inside she hoped
her parents would appear, smiling and telling her it had all
been a mistake; it was time to go home. But they didn't.
Now she needed to take care of herself, and for the moment
her options seemed limited to one.

"Excuse me," she said to an official-looking man with a
clipboard. "How can I arrange to have my bags delivered?"

The man looked down at her over his half-moon
spectacles. "You'd need to talk to Fred, Miss." He yelled over

his shoulder. "Fred, there's a young lady here, wants her bags delivered."

A young man in dusty overalls and rolled up shirt sleeves appeared in the doorway of the freight shed. "And where would that be?"

"To my aunt's." The girl took the slip from her pocketbook and handed it to the man with the clipboard.

"You might want to take Henry Henry with you," the man called to Fred as he read the slip. "Her aunt is Miss Lily."

Fred groaned and kissed the cross that hung around his neck. "I knew my day would come. I just didn't expect it so soon."

"None of us do, Fred, none of us do."

The girl watched in disbelief. "She can't be that bad."

"Believe what you will," the man said as he checked off the boxes being unloaded from the train, "but those of us who've spent time with her can think of no worse fate."

Almost drowning in panic, the girl took back the slip of paper. She looked at the words her mother had written. They gave no indication of anything wayward or wicked. The script was in the same easy flow she was used to. The people in this place must exaggerate, she thought. Surely her parents would never send her to an aunt so foul.

In no hurry to find out, the girl decided to take a look at the town instead. She wanted to ask the man with the clipboard if there was anywhere she should avoid, but she anticipated that his only response would be her aunt's house. Taking a deep breath, the girl steeled herself. If she were going to survive this adventure, she would actually have to participate in it. She rounded the corner of the station mumbling the thought as if it were a mantra.

Main Street was like no other she had seen. The fact that it ran directly behind the train station was the only thing that made it unremarkable. One side of the street was plain with one-story wooden buildings. The stores matched the patrons who mingled in front of them, appearing practical and hard working. Dray horses and wagons were tied to hitching posts that lined its walk. The other could be only described as ostentatious. Brick buildings two and three stories high towered over their poor wooden cousins huddled together across the way. The people there, in gleaming white gloves and fashionable clothes, looked as if they had been transplanted from the streets of Paris. There were no dray horses or wagons lining its walkways. It was reserved for buggies and shiny new automobiles.

The street even had two names. The signpost on the wooden side read Main Street, but the one on the brick, read Grand Avenue. Avenue and street not just running parallel but facing off as if there were some type of unspoken challenge. The bank, post office, and any building looking somewhat official cozied up to Grand Avenue like kittens in the cold. A haberdashery, bakery, and somewhat ritzy looking cafés filled in the spots that were left. The only steeples the girl could see rose from the lazy slope that climbed behind Grand Avenue, as if God too had taken sides.

This was all juxtaposed to Main Street. A livery stable, Chinese laundry, grocer, and any other establishment that hired help or those with little disposable income would patronize. The train station seemed to take a neutral position at the head of the street, no closer to Grand Avenue than it was to Main Street.

In all her travels the girl had never seen such a thing. How was she supposed to find anything if streets and avenues didn't intersect? Directions would be impossible to follow. The first lane that trailed off of Main Street and Grand Avenue didn't dispel the girl's misgivings. The sign that lead away from the brick read, It Was the Best of Times, its corresponding counterpart, leading away from the wooden read, It Was the Worst of Times. At the next intersection the street signs sniped To Be and Or Not to Be. The print was large enough to be seen from where she stood. What were her parents thinking sending her to such a place? It was unlike any other town she had been to or even read about.

The girl tightened her grip on her pocketbook. She

wondered to what side her aunt belonged. Her mother was most certainly a brick; she couldn't imagine her any other way. As for herself, the girl knew she wasn't dressed for the ostentatious side. Her travelling frock was rather plain and somewhat rumpled from her journey. She couldn't understand why her mother had insisted on it, but she had been too numb to argue. The dress was far more suitable for the help. That in mind, the girl knew that the wooden side would have to do.

She hadn't walked far down Main Street when she realized she had a follower, Harriet Simpson. The older woman trailed her at a safe distance, seemingly cautious not to get close enough to let their shadows touch. At first, the girl found it comforting, as if her new acquaintance were watching over her. Then Harriet spoke. She had paused in front of a man lighting a pipe. "You see that girl?" Her words were loud enough for all to hear.

The man bit hard on the stem and squinted. "The one that has a bemused look about her?"

"That very one. I call her the *poor puffy-eyed girl*. I don't know her name, but now it seems of little importance. She'll be dead soon. I'm sure of it."

"How can you say such a thing?"

"She's Miss Lily's niece. Going to live with her."

"Little spit of a thing," The man looked at the girl more intently. "Won't need much of a coffin will she?"

"No, she won't."

The man cursed, and Harriet placed another pox on the girl's parents. "Never has a more grievous thing happened; so young, so innocent." Harriet's hands began to flap as the girl continued to walk and the distance between them lengthened. "I must be going. She's getting away on me and there are others I need to keep abreast of the situation."

Harriet and her remarks followed the girl as she made her way down the street. It was like having a town crier baring all. Even the echoing thud from the girl's footfalls on the wooden walkway didn't drown them out. For a moment, the girl considered going to the brick side, but the people there had already turned to stare. Harriet's voice carried like that of no other.

The girl couldn't take it any longer. Soon all of Forget would know of her ill-fated predicament. She had to find her aunt and face whatever the outcome. It couldn't be worse than this. It was then the girl saw a woman standing in front of the post office with her mail. She was dressed for the wood side but had planted herself in the middle of the walkway on the brick side. As she flipped through the envelopes in her hand, the bricks had to part around her like the Red Sea. Her mother would have called her an oblivious suffragette, not caring what her betters thought. The woman looked ancient — at least fifty. There was hardly a hint of colour left in her hair, and her sharp features and widow's hump made her look like a vulture. Had they been in closer proximity, the girl would have leaned over and pushed up the woman's spectacles perched precariously on the tip of her nose.

Despite Harriet Simpson's loud pronouncements of doom, the suffragette did not incline her ear. She picked her way across the street with a distracted or perhaps just disinterested air. The girl was relieved to see someone sane and approached her elder with some urgency. "Can you help me?" she asked. "I'm looking for my aunt."

"I'm not a mind reader," the woman said, rather irritated. "Who's your aunt?"

"Lily."

"Any fool knows where she lives. If you'd come to visit occasionally, you would too. What kind of a niece are you?" The woman, sized the girl up, first with her right eye, then with her left. "Leaving that poor, sainted woman to suffer. Mm, mm, mm, you don't deserve her, but I'll take you there."

"You heard me say Lily didn't you?"

"I heard what you said. I may be old, but I'm not deaf." The old woman hooked her cane into the crook of her arm and scurried off down the street. It was all the girl could do to keep up. Harriet Simpson didn't even try. The suffragette never spoke, nor let up, and the girl spent much of her time trying to match her stride.

The girl tried to memorize the sign-posts as she passed but it seemed an impossible task. Her mind was too muddled. When the older woman led her past a meadow, which contained the bulk of the spring runoff, the girl gave up all together. Around the water's edges, interspersed between the willows and last summer's dried grasses, were children. Some barefoot and untucked, others looking as if they were off to meet the pope. Even though their attire was quite different, their focus was united. A raft, resembling an old barn door, bobbed at the water's edge next to some cattails. The old woman stopped and stood ramrod still as she saluted it; the children did likewise. It was like the contraption was part of the Royal Navy.

Three dishevelled boys stood on the raft. One tied a ragged shirt to its rickety mast while a primly dressed young woman bashed its side with a mason jar. "Today we christen thee the *Scourge of the Seven Sloughs*," she proclaimed. Her voice was calm in spite of the fact she was being dive bombed by a red-winged blackbird which must have had a nearby nest. The children cheered and banged pot lids together. The old woman wiped a tear from her eye. The girl stood dumbfounded.

"Much obliged, Miss Poppy," the tallest boy with re-patched pants said, doffing his cap and bowing slightly at the waist. "We have never received a better send off."

"Alexander," the boy next to him said as he jabbed him in the ribs with his elbow. "Let's toss her in."

Alexander eyed the young woman for a moment as if considering the suggestion, which gave Miss Poppy enough time to scramble safely ashore.

A little red-faced and out of breath Miss Poppy clapped her hands. "Class dismissed."

It took a minute for the girl to take in what had just

happened. Miss Poppy was a teacher, the children around the pond's edge her students, and she was christening a raft as if it were a class project. The whole situation seemed preposterous. Surly something like this would never happen in an Ontario school.

As the children began to disperse, Alexander called to them. "Come brave the waters, come smite a sea monster."

The old woman, who had been taking the girl to her aunt's, curled her back. "I'd not shrink from that challenge boys," she said. "Black Beard himself will get the cowardly soul who does."

The children stared with what the girl thought was longing. She was sure they wanted to be as free as the boys on the raft but there was something holding them back. The old woman that shouted Black Beard's curse didn't help matters. A well-dressed boy in short pants drew a cross in the dirt with a stick while he muttered, "Matthew, Mark, Luke and John, God bless the dirt that I stand on." Other children followed his lead. Soon the muttering turned to chanting, drowning out the blackbird's cries.

"That won't save you from the curse," the old woman warned as she rubbed out a cross with her cane. "One of you has to take the challenge. One of you has to board the raft. It's how it has always been done."

A small boy dressed in a crisp linen shirt, velveteen pants, knee socks and brown leather boots that buttoned on the side, stepped forward. He couldn't have been more than six or seven. Whether it was a voluntary step the girl couldn't tell. His hand shook a little. The boy was obviously from Grand Avenue, a brick.

Alexander clasped his hands together. "Come here, laddie," he said. "Today you become a man." With two fingers of mud Alexander painted the boy's face. The boy was knighted a pirate and everyone spat in the dirt.

The old woman swatted the girl on the behind. "Let's be off before some tattletale goes and fetches his ma. There's no need to be dragged into another scandal."

22

Blinking, the girl hesitated; her new companion was certainly not a suffragette. But in spite of this revelation the girl followed the old woman out of the clearing. She was led to a street named Roland le Peteur. The two-story wood framed houses were placed well back on lots, with ample room for a small number of livestock. There were stone walkways and picket fences. Neglected houses with peeling paint that appeared sleepy and quiet. On some porches, swings creaked in the wind. They had the sound of old bones and tired limbs.

Roland le Peteur had no significance to the girl. She had recognized all the other street names to either have a biblical or literary reference. But this street was just a name. "Who is Roland le Peteur?"

The old woman stopped mid-stride and turned to face the girl. "You don't know?"

"Why would I know?" The girl wanted to pull out someone's hair; whether it was her own or the old woman's, at this point it really didn't matter.

"Your education is clearly lacking. I guess I'm somewhat obligated to change that." Her lips tightened. "He entertained in the court of Henry II. Quite notable for preforming the *Unum saltum et siffletum et unum bumbulum* at Christmas."

"I have no idea what that is," the girl muttered as she looked down to dodge a spring puddle. When she looked up again the old woman was gone.

The girl wasn't sure what to do. In a strange town with even stranger people, her only thought was to lie down in the middle of the street and wait to be run over. But to her relief the old woman reappeared. "What are you waiting for? I'm not getting any younger!" she yelled, waving the girl into a flaky white house with a wide veranda.

As the girl approached, the old woman's head shook. "You're not what I expected. You look a lot like your father." The girl thought she looked nothing like her father but thanked her anyway. "Your room is at the top of the stairs."

The stranger continued examining her mail. "When you're settled I expect you to come down for tea."

"I have come to stay with my Aunt Lily. Not with you."

"I am your aunt, you ninny!" She poked the girl with her cane. "I can't believe you're so daft."

Chapter Four

FRED HAD already delivered the girl's bags, now in a heap on the back step. Hauling them upstairs and into her new room made the girl feel heavy inside. None of this had been her choice. She felt so helpless. Her parents had said she could contact them in a few weeks—eight to be exact. If things weren't going well, she could write their solicitor but they assured her it probably wouldn't be necessary.

"Whatever you do, don't make her cross," her mother had said that morning in the Saskatoon train station.

"That's right," said her father. He placed his arm across her shoulders and pulled her close. Crowds of people jostled around them. "That one can be cruel and unrelenting. Best stay on her good side."

"Harold, my sister is not cruel. She's eccentric."

The girl looked from her father to her mother. "Why am I going to stay with her?"

"I've already told you, darling," said her mother. "To get acquainted. As long as you do as she asks you'll fare well. But remember to do as she asks even if you think her logic is a bit muddled. It will keep her calm and make your stay bearable."

As her mother's words filled her mind, the girl's eyes welled with tears. Her aunt didn't look like someone she wanted to acquaint. The woman scurried around like a rabid rodent. As she had followed her home, the old woman had only used her cane once, and that was to splash some children standing too close to a puddle.

Despite her parents' advice, the girl was sure, in this place, giving her aunt a chance would take a relatively short amount of time. Mechanically, the girl started to unpack her things into a large highboy in the corner. When she tried the closet door, it was locked. No matter; her mother had packed practical clothes. It was depressing just to look at them. So what if they got wrinkled in a drawer? What had she done to deserve this? Turning, she faced the room. It was spacious enough. There was a white iron bed with a hand-stitched log cabin quilt folded at its foot. A braided rug and wallpaper in a pattern of interwoven pink roses coloured the room.

On the far wall, next to a dressing table, was a window seat, cushioned and inviting, waiting for someone to enjoy the view. She walked over to it and ran her hand along the window's wooden sill. The words I hate Lily had been carefully carved into its painted frame. This must have been my mother's room, she thought. She looked around and wondered what else her mother had left behind. So many things had been kept from her.

The girl took out the bundle of letters from her bag. There were eight in total, tied with a bright yellow ribbon, one for every week she was to stay. Perhaps they held the answer. She slipped out the first letter.

Open upon arrival, was written in bold print on the envelope. The girl turned it over in her hands. She wasn't sure if she wanted to open it. She wasn't sure if she was ready for any answers.

Ready or not, it would have to wait. The hard tip of what she assumed was her aunt's cane banged on the ceiling below. "Are you coming downstairs?" came her aunt's raspy voice. "Or shall I pour the tea out?"

"I'm coming." She would open the letter later. For now the answers to this remarkable but trying day could reside in the top drawer of the highboy. She left the room and closed the door tightly behind her.

She found her aunt in the sitting room, dusting out china teacups with an old feather duster. "Oh there you are" said Aunt Lily tipping over a teacup to allow a dead spider to fall out before setting it down before an over-stuffed chair; the one intended for the girl. "Come sit."

The girl's mouth tightened while Aunt Lily's face carried a look of relief, as if the creature dying in the company cup was a sign of loyalty. The girl took her seat under silent protest.

Aunt Lily smiled and poured the tea. "What's your name, dear?"

The girl looked up in surprise. "You don't know my name?"

"No, your mother and I haven't been on listening terms for years."

"Listening terms?"

Her aunt looked at her with a fair amount of disgust. "Oh God, where do I begin? If we aren't speaking, how can we be listening? It's fairly self-explanatory." She paused, fanned herself with the feather duster before again asking the girl her name.

"I was beginning to wonder if anyone cared," the girl said. "You don't know how worried I've been. This is such a strange place. It was only this morning that I heard of it. Before that, I thought my mother had been born overseas and lived there until she met my father."

Aunt Lily rolled her eyes as she added sugar to both cups of tea. "Oh, the way you blather on and on. No wonder your parents sent you away. I only asked you your name. I didn't ask for your life story."

"I'm not sure I want to tell you now."

"Oh, it doesn't matter. I'll never remember anyway.

Probably it's something quite dull and unimaginative; that would be just like my sister. Murgitroyd or Ichabod no doubt. I've always hated those names. Likely I'll hate yours just as much."

Aunt Lily dipped a biscuit into her cup and looked thoughtful. "It's hard enough naming new things. Things that haven't been worn by time. But to have to name something that is all ragged is something quite different; a very difficult task indeed. I didn't expect that, at my age, I'd be naming half-grown people. You can well imagine the kind of grief you are causing me. I might need the smelling salts."

"You don't even know what my name is. I'm sure you'll like it."

"It doesn't suit you." Aunt Lily dipped another biscuit before handing it to the girl. "I can tell just by looking. The name doesn't sit well on your skin, makes you all sallow and unattractive. I'll think of a new one."

"What if I don't want a new one?" The girl re-dipped the biscuit before handing it back. A few crumbs were left floating in her tea.

"I don't remember asking you if you did. Do you remember me asking if you did?"

"No."

"Then, apparently, I don't care." Aunt Lily reached out and touched the girl's arm. "But don't think that I don't care in an uncaring way. That would only make me heartless and uncharitable. There's nothing good to be said about people like that. No, that's not me at all. I don't care more in the way that I don't think it's really that important."

"What will you call me then?"

The old woman looked at her for a while. "Stand up and turn around."

A little hesitant, the girl stood and turned.

Aunt Lily groaned and banged her cane on the floor. The teacups rattled on the table. "What's wrong with you? Don't turn that way! No one can name a thing that turns counter-clockwise. It goes against the sun, and the sun used to be a god you know." She rubbed her palms on her forehead. "Here for ten minutes and already you're trying to upset the has-been gods."

The girl paused before turning in the opposite direction. She hoped this naming thing wouldn't take long. She was starting to feel nauseated.

Aunt Lily dropped her hands and squinted at her niece through her eyeglasses. "Girly. I will call you Girly."

"I don't like it."

Aunt Lily shrugged. "I don't care. Besides, would you rather I call you Murgitroyd?"

"No."

"Then Girly it is."

Chapter Five

SO GIRLY it was. She closed her bedroom door. If she had a key, she would have locked it. Instead, she braced it with a chair she borrowed from the hall. She was at a loss what else to do. After the naming, her aunt dismissed her and told her to get some sleep, that she'd be needing it. What did tomorrow hold in store? The thought frightened her; only God knew what the old woman was capable of. And according to Harriet Simpson, whatever that was, it wouldn't be good.

Her new name joined the other confusing and preposterous events of the day. Girly. What kind of name was that? It was more of a description. She said her new name over and over again. Girly. Girly. Maybe it was good to have a different name. A name that would divide her life into two separate realities, one that was envied and another that was inconceivable.

Girly's gaze fixed on the highboy. In the top drawer, the letters waited for her. She thought back to earlier that day, when her mother handed the packet to her. "Don't read them all at once," she'd warned. "It will be too much for you. Follow the instructions on the envelopes."

The bundle had seemed heavy in Girly's hand.

"Did you hear me?" Her mother raised an eyebrow. "You need to promise me."

Girly made the promise without really thinking about what she was saying. She was dazed and her tongue felt swollen. Now, she regretted her promise. How could a bundle of letters have made that much difference? Her life had changed so much, letters or no letters.

Retrieving the bundle, she flopped on the bed and untied the yellow ribbon that bound them together. The first envelope read *Open upon arrival*. The second read *Open me in seven days*. The third read *Open me in fourteen days*, and so on. A letter a week is what her mother intended and Girly, in spite of herself, felt obligated to comply.

Tearing open the first envelope, Girly unfolded a sheet of her mother's monogramed stationary, the stationary she had never been allowed to use.

> *My darling daughter,*
>
> *I can imagine how lost you must feel; your father and I feel the same. It was difficult sending you away. More difficult than you could possibly know, but I didn't have a choice. Your aunt needs you, and I felt I had to consider her after so many years of neglect.*
>
> *Believe me, she is not as odd as she seems. In time, I'm sure you will realize that and maybe even grow to care for her. I'd like that.*
>
> *Please think of us often and know there isn't a moment of the day we aren't thinking of you.*
>
> *With all my love,*
>
> Your Mother

Girly refolded the letter and put it back into its envelope. It was more of a note than a letter. Disappointment filled her. She wanted more, some kind of explanation. Anything that would stop the sinking feeling inside. She was so tempted to open the next in the stack but was afraid it would be as empty as this one. Besides, there were only eight. If she were to read them all at once there would be nothing left to sustain her, nothing for her to hope. Retying the bundle, she placed it back into the top drawer of the highboy. If she could, she would bury her face in her pillow and weep but she was too tired. As it was, she was sure she had enough sorrow in her to drown the world, and sleep seemed the only sane response to this insane day.

Chapter Six

IN THE morning Girly stayed in her room as long as she could. She sat on the window seat and scanned the neighbourhood that would be her home for the next eight weeks. It was at the edge of Forget. The back of her aunt's lot bordered a pasture. Poplar trees were losing their early spring green, deepening to full leaf and shade. Nests were either being built or occupied. Jenny wrens, barn swallows, and crows winged past her window. In amongst the hodgepodge of avifauna mating rituals, a gaggle of rubberneckers stood on the other side of Aunt Lily's picket fence pointing at Girly's window. She drew down the blind.

If there had been a chamber pot under the bed she would've taken up permanent residency in that room, avoided anyone who had anything to do with this place. As it was, she could only cross her legs for so long, and taking a deep breath she removed the chair from her door and stepped out into this unknown life. Aunt Lily was waiting at the bottom of the stairs. She tapped the tip of her cane on the banister as Girly descended. "You look like you're in pain; best head out back to the outhouse."

"Outhouse?"

"It's either that or the five-gallon pail in the cellar."

Girly felt somewhat indignant. All night she had held her water and now, when she could no longer hold it, she had to choose an outhouse or a spider infested pit. At home they had indoor plumbing; no one peed in a bucket.

Aunt Lily was in the sitting room peeking through her lace curtains when Girly emerged from the bowels of the house. "What the hell took you so long? You think I have nothing better to do with my time than to wait for you?"

"I didn't know you were waiting."

"Well, you're going to have to learn how to anticipate aren't you?" She turned back towards the window. "Curious bunch of beggars aren't they?" Aunt Lily pointed at the Forgettians just beyond the fence. "You'd think you were a freak show from the circus. I don't think any of them believe I can have a niece that walks upright."

Girly didn't find the neighbours assumptions too far off the mark. If she hadn't been Aunt Lily's niece, she'd have the same thought. "Who are they?" she asked as she joined her aunt at the window.

"Well the two old biddies on the left are the Ford Sisters. They live next door in that yellow house." Aunt Lily jutted out her chin so she could peer through her spectacles perched on the end of her nose. "And the ragged bunch are the Tuckers; three of the boys were on the raft you saw yesterday. The tall lanky one's Henry Henry; that man will fetch and tote almost anything. The most interesting thing about him is he has a secret in his pocket. I've always wanted to see it. That little one who can barely see over the pickets is Wilber. He's a member of the National Association for Crippled Midgets."

"I've never heard of it."

"He's the only member. And there's—oh my God." Aunt Lily took a deep breath and dropped to her knees. "That's Harriet Simpson. Her and her stupid Magna Carta."

Girly crouched down on the floor beside her aunt. "I think it's her magnum opus."

"Magna Carta, magnum opus, with that woman, does it really matter?"

Girly wanted to tell her that they were very different but after the look her aunt shot her she thought better of it. "I suppose not," was all she was able to muster.

Aunt Lily grunted and after what felt like of a lifetime of peeking and crouching under the window ledge Girly asked, "Why are we hiding?"

"That woman, Mrs. Harriet Simpson, will place a pox on me and my cat."

Turning her head Girly looked for a cat. She hadn't seen one since she arrived. "Where's your cat?"

"Dead, but that's not good enough for Harriet Simpson." Aunt Lily crawled towards the davenport. "No Harriet's not satisfied until it's cursed as well. A dead cat that has been cursed, can you think of anything worse?"

At the moment Girly couldn't think of anything. She crawled after her aunt. The morning was turning out to be as strange as the day before.

"I made you toast," Aunt Lily said as she climbed onto the davenport, "thought you might be hungry."

"Thank you." Girly followed her aunt's lead and climbed on the chair opposite of her.

"It's on the table in the dining room, you'll have to crawl to fetch it. Harriet might see you if you stand."

The hunger Girly felt when she first woke now dissolved. She didn't want to crawl across the room to eat hidden amongst the table legs. "I'll eat it later."

"Suit yourself."

Girly folded her hands in her lap. There was an awkwardness that filled the space. It was almost a relief. Girly had avoided awkward moments in the past but now she felt like embracing them. It was better than the bizarre.

The seven-day clock on the mantel counted out the seconds. How long had they sat there not speaking? She wasn't sure; it seemed like forever. Girly looked around. The room where they sat was comfortable. She was sure the furnishings hadn't changed since her grandmother's time. Old photos and doilies dotted well-dusted pie crust side tables. There was a large square area rug placed in front of a fieldstone fireplace. A rocking chair, davenport and two armchairs formed a U shape around the hearth, with side tables separating each piece. There was a barrister's bookcase nestled between the two six-paned windows that faced the street. And a writing desk strewn with, what Girly could only describe as an unorganized mess, positioned on the opposite wall.

"Isn't that the same dress you wore the day I met you?" Aunt Lily interrupted Girly's perusal. She looked particularly pleased with herself. "I have a good memory for such things."

"You met me yesterday."

"Even so, you must admit I'm very observant." Aunt Lily picked up her knitting. "Do you knit?"

"No."

"You should start. I knit socks for the boys that have made it home from the war. I've supplied more soldiers than any other woman in Forget, although the war department has written me to cease and desist. They're so funny. I'm going to get a plaque."

"Who?"

"Who what?"

"Who's going to give you a plaque?"

Aunt Lily put down her knitting and looked thoughtful. "I haven't decided yet."

Girly rubbed her temples with the palms of her hands.

"Don't do that," said her aunt. "It gives one the impression you're frustrated." She patted the spot beside her. "Come sit and I'll teach you how to knit."

The rest of the morning Girly spent dropping stiches and listening to the sound of the click of knitting needles. Sandwiches and cookies were fetched from the icebox and

Girly could feel herself relax. Maybe eight weeks wouldn't be that long. She hadn't had a chance to tell her friends where she was going but perhaps she could write them. Girly imagined regaling them with tales of just the past two days. Her friends, especially Daphne, would think she had stepped into a Mark Twain novel. When she got home they could lie on her bed and giggle at the absurdity of it all. Aunt Lily was nattering on and on as Girly's mind wandered. They sat side by side, content, each in their own way.

"And of course, you'll be my gardener, maid, cook, butler and historian."

Girly snapped out of her repose. "I beg your pardon?"

"You'll be my gardener, maid, cook, butler and historian."

Images of raw hands and endless hours almost brought Girly to her knees. She began to cry into the half knit sock.

"Oh dear," said Aunt Lily, "that's not how we do it here but it's a nice sentiment."

Girly looked up.

"Tears mixed with a soldier's sacrifice. That's a touching thought. I'll have to tell the committee."

Girly resumed sobbing and Aunt Lily patted her on the back. "Think of how delightful it will be to be a jack of all trades. The neighbours will envy you I'm sure. I know I will." Aunt Lily gave an unconvincing smile. "Did I mention that the positions were more for show than anything else? The laundry will still be picked up and taken to the Chinese laundry. The laundress is an amazing woman. She wears pants. I still marvel every time I see her." Aunt Lily picked up a sandwich before she continued. "Mail needs to be fetched and posted once a day, which you will do. The diner will drop off our supper but you, as cook, will be expected to plate it. I think even a city girl can handle that. The bread and baked goods will also be picked up from the bakery twice a week by the cook. Not the maid, not the butler, the cook. Do you understand?" Aunt Lily looked at her niece. "Don't just sit there like a lump. Nod if you do."

Girly sniffed and nodded. What else could she do? Her mother's words echoed behind those of her aunt's. As long as you do as she asks you'll fare well, but remember to do as she asks even if you think her logic is a bit muddled. It will keep her calm and make your stay bearable. Girly didn't know if she wanted a bearable stay but she had no money, no options.

"Market day is Wednesday," Aunt Lily continued. "That's when you'll pick up the dried goods. Other than that we'll play it by ear."

Girly wanted to ask her how she could afford such luxuries. Prepared meals, bakery goods, the Chinese laundry; her parents must have sent Aunt Lily money. That's the only thing that seemed logical. But how could this old woman not only demand their money but their daughter? There had to be something no one was telling her. Something she had to find out. Girly sniffed again.

Aunt Lily laid her crust on the sandwich plate and dabbed her lips with a napkin. "The washing of floors, wall and heavy cleaning has always been hired out, even in my mother's day. So has the gardening. Before we rise in the morning, Tucker will stoke the fires that need stoking and bring in fresh wood. I expect you to master the feather duster and broom. There will also be some washing up to do after meals and preparing breakfast and simple lunches, —sandwiches and such. And of course creamed onions. I can't live without creamed onions. You'll have to learn how to make them."

Girly ground her teeth; her mood was changing. She wondered if her parents had been privy to her aunt's plan. The very thought made her boil inside. She felt so betrayed. Mopping up after a senile old woman was not how she had planned to spend her time.

"Good it's all settled," said Aunt Lily as if the scheme had been agreed upon. "I laid out the uniforms on your bed while you were occupied in the cellar. We'll start training for your new posts later this afternoon."

Chapter Seven

Just as had been promised, Aunt Lily had laid out different attire for each of Girly's roles. They were spread on the bed with a paper pinned to each collar identifying which was which. The maid's was a simple mid-calf black dress, stockings and a frilly white apron and cap. Aunt Lily assured her she needn't worry; the set of keys that went with the outfit didn't fit any of the locks. Girly thought she could stomach wearing it if she didn't have to wear that ridiculous lace cap in public.

The butler was to put on the maid's dress minus the apron and cap. A mousey grey shapeless frock was what the cook was supposed to wear; if she didn't know better, she would have sworn her mother's upstairs maid, Esther, picked it out. The gardener's attire consisted of a hat with a veil—presumably to protect against insects—gardening gloves, rubber boots, a stiff pocketed apron that contained a variety of gardening essentials, and a dress that Girly was convinced was sewn from a set of old drapes. She wanted to burn it on the spot.

Girly's unpaid-help-in-training started later that day. Aunt Lily sat on the porch swing and fanned herself with a faded newspaper, having summoned Girly. "I didn't call Girly

Gardner," Aunt Lily said, looking Girly over as if she'd lost her mind. "I called Girly Maid."

Girly was tired and didn't feel like complying. She pushed back her veil with her gloved hand. "Can I help you?"

"No. I need Girly Maid. You can't do her work for her. It will only teach her to shirk her duties."

Rolling her eyes, Girly went back upstairs to change. She reappeared with her buttons unevenly done and apron loosely tied. "Yes?" she said through tight lips.

"Oh, there you are. I've been calling and calling. Do you know where the cook is?" Aunt Lily put down the newspaper and picked up an empty water glass. "I can't find her anywhere."

Girly walked back into the house and slammed the screen door behind her. She could hear her aunt click her tongue as she called after her, "Poor dear, the cook frustrates her as much as she does me."

By the third day Girly thought she might be able to manage. Before she opened her eyes that morning, she promised herself she would, for the first time since she boarded the train in Saskatoon, try to get through a whole day without bursting into tears. She had to. There was no one there to pat her hand and tell her that everything would be all right. Girly was on her own.

As she stood and stretched, Girly could hear the tick of the hall clock. She had no idea what time it was. The day had to be well on its way. It seemed like hours ago since she heard a pair of hard shoes clip down the hall and stop outside her bedroom door. She knew it was her aunt but ignored her even when the doorknob jiggled.

Out of her bedroom window the sun had long ago begun its steep climb. Handfuls of clouds dotted the sky waiting to be burned off. It was a perfect morning. Her mother would have said there was enough blue in the sky to cut out a pair of pants. Girly leaned against the window frame and traced the words 'I hate Lily' with a fingertip. She smiled and wondered what the day would bring.

Her peace was disturbed when a motley troop of boys came careening down the walk, each bearing a well-used gardening implement. Girly had seen the throng before; they were the Tuckers. Rakes, hoes and shovels lay across their shoulders like weapons. And the noise that accompanied them chased off any semblance of peace. Birds had either stopped their songs or flew to destinations unknown. Girly watched somewhat bemused. It was hard to believe they were brothers the way they argued and prodded one another. Or maybe that's how brothers were. Girly didn't know, being an only child. It was as if war was imminent. She could hear them through the glass. Girly knocked on the pane. If her aunt heard them, Girly was sure she would beat them with her cane.

It may have been happenstance or perhaps a keen set ears that caused one of the boys to glance up at her window. He pointed, and as if on queue, the troop looked up and in unison, stuck out their tongues. The cheek unraveled Girly; she dressed haphazardly and raced down stairs. She wasn't aware or even cared what Girly she was until she stepped into the kitchen and her aunt addressed her.

"Come to join the land of the living?" Aunt Lily said somewhat lackadaisically before she turned to examine her niece. The softness of her face changed and hard lines appeared. The look of disgust was unmistakable. "What kind of Girly are you? Hodgepodge? Who in their right mind would name a Girly that?" She shook her head. "City people."

Girly looked down at what she was wearing, the gardener's boots, the cook's dress with the maid's apron. She didn't think her attire mattered; her mission was to intervene between the Tuckers and Aunt Lily. What she was wearing seemed to be of little importance at the moment.

"You need to change. You're giving me the vapours and God help you if I get the vapours." Aunt Lily turned back to the window.

Despite the warning, Girly wanted to step in front of her

aunt, to draw attention away from the Tuckers who had
leapfrogged the gate and were laying siege to Aunt Lily's
garden like a cloud of locusts. Girly imagined an outburst
that would shake the foundations of the universe, but it
never came. Instead her aunt's peaceful countenance
returned, and she cooed as if she had been handed a tiny
baby. "Have you ever seen anything more marvellous?
They're a sight for sore eyes."

Not knowing how to respond Girly retreated to her room
to change.

Girly Cook and Aunt Lily munched burnt toast as they
watched the Tuckers through the kitchen window. Between
throwing dirt lumps and earthworms at each other, the boys
attacked the garden with surprising precision. The grass
was raked, weeds were shorn off at the root, the chicken
coop was cleaned and the compost pile turned. Even the
smallest Tucker seemed up for the task.

"They're my odd job squad." Aunt Lily waved at the boys
through the window. "They've been coming here for years.
Ever since they were old enough to hill potatoes and gather
eggs."

The boys saluted Aunt Lily in the same manner they saluted
the barn-door raft. A rag-tag bunch interspersed between
rows of emerging vegetables. All were barefoot and blond.
They ranged in height from a head taller than Girly, to
just above her waist. Girly reasoned the oldest must be a
little older than her and the youngest no more than five
or six. Their bodies were straight and lean, with enormous
hands and strong fingers that grew like crooked roots. Their
hair was uncombed and flopped across their foreheads. To
Girly they looked as if they were one and the same. Each a
younger or older version of the others.

"There's more at home," said Aunt Lily.

"More what?"

"Tuckers."

The thought of more blond boys scampering about in the
breeze made Girly feel a bit uneasy. She had never seen so

many free spirits. It seemed they never stopped to take a breath. "How many?"

"Oh, I've lost count. But I swear it wouldn't hurt that woman to fake a headache every once in a while. It would be the immaculate non-conception." Picking up a tin of prize cookies from the back of the cupboard, Aunt Lily opened the screen door and called the boys over.

They lined up in order of height, as if that were the way it was always done. Their shoulders were pinned back as they stared off in the distance. "You know what to do," said Aunt Lily.

The line of boys became still and serious. As each boy spoke Aunt Lily pelted him with a cookie. The tallest Tucker stepped forward. "My name is Alexander the Great, the undefeated warrior." As he stepped back, the boy next to him stepped forward.

"My name is Socrates, the thinker."

The next boy had to be prodded. He was drawing in the dirt with a stick and wasn't paying attention. "My name is Leonardo de Vinci, the creator."

Bringing himself to his full height, the next child thumped his chest. "I am Napoleon Bonaparte, I will rise to greatness. Vive la France."

Stepping forward before Napoleon had stepped back, the next peered around his brother. "My name is Romulus, son of the god of war."

"William Godwin," said the next. "My name is William Godwin, I speak out for justice and social change."

The last Tucker smiled as he moved forward. "Joseph."

"Joseph what?" asked Aunt Lily.

"Joseph of Many Colours Tucker and I will become a nation," he said. The boy's smile was wider than those of his brothers. "But most folks call me Mean Dog Joe." He stood on his tiptoes as if to emphasize the point.

"Very good," Aunt Lily smiled. "Your mother has named you well."

"Thank you," said Alexander. "And we will do our best to live up to our names."

The line of boys held their position a moment longer, almost as if they were stamping it into Girly's memory. Then they scattered and were gone. The only sign that they were ever there was the pile of weeds in the compost. The experience made Girly feel strangely elated, and more than that, she had yet to burst into tears.

As Girly readied herself later that morning to post the mail, her aunt gave her a list of instructions. "Don't take all day," her aunt scolded. "I don't have any patience for dawdlers."

"I'm not a dawdler."

"Perhaps not now, but if you're anything like your mother, it's something you will aspire to." Aunt Lily raised her eyebrows as if it had been a warning. "And after you post the letter," she continued, "you must wait for the postmistress to put her mark on it. I'll know if it's not done right."

"Yes, Aunt Lily."

"You can go to the post office as the maid today. Don't want anyone to think I don't have a vast staff."

Girly closed her eyes and took a deep breath. She envisioned the map her aunt had drawn. First she'd weave from Roland le Peteur to Beggars Can't be Choosers. Then she'd slip down Love Thy Neighbour as Thyself, skirt the side of the meadow to This Boy is Ignorance and This Girl is Want. That should lead her to Main Street, which she would cross to Grand Avenue dressed as a maid. It was simple enough in its own convoluted way and at least it got her out of the house.

As soon as Girly left, she slipped off the maid's cap and put it in the pocket of her apron. She made her way towards the post office greeting everyone she met. They all seemed to know she was Aunt Lily's niece and which 'Girly' she was. "Girly Maid," said the man with a pipe, "nice to see you're not dead yet."

Girly waved back and replied she too was relieved. In Toronto, Girly never wandered the streets alone. Strangers may have acknowledged her with a nod but they never spoke or hollered across the street, and no one addressed her by her first name unless they were very familiar. It would have been considered vulgar. A feeling of unease filled her. To be known by so many—not just strangers but strange people—was unthinkable. By the time she had retraced her steps back to her aunt's house she felt rather overwhelmed.

Girly barely walked through the door when Aunt Lily snatched the mail from her hand. It was a letter that Aunt Lily had written and posted to herself. "Oh, I'm so pleased to hear from myself," she said as she skipped to the davenport. "I'm so dependable when it comes to correspondence. Girly Maid, you could learn a lot from me. Well, you all could. Have you seen Girly Gardener's penmanship? It leaves a lot to be desired."

Aunt Lily fluffed out her dress as she sat down. Putting on her eyeglasses, she cleared her throat and opened her letter. "I wonder what I have to say. Haven't heard from me since yesterday."

Girly Maid sat on a chair across from her.

"Where are the others?"

Girly shrugged.

"It's so hard to keep track of all of you. None of you can be in the same place at the same time. I'm forever looking. It would be so much easier if I had only one."

Aunt Lily opened the letter. It was short; just half a page. She snorted and shook her head in disappointment. "Well, all my letters can't be ten pages long. Let's see....

"*Dear Myself.*" Aunt Lily paused. "All the letters start that way. They always have. So predictable I have it memorized. I'll have to mention it in my next letter.

"*So much has happened since last I wrote. As I have already informed you, my niece has come to stay with me. She is a strange thing, forever changing her clothes. I don't know what's to become of her. So glad I have a maid what with all the extra laundry.*

"*When you get as long in the tooth as I, you become a keen observer. Such as the other day, I noticed Girly talking to herself. How odd, I thought. The young thing already so close to senility. Who will want her then? Not many,*

45

I wager. There is little demand for girls who have lost their minds. A pity really; for some it is quite an improvement.

"The thing that troubles me most is the way she cries in the night. Such a longing in her sobs. I remember feeling that way once. One day, perhaps, I will tell her of it.

Best regards,

Me."

When the letter ended, Aunt Lily folded it up and put it back into the envelope. Then she clicked her tongue. "I'm so disappointed in myself, going soft in my old age. I shouldn't put up with all that nonsense."

Girly stared at her aunt for some time. She didn't think the old woman had gone soft. That first night she arrived her aunt had yelled, "Stop your blubbering." It hadn't sounded caring or soothing. But then again, Girly thought, she was just getting used to the place.

Chapter Eight

IN A long, black dress with a stiff lace collar, Girly stared at herself in the mirror. Girly Historian. She scowled. She had been at her aunt's for nearly a week, but it was the first time this Girly was called for.

The sleeves were the garment's only redeeming quality—full at the shoulder and tight from the elbow to the wrist. She had always had a weakness for puffy sleeves, outdated and old-fashioned as the dress was.

The dress itself had been significantly starched and could stand on its own without any assistance. Girly had winced when she put it on. Even with a slip, it was like putting steel wool next to her skin. When she looked at her reflection, she had aged. Black suited her, but the style of the garment was for someone much older. If her mother's words of warning hadn't been burned into her every thought, she would have taken it off. As it was, she knew she had to appease the dragon. She could hear her thumping the ceiling with her cane.

As Girly descended the stairs, her neck was already red from chaffing. Aunt Lily clapped with delight. "You look so severe, so dower, perfect for the job. Historians always look like death warmed over, but you outdo them all. You just look like death."

Girly gave a wan smile. Since her arrival, that was the closest thing to a compliment she had heard. They sat in the sitting room. It took Girly some time to settle. The dress didn't move the way it should and it cut into her, scratching her body with its rough edges.

Aunt Lily sat on the davenport and hummed as she rummaged through the pile of notes in her lap, paying no mind to her niece's predicament. Girly sat as patiently as she could in front of the mail order typewriter.

"As I've already told you," Aunt Lily said, "as historian you will record the town's shameful past. We will skip the triumphant parts; there are only a few of those. For the most part, they only include me. Can't always be tooting my own horn. No, we will stick to the things the curious will want to read, the things that can't be talked about in polite company." Aunt Lily took a sip of water. "Thank God there is no one that polite in Forget." She continued to sift through her pile of papers while Girly scratched.

"Here we are, Harriet Simpson. That woman could take up the better part of the book, but that would only go to her head and make her more unbearable. Type this instead:

Harriet—noun—meaning hairy woman.

Simpson—verb—meaning simpleton.

First and last born to a very disappointed couple.

Never married and produced nothing but discontent.

Reasons for going to hell—many.

Girly looked up at her aunt. "Are you sure that's what you want me to say?"

"I don't want you to say anything. I want you to type it." Aunt Lily examined her fingernails. "That's what historians do."

"But I think historians are supposed to be truthful."

"You are being truthful. Her name is Harriet Simpson isn't it?"

"Yes."

"Really, that's all a historian needs."

Girly pressed several keys at once and let out a deep breath. She felt like she had been holding it in since she had arrived. To frustrate her even more the type-bars had jammed into a tight ball. She grunted as she pried loose the individual bars. Girly wanted to tell her aunt just because she dictated something to her so-called *historian* didn't make it irrefutable. In fact, she was fairly sure anything her aunt dictated was fabricated at best. Since she had come to Forget, she had encountered such bizarre behaviour that it made Harriet Simpson's emotional deluge on the train seem commonplace. For Girly, the whole experience had the same effect as if she had taken a little too much of her mother's laudanum.

"Oh, we mustn't forget to mention her third nipple," Aunt Lily continued.

Girly blushed. She couldn't imagine typing that. It would be indecent. "How would you know such a thing?"

"Anyone that deranged has to have a third nipple. It's what sets them apart."

Chapter Nine

GETTING OUT of her historian dress was a relief. By the end of Aunt Lily's dictation Girly's fingers were so sore from pounding the mail order typewriter she wasn't even sure she typed real words. It didn't matter; Aunt Lily seemed pleased. "You're writing in code," she chirped as she perused the finished pages. "The Huns will never be able to decipher this."

"The Huns," Girly muttered as she crawled between the cool sheets. "They had no idea what waited for them on this side of the Atlantic." She envisioned her aunt crawling, belly to the ground, a knife clenched between her teeth. "They were lucky they never invaded."

Girly curled into a ball and pulled the blankets around her ears. She had never felt so small and alone. The room seemed larger in the dark, the shadows at its edges still unfamiliar. After awhile she could hear her aunt snore from down the hall; at least she wasn't crouched in the hallway ready to pounce. That was somewhat of a relief.

Her gaze wandered over the shadows in her room, lingering on the highboy. The letters there remained untouched since the day Girly arrived. She wasn't sure they contained answers or misery. In fact, she went out of her way to avoid them, opening the dreaded top drawer only when she had to. If it hadn't been for her last memory with her father, she didn't know if she would have survived.

While her mother had given her instructions at the train station, her father had draped an arm over her shoulders and pulled her close. Girly had slouched under his embrace. It was unusual for him to show any public affection. Girly had watched her mother as if she were a stranger. Her mother hadn't been herself since before they left Toronto. Esther, the upstairs maid, usually prepared their bags for travel. But for this trip her mother wouldn't have it. She had insisted on doing the task herself. Her hand lighting on one thing then another. Girly hadn't seen her like that before; her behaviour was frenzied. She was even perspiring.

Esther, who had lips that were permanently pursed, always looked as if she disapproved. Girly thought she probably did. A stray hair or a piece of wayward lint would send her into a tizzy. Girly wondered what Esther had thought as she watched her mother pack. Even Girly knew her mother didn't do it right. The clothes needed to be stacked and folded in a certain manner to avoid wrinkling and her mother had struggled with the task. But Girly hadn't cared. Everything being packed had been purchased by Esther; various shades of bleak. Her mother had claimed it was because they were going on a grand adventure and her daughter needed practical, everyday clothing.

"Your aunt doesn't run in the same circles," her mother had said above the bustle of the station.

"What kind of circles does she run in?"

"Well, I wouldn't really call them circles." Her mother had scanned the platform as if looking for somewhere neutral to rest her gaze. "I'd call them fragmented bits."

Her mother's concern with social status was something Girly had always found amusing, but she had never understood until now; now that she had met Aunt Lily. Her father was just the opposite. He shunned social constraints. Her mother obviously had no such luxury.

At the station everything had whirled around Girly as if she were in some kind of kaleidoscope. She had felt like she was being pulled apart. To be alone was all she had wanted, then perhaps she could've made sense of things. When she had boarded the train she had looked for her mother, but she was nowhere to be seen. Her father had been there though. He had taken her hand and stroked it. "I can't say goodbye," he had said. "It would be my undoing."

She had thrown her arms around his neck. She could feel the rough wool of his tweed jacket against her cheek. The smell of his pipe had tickled her nose. She had wished she could inhale him. "Don't say it then."

Her father had trembled. "You are a better man than I am, Gunga Din."

If she could step back in to those moments, she would. No one would be able to stop her. She closed her eyes and pulled her knees closer to her chest, listening harder for her father's voice. It was somewhere, she only had to find it, or let it find her, bleed its way between the glass and window frame.

Tho' I've belted you an' flayed you,

By the livin' Gawd that made you,

You're a better man than I am, Gunga Din!

Chapter Ten

"GIRLY COOK," called Aunt Lily as the screen door closed, "have you got the bread?"

Girly rolled her eyes as she placed loaves in the breadbox. "Yes."

"Good," Aunt Lily yelled back from what Girly presumed was the sitting room.

If today was going to be anything like yesterday, Girly thought she would scream. And not a Toronto scream either, a scream that would put Harriet Simpson to shame.

First she was sent uptown to post a letter as Girly Maid. When she arrived back at the house Aunt Lily had her change into the cook's attire to go downtown, the opposite side of the street to uptown, to check to see if her aunt's best dress had been sent to the laundry. Why a cook would be checking on laundry was a mystery to Girly.

"Can you get the gardener to check to see if the weeding has been done properly? I don't quite trust the boys I've charged with the task."

Girly trudged up the stairs to change. As she went she muttered something about why her aunt would hire the Tuckers if she didn't think them capable of weeding a simple garden. She thought, to find peace she might misplace her aunt's spectacles. Then the old woman wouldn't be able to tell if anything was amiss. But if she did, Aunt Lily would just force one of the other Girlys to find them again.

"Before you start weeding," Aunt Lily said as Girly Gardner stepped into the doorway of the sitting room, "help me move the rocker."

Girly Gardener stared at her aunt. Her feet were already sweating in her rubber boots and if she spoke she was sure the veil from the hat would stick to her teeth.

"Well?"

"Aren't you going to get out of the rocker first?"

"So I can sit back down again once it's moved? Honestly where is the sense it that?" Aunt Lily glanced down at the needlework in her lap and lowered her voice. "No wonder some are just the hired help."

Girly inched the rocker across the room. Twisting it first to the right and then to the left. Progress was slow and the soft grips on Girly's rubbers boots didn't help. Aunt Lily leaned forward in the rocker as if the shifting of her body would influence the chairs progress. "Just a little further," she said, "a little further."

With the toe of her boot Girly kicked the area rug out of the way.

"That's a girl," said Aunt Lily. "Get rid of all the obstacles." The only obstacle that Girly truly wanted to get rid of was her aunt.

By the time the rocker was positioned in front of the sitting room window, Girly was ready to toss her aunt out of it. The only thing that prevented her from doing so was that she was too exhausted.

"This doesn't feel right," said Aunt Lily as she wiggled in her chair. "It's too close to the window."

Girly took a deep breath before she twisted the chair a few inches back.

"Now it's too far."

Girly sighed and nudged the rocker closer.

"A little more to the left."

Girly tapped the rocker's runner with her boot.

Aunt Lily clapped her hands. "The sweet spot."

Girly rolled her eyes. There was nothing sweet about the spot. It's where the old woman wanted to keep her vigil — Girly Gardener's unwanted companion. But at least they had the glass separating them. Girly could ignore the constant rap of her aunt's cane on the window frame, the signal that she was displeased. Sadly for Girly, her aunt was often displeased. Once the screen door closed behind her though, she was Girly Gardener, the inept and slightly deaf grounds keeper. Girly liked the slightly deaf part best; it gave her a greater measure of freedom. Dropping to her knees, Girly took off her gloves and sank her fingers deep into the soil until she could smell the earth. It was a smell her father said contained all the secrets of the universe. Girly smiled. It was as if her father had joined her in the garden.

"What are you doing, Gunga Din?"

Girly wrinkled her nose. "*Waiting for you.*" All the hours she and her father had spent wandering through fields and meadows seemed to be held within that moment. A spider's thread stringing them together. She remembered her mother's anxious expression as she stood on the back step, Esther in the background, her lips more pursed than usual. "Harold she is not a boy; you can't traipse all over hell and yonder. What will the neighbours think?"

"They will think what they like."

Her father squeezed her hand as they raced for the rise of the hill. Her thighs burned but Girly didn't stop. As she ran she could hear the distant sound of boys playing ball, of old women calling to each other, it all seemed so real. When they had reach the summit, Girly bent over and plucked a blade of grass to chew on the root, her father ruffled her hair. The air smelt good and it was then, when she turned her head, she saw him come whistling out of a cloud. Girly smiled and waved at him.

He cleared his throat.

Girly stopped waving. This didn't feel real anymore, this *was* real. She spit out whatever she had been chewing on. It was far too gritty to be a blade of grass but she refused to drop her gaze to examine it. She didn't need to know.

In front of her stood a man that she thought looked crisp. His clothes were all white and pressed; they seemed to salute him. He stood out on the dilapidated street; he was the kind of man who knew his station. Such a contrast to her curtain dress and preposterous veil and hat. It made it all the more humiliating.

The stranger leaned on the garden gate, his feet casually crossed as he whistled into the breeze. He let his eyes leisurely pass over her. Then, with the gall of the devil himself, he asked, "Do you have a rose for a beautiful girl I know?" An impish boy grinned from that man's face. Girly wasn't sure what to make of this bold intruder.

"A rose from this garden?" Girly said picking the veil from between her lips.

"Yes, for a beautiful girl."

She cut for him the closest rose. "Will this do?" she asked handing it to him. His hand brushed her garden glove. Girly was sure if she hadn't been wearing gloves she'd have fainted. She'd write Daphne about it.

He smiled, held the rose lightly in his fingertips, then raised his brow and with a half grin handed it back to her. "Hello, beautiful."

"Goodness me."

Leaning further into the garden, he almost touched her, his voice dropping to a whisper. "Do you have a rose for a woman of unequalled beauty? For a woman who is a rare find? Would you have such a rose?"

"A rose?" she gasped.

"Yes, for the woman who haunts my dreams."

"Oh."

His words took her breath away. She searched and clipped for him the best rose she could find. He seemed pleased with her choice, and after lifting her veil, he ran the rose tenderly across her cheek. Girly waited, wondering what would happen next. Then he nodded as if a spell had been broken, thanked her and continued on his way. Slipping the rose into his lapel, he whistled even louder.

As he passed, the rose thief tipped his hat to all the old ladies, and they twittered like young girls.

Girly watched him disappear around the corner. To him, she was sure she was a foolish girl playing dress up in her aunt's garden. Maybe that's how all of Forget saw her. Aunt Lily's understudy. What would Daphne say? He was the kind of man that caused women to lie awake at night. The kind they would bat their eye lashes at and then giggle about in the dark. But he hardly even saw her; he was after the woman who haunted his dreams. One day, though, Girly vowed, she too would haunt dreams. Perhaps even his.

Chapter Eleven

GIRLY DREADED entering the house later that afternoon. She heard her aunt's continuous rapping on the windowpane but had chosen to ignore her. The woman rapped as if it were a compulsion and she thought it best not to encourage her. When she entered the sitting room, she found Aunt Lily perched precariously on the windowsill, her hair somehow caught on the window latch. It was twisted and matted in the most unbecoming style. The old woman's needlework and glasses lay on the floor at her feet. "What an unproductive afternoon," Girly said removing her gardening gloves. "You were unable to spy on me or do your needlework."

Aunt Lily, who had seemed lost for words when Girly came into the room, found her tongue. "For the love of God, release me!"

For a moment, Girly wasn't sure if she loved God.

"Didn't you hear me knocking? Banging?"

Girly bit her lip. "I thought it was a woodpecker. Besides, couldn't you have called Girly Maid or Girly Butler?"

"I won't dignify that question with an answer."

Girly narrowed her eyes. With her altered vision she imagined her aunt a beautiful foreign dancer, delicately moving to an overpowering piece of music. It was touching.

Her limbs moved in perfect unison. Her face was soft and tender. This graceful woman she would save. Unfortunately, when she widened her eyes, her demented aunt still remained.

As Girly stood there, a sense of power overcame her. All the notes she had typed as Girly Historian came to mind. Giving no credence to her aunt's dilemma, and in a calm, emotionless tone, Girly said, "Aunt Lily, the minister and his new bride have just arrived for tea. Shall we take it in the dining room or the sitting room?"

The colour drained from her aunt's face. A blank look of awkwardness came over her dishevelled being. After a time she groaned, and effortlessly words spewed from her mouth. "That impertinent old man! I have no intention of indulging him and his iniquity." Aunt Lily's wiry voice and flailing arms scratched the air as she spit out her words. "His first wife is not yet cold in the ground and he dares to flaunt that new thing that warms his bed. Tell him I am not up to entertaining, but if he should desire entertainment, I'm sure his less than innocent bride will oblige him."

"Very well." Girly left the room long enough to excuse the invisible guests. She smiled to herself. Aunt Lily would regret her words especially on Sunday; the realization would come to her in the night. Girly longed for the night, but not in the way she longed for the Sabbath. For now, though, it was time to release the red-faced demon.

"I was just going to politely tell him not to bother my gardener," Aunt Lily explained as Girly began the almost impossible task of untangling her aunt's hair from the latch.

"Tell who?"

"That boy made of starch. Oh, I think his name's Bill. Around here though we call him Lothario. The weasel in costly shoes." Aunt Lily let out a small cry.

"Sorry. Your hair is so twisted."

"He wouldn't have come down here on purpose," Aunt Lily grimaced. "Must have taken a wrong turn."

Girly looked at her aunt and sighed. "I'm sure he's harmless. He just wanted a rose."

"From my garden?"

"Yes from your garden."

"And you gave it to him?"

Girly wasn't sure how to answer.

"I only give my roses to the dead." Aunt Lily was almost vibrating. "They are the only ones that can truly appreciate them."

"I'll try to remember."

Aunt Lily went silent but as soon as she was freed, she gave an indignant grunt, marched out of the room and slammed the door, only to reopen it to retrieve the misguided skirt that had the audacity to lag behind her. Girly left a few strands of hair in the latch, so if Aunt Lily happened to see them she might laugh at her mishap. She didn't.

Chapter Twelve

THE WAY Aunt Lily looked at her sideways, Girly was sure she was still angry about the roses. It was apparent each time they passed one another. Aunt Lily would snort as if Girly had forgotten to button her blouse or had the hem of her skirt tucked into her waistband. Girly wished she would just say what was on her mind. It was better than constantly checking if she were properly dressed or had something stuck in her teeth.

It was almost a relief when Aunt Lily spewed her venom. She was on the front porch swing fanning herself with the feather duster, "You know even when your crouched behind the peonies I can still see you."

Girly pushed back her gardener's veil and glared at her aunt, "I wasn't hiding."

"Maybe you should. At least then you couldn't give away my roses."

"We've already gone through this."

"That maybe so but I'm not convinced that you understand the significance of what you did. You gave a rose to Lothario. Lothario. You shouldn't even talk to Lothario let alone give him my roses."

"I didn't talk to him. He talked to me."

Aunt Lily ripped a feather from the duster. Girly thought by the look on her aunt's face she would pluck the whole thing but somehow Aunt Lily steeled herself and began to gently finger the locket that hung around her neck. Her voice softened. "I once knew a fellow like that," Aunt Lily began. "He was charming and bright, but he wasn't real. He was made of starch. Oh, he called me his pet and brought me wild flowers and chocolates, but I think he did that with all the girls — even the fat ones. His intentions weren't bad, just careless. You want a common man, one with good character. That is better than any amount of charm."

Girly sat in wonder as she listened. It was just like some of her aunt's letters. Aunt Lily wished good things for her, but then the chilling breeze of her true personality swept back into the room. Her aunt let go of her locket and the moment was lost.

"I doubt that boy will ever remember you," she continued. "There are many pretty girls; girls of substance—and you, my dear, are not one of them." She smiled. "To him you would be no more than a scullery maid, and who would care for a scullery maid? Not him." With that, Aunt Lily gave her niece a sly smile before raising the duster as if it were some kind of Victorian fan. There was a smugness about it that needled Girly. What made it worse was Aunt Lily peeking through the feathers as if measuring her response. Girly wanted to rush across the veranda and rip the duster from her aunt's hand. Instead she just glared at her.

Aunt Lily was wrong. She was more than a ridiculous maid. Therefore, Girly had no choice. At her next opportunity she would have to spit in Aunt Lily's tea.

Chapter Thirteen

ON WEDNESDAY mornings, Girly took the wagon to the grocer's. It had three functioning wheels, with a fourth that twisted uncontrollably whenever she pulled it. It didn't only twist it squeaked. Chirping at her with every step. Always reminding her that she and Aunt Lily were eternally connected. She hated that wagon and even told Aunt Lily so.

"It's not a wagon, it's a trolley," Aunt Lily said quite taken aback. "All the moneyed people have trolleys! If you read more you'd know that.

"You're missing the point," Girly's mouth twitched. "It's broken."

"It's not broken, merely injured. And if you were a God-fearing Christian, you'd be thankful for an injured trolley, and be glad you didn't have a broken wagon."

Girly was a little dumbfounded and couldn't think of a response. Besides, she was a little scared if the conversation continued she might actually agree.

On this particular Wednesday morning, Girly had arisen early, before her aunt emerged weary from her bed. It was Girly's hope to catch a glimpse of the Rose Thief—she couldn't bring herself to call him Bill. She hadn't seen him since that day in the garden, but had spent many hours imagining what she would do if she did. Not only that, she longed to speak with Harriet Simpson. She had so much to tell her. Life at her aunt's was unconventional to say the least and Girly hoped Harriet would help her make sense of it. With a scrawled grocery list in hand, Girly stepped out of the house and into the sunlight.

Girly wore her best shoes, her aunt's Sunday hat, and a periwinkle dress in which the family had planned to bury her cousin, Dead Hilary. Dead Hilary was apparently notorious in Forget. The first Sunday Girly went to church, Girly's likeness was compared to that of her almost dead cousin. It was a relief to Harriet Simpson that the likeness was slight. She said that it probably made the stoning of Girly less likely.

"What did Hillary do?" Girly had asked.

"Well, she didn't die for starters. It was quite scandalous, shunning heaven like that. Never seen anything like it before, rising from her death bed as if she were Lazarus. Didn't even consider her parents and the minister, who had taken so much time and consideration planning her funeral." Harriet shook her head. "And to top it all off, she ran off with the organist's husband."

"A shame," Aunt Lily had chimed in. "Hilary would have made a beautiful dead person."

"That left the church in quite a quandary," Harriet continued. "At Sunday meetings, we now had an organist who was inclined to weep while she played off tempo. Some said it was spiritual, but I didn't agree. Listening to a broken-hearted organist playing some uplifting song about hell and damnation frightens me."

"I usually sleep through that part of the service," Aunt Lily said. "If I wanted to go to a circus I'd buy a ticket."

If Aunt Lily really wanted to see a circus, she didn't have to buy a ticket; she'd just have to watch Girly pull the injured trolley. It didn't seem to matter what she did, the trolley fought her. There was no getting around it, it was going to be another arduous journey to the market. Periodically she looked up at the other homes in their quarter, curious if they had their own version of Aunt Lily but just hid them better. If so, she thought a curse be on them all.

Girly shuddered at the thought. Where had her parents sent her? Her aunt had told her at least one story to go with each of the houses. She had heard some as Girly Maid, others as Girly Butler, but most as Girly Historian. Aunt Lily rarely talked to Girly Cook. She said she didn't want to distract anyone with such limited talent from her duties. Girly Cook was relieved.

The home directly to the north of Aunt Lily's housed the gangly Ford sisters, Emma and Ella. One was close to ninety, and the other was five years her senior. Aunt Lily had it in her head the sisters were Communists. In the summer, she'd picket their front lawn, which delighted the Fords. They'd serve brandy and scones.

Girly remembered her aunt's dictation regarding them.

Emma—noun—meaning thin without much for a bosom.

Ella—noun—meaning—same as Emma.

Ford—verb—meaning—will get on one's nerves at any given opportunity.

Could have been twins if they hadn't been born so many years apart. They have a tendency to see the good in things. Bad trait that cannot be trusted.

Girly smiled as she looked at their house. According to Aunt Lily the two toothless women had lived in Forget their whole lives and did nothing more than gossip and flirt with younger men. They were the closest things the town had to saints. They were on every committee and they knitted for orphans in their spare time.

There weren't any orphans in Forget, but Aunt Lily said that didn't discourage the Fords, God bless them. It had always been their dream, that one day the town would be full of little, well-dressed, weeping, parentless children. A dream, sadly for the sisters, never realized.

Kitty-corner to the Fords were the Harrisburgs. Aunt Lily

had little to say about Mr. Harrisburg. She seemed to take no notice of him, as if he had already died. However, Mrs. Harrisburg was different. Aunt Lily saved a special kind of gentleness for her.

Jane—noun—meaning— ilent spring rain.

Harrisburg—verb—meaning— vaporator of life.

Could have changed the world, Miss Jane could, if her wings had not been clipped at such a young age.

Girly had asked how Mrs. Harrisburg's wings had been clipped, but Aunt Lily only waved her hand. "We will do definitions now," she said. "Details will be filled in later."

"But you've told me all about the Fords."

"True. Terrible misstep. Forget everything you've heard." Aunt Lily narrowed her eyes and looked at her niece. "Have you forgotten what I told you to forget?"

"Pardon me?"

"Oh, that's my girl."

It was to Girly Maid that Aunt Lily spoke regarding Mrs. Harrisburg but only after making her promise not to breathe a word of it to that nosey Girly Historian. In contrast to the Fords, the Harrisburgs kept predominantly to themselves. Their shades were modestly drawn, showing nothing but quiet to the outside world. Mrs. Harrisburg had been injured as a young girl, making her barren and slightly disfigured. Despite her injury, she was still rather breathtaking—but not to her father. However remarkable Mrs. Harrisburg may have been, her father saw her as if she had been purposely marked. Aunt Lily said he couldn't look at his daughter without angry eyes, and when she was fifteen he had exchanged her for some fieldwork that needed doing.

Mr. Harrisburg was all too happy to claim his young bride. He had been on his own for many years and was glad for the company. Girly heard her aunt say Mr. Harrisburg was older than Mrs. Harrisburg's father. Girly had seen Mrs. Harrisburg on a few occasions. Aunt Lily hired her to do what she referred to as the heavy cleaning. As far as Girly could tell, after the scrubbing and straightening was done, most of her time was spent drinking tea with her aunt, tea that Girly served but in which Girly was not invited to partake. The thing that irked her most though, was the fact Mrs. Harrisburg could wear whatever she pleased to work.

Girly paused at the end of Love Thy Neighbour as Thyself Street before skirting the edge of the meadow. Such a wonderful place for play and imagination; when the spring runoff dried up it would be a fine shortcut to the market. Girly swore it contained magic. The trees at its border had heavy boughs that draped over her as if she was a fairy princess away to her coronation. Their scents permeated her hair and made her feet feel as if they floated over the worn path. It felt like a celebration whenever she walked beneath them.

The market, when she arrived, was as usual full of common, early morning gossip. Some of the more devout members of the church's congregation had come to discuss that week's prayer list. At least the members from the east side of Main Street. The Woods, as Girly liked to think of them. The Bricks would never cross over to the wood side unless something dire was about to occur.

With all the concern, Girly thought she could get quite an education if she should happen to linger too long among the canned goods. It was there the loudest whisperers liked to gather. And that's where she found Harriet Simpson.

"Oh, there you are, dear," Harriet said, looking up from the can of tuna in her hand. "I was worried about you."

"I'm fine."

"You look good." Harriet leaned over and lowered her voice. "There aren't even any visible pustules."

Girly felt self-conscious. Now she understood why everyone seemed to examine her skin so closely whenever she entered the grocer's. They were looking for the plagues.

Harriet put the dinted can back on the shelf. "And what of the letters?"

Girly didn't want to talk about the letters. The first one had been a disappointment. To admit her mother could give so little an explanation only hurt. She could feel her shoulders slump when she answered. "I've only read one and it didn't really answer any of my questions."

"Well, maybe you're asking the wrong questions." Harriet poked Girly in the nose. "I think it's time you read another one, don't you?"

Girly nodded.

"How long have you been staying with Miss Lily anyway?" Harriet closed her eyes as she counted on her finger. "Just over a fortnight. Must feel like forever."

It did feel like forever. Girly still had six weeks left with her aunt. She didn't know how she was going to survive.

"Second letters are often more enlightening than firsts," Harriet continued. "Especially if the composer has been drinking. But disregard the third letter; by then they have drunk so much nothing makes sense."

"My mother doesn't drink."

"Well, you're in luck then, open two. You've been here long enough."

It was true the next letter might shed light on her situation. Though Girly didn't think there was any explanation in the world that would justify sending her to her aunt's. As soon as she finished her duties, she promised Harriet she would open the next two letters. In fact, she said she'd skip the shopping altogether if she could, but Aunt Lily would see that as an unmitigated act of treason.

She picked her way through the aisles, dispatching Aunt Lily's list. The items never changed from week to week and after the grocer had charged the purchases to Aunt Lily's account and placed the packages on her wounded trolley, Girly gave a sigh of relief. She checked the list one last time. Missing anything would send her aunt into hysterics. Last week she had forgotten the canned beans, and Aunt Lily had wailed that at night she would never be warm again.

Confident everything was at hand, Girly said goodbye to

A Town Called Forget

Harriet Simpson and moved towards the door. That's when she saw them. Through the oval window in the door she spied a couple across the street. They were standing in front of a brick monstrosity. The gentleman, she was sure, was The Thief. She stepped closer and brought her face to the glass. It was him. He was with whom she assumed was the girl who haunted his dreams.

"Mrs. Simpson," she said. "Who's that girl in the lilac dress?"

With a gentle shove Harriet moved Girly from her post. "Oh," she said rubbing her hands together. "You mean the one with the bob standing next to poor Lothario Bill?"

Girly looked closer at The Thief. He seemed all right to her, although the way he swooned and fawned over Miss Fashionable Hair might have been the result of a fever. "What do you mean poor?"

"Your aunt hasn't told you?"

"No."

"Well," Harriet emphasised the word as if it carried the fate of all mankind within its letters. "He suffers the same fate as most of the bricks, flat feet. His dream of fighting overseas dashed, Bill was relegated to protecting the home front." Harriet shook her head. "Poor Doc Dippel—it was exhausting for him to write all those letters explaining the boy's conditions."

"All the bricks?"

"Almost every last one, except for Lothario's older brother, of course; he was killed on the first day of training camp." Patting Girly on the arm, Harriet took a deep breath. "But here I go off on a tangent when all you wanted to know is who's the girl in the lilac dress."

Girly nodded. Harriet's last words seemed so unimportant following the previous ones that had fallen like stones.

Harriet's voice turned into that of a commentator. "You mean the girl in the frock fashioned from the purest silk and accented with handwork of baby Irish lace; lacework

69

crocheted by the slender spidery arthritic hands of praying nuns?"

"I suppose."

"That's Lottie Smith." Harriet scrunched her shoulders. "I've been reading *McCalls*. Now I feel like the queen of fashion."

Girly wasn't sure if she should commend Harriet on her reading repertoire. The woman was kind of an enigma. "Lottie Smith, I've heard of her," Girly said. "Actually Girly Historian has, but that's neither here nor there." She tapped her lip. "How did Aunt Lily describe her?" Girly pictured herself in her black historian dress sitting at the mail order typewriter.

> Lottie—noun—meaning—could be described as attractive but also vain and shallow; with bosoms the size of a small man's head, which gives her a smothering personality.

> Smith—verb—meaning family should move away.

Although she had a common last name, it was apparent to Girly that Lottie wasn't all that common. Girly could hardly breathe. It was just as Aunt Lily had said—Lottie was beautiful and voluptuous. (The latter was a quality Girly could, under no circumstance, tolerate.) Lottie came from a well-to-do family and the way she carried herself was as grand as the side of the street on which she stood. Aunt Lily had said that when the Smiths' name was spoken, it was immediately recognized as one of power and influence. The Smiths thought everyone should be eternally grateful they chose to live in Forget. After all, the Smiths thought they owned the town, and with the town came all the people.

According to Aunt Lily, that's all Lottie was—a name. She was never known to be kind or generous, particularly witty, or even talented. She didn't have to be. She was beautiful and she was rich; that was all she needed. As far as Aunt Lily knew, she never tried to be anything more.

The sight of The Thief and Lottie together made Girly knock her head against the pane. Lottie seemed to hold his attention as he had held Girly's in the garden. Girly wondered if her beautiful rose had been given to Lottie, and if he had run it gently along Lottie's cheek before leaving it to rest on her fingertips. Maybe Aunt Lily was right; maybe Girly was nothing more than a scullery maid.

Her thoughts were rudely interrupted when she heard a voice announce, "I think that's Dead Hilary's dress. Yes, it is Dead Hilary's dress. I sold it to her mother you know." Girly turned to see the grocer's wife standing behind the counter and pointing directly at her. That woman had a smile so sharp you could cut your fingers on its edges. Girly tried to remember Aunt Lily's dictation regarding her.

> Grocer's wife—neither noun nor verb, nor is she vegetable, mineral or animal.

> Has a category all her own: heartless.

"She's not dead," Girly said pulling herself away from the window.

"Oh, that's right," answered the grocer's wife putting her finger to her chin. "She's an adulteress."

"Well, she was almost dead," Girly returned, hoping that small sacrifice would be enough to appease the hungry crowd. It wasn't.

The other patrons were appalled, even Harriet Simpson. "That's true," one said. "An almost dead adulteress."

"That dress is such an unpleasant reminder. I can hardly bear to look," said another.

"And the morning was going so well."

They stared and hissed, like old hens poised, ready to peck. How one dress could cause such a fuss Girly would never know. Her only comfort was Dead Hilary was her distant cousin. She tried to slip away quietly, leaving the old birds to feed off Dead Hilary's haunting memory, but a quiet departure was not to be.

There was no discreet way to leave the market. In the excitement, her trolley succumbed to its injuries, Aunt Lily's hat seemed to have grown, and the heel of Girly's shoe caught between two rotting boards. Lottie and The Thief broke their conversation and turned towards the commotion. The voluptuous wench glowered. Fleeing the ravenous birds of the market only to be scorned on the street didn't seem much like the coronation of a fairy princess.

Girly locked gaze with The Thief. She dared him to think of her as a scullery maid. She was no less than his sweet Lottie! His face wrinkled as if he were puzzled. But Girly was not dissuaded! She could turn his fair-haired melon her way if she longed to, except at that moment she didn't long to. If he wanted to slither into indiscretion, he would have to do it with his vixen Lottie. Inspired, Girly dislodged her shoe, straightened, as best she could the bent wheel of her trolley, pushed back the hat and marched home.

Chapter Fourteen

ON HER way home, Girly let herself disappear. It was her only escape. Now she was always Aunt Lily's niece, or Dead Hilary's cousin, but in her mind she still had her old name, her own identity and place in the world, and she was cared for. Daphne's arm was draped in hers while they passed judgment on all who went by. Things felt the way they used to. Girly was a brick again. Her skin prickled. She wore short black gloves with a fitted riding jacket and britches. Quite a rebellious look, as she was not at the stables. What was more important, she could cast a shadow even the grocer's wife would envy.

As her imagination filled her thoughts, her world changed. It became fuller and somehow familiar. Forget faded and her home in Rosedale came into view. She could see the manicured flower beds and trees. The smell of sweet peas and petunias. Hired help gave her and Daphne a wide berth. They knew better than to approach them.

"Good morning," she said to the imaginary group of young men as she passed. "Lovely day isn't it?"

"Yes it is, Miss," one of them answered, doffing his hat.

Girly and Daphne greeted several admirers in the same manner, they waved to some, and others they let kiss their gloved hands. It was quite exhausting. Girly led her beautiful, but lame white mount, which of course was the injured trolley. She felt grateful, she only had to stop twice to tend his needs.

Girly twisted her body back and forth to match the rhythm of the breeze. She breathed deeply and hummed with the birds. It was a great day!

When she realized she had an observer, it was too late. He was waiting for her by the front gate, and he was whistling.

Chapter Fifteen

As he swung the gate open for her, The Rose Thief, Aunt Lily's Lothario, smiled and raised a taunting eyebrow. Girly knew he had been watching. At that moment, she wished Lottie and her ever-expanding hips would be his for eternity, but her attention was quickly drawn away.

"O for a Muse of fire, that would ascend the brightest heaven of invention. A kingdom for a stage, princes to act and monarchs to behold the swelling scene!"

There on the front veranda, for all to see, Aunt Lily was reciting Shakespeare! And she was reciting it loudly! Girly froze. How many times a day could she be mortified?

The Ford sisters and a few of the neighbours were standing among Aunt Lily's prize roses. Girly thought they were brave. A misstep to the left or right might cause one of them to trod on an unsuspecting plant and thus to lose a limb—or to be more specific for her aunt to take one. Bright handkerchiefs waved through the air in her aunt's direction as the pack vibrated with what Girly could only assume was excitement. She supposed there hadn't been much live theatre since the war, as they appeared enthralled by Lily the Actress. Even though this was late morning, Girly assumed brandy had been their beverage of choice.

"Then should the warlike Harry, like himself, assume the port of Mars; and at his heels leash'd in like hounds, should famine, sword and fire crouch for employment." Aunt Lily took care to enunciate each syllable, pausing at times for dramatic effect. Her hands were like claws, holding the kingdom of which she spoke.

"I think that's *Henry V*," said The Thief, seemingly impressed.

"Don't encourage her," Girly said, and then she added more to herself than to her companion, "At least she's not nude, that's a comfort."

"A horse, a horse! My kingdom for a horse." Aunt Lily dropped to her hands and knees and could only be seen though the slats in the railing. She crawled to the entrance of the veranda. Her eyes nearly bulged out of her head.

"No, it's Richard the III."

"Or perhaps she's delirious," Girly snapped. She looked her companion up and down. "How would you know? Who made you an expert on Shakespeare?"

"I live beyond Grand Avenue," he said as if the answer should be obvious. "It's almost compulsory."

Aunt Lily stood, arched her back and walked on her tiptoes across the length of the veranda. Her arms were curved in the air above her head, fingers pointed.

"Or maybe it's ballet."

"Oh just shut up."

With an abrupt turn Aunt Lily's eyes narrowed and her voice rose in wild shrills toward the heavens. Her arms waved frantically and her untamed hair fell in heavy heaps upon her shoulders. Girly wondered if her aunt was having some kind of fit.

"Uh, opera?"

Girly had had enough. Her parents couldn't expect her to idly sit by while her aunt went out of her way to humiliate her. They wouldn't have put up with such behavior. They'd have had Aunt Lily committed. Girly was about to strangle someone when the Thief leaned over and whispered, "You and your aunt have quite a bit in common."

"We do?"

"I hope you're not offended," he apologized. "It's just you're both such stimulating women."

"Stimulating. Is that what you call it?"

He opened his mouth and then closed it again. It was as if words had failed him.

Girly could feel her temperature rising and the red in her cheeks deepening. Her eyes narrowed and he blushed. He didn't appear quite so clever, and she didn't feel quite so dreamy. It wasn't the way Girly imagined their next encounter would be, but it was consistent with everything else in her life of late. In her opinion, there wasn't a lot to be said for consistency.

At that moment, Aunt Lily came bounding off the step. "Lothario, Lothario, where art thou Lothario?"

A little confused the Thief dropped to one knee. "But soft, what light through yonder window breaks? It is the east and Lilyiet is the sun!

Rolling her eyes, Girly bit her lip. Would this morning never end?

"Do my eyes deceive me or is my Sunday bonnet atop a strumpet's head?" Aunt Lily took the tone of one of Macbeth's witches.

Girly gasped and brought her hands to her throat. This wasn't a line from any play she had attended. Even the old bard couldn't have been that accurate at foreshadowing.

"Yet there it sits, with no qualms for the lice ridden pate for which it has so well acquainted itself." Aunt Lily leaned over and flicked the hat with the tip of her finger. "Can such an offence go unnoticed? Who will rise and defend the hapless bonnet?"

The Thief stood and brushed the dirt from his knees. "But doesn't even a lice-ridden head deserve a reprieve from the sun? Does thou not have that much grace?"

Girly jabbed him in the ribs.

"Ouch. What did you do that for?"

"She's talking about me."

"I thought we were just bantering."

Aunt Lily dropped her gaze. Her fingers curled and as she spoke her words were peppered with spittle. "And of the dress! What say ye of the dress? Is it too a protection from the sun or is it a dishonour to the nearly dead?"

Hands clasped behind his back the Thief circled Girly. "I'd say the dress favours the girl. It could not do as much for the almost dead."

"So tell me this, why does the wearer blush? Dost she not feel the disgrace of her actions? The prick of her ill intentions?"

They both turned and faced Girly. If she was blushing before, she was boiling now. She didn't want to be a part of their impromptu performance. It was humiliating.

Aunt Lily blinked slowly. "Do you feel no shame?"

"I do now!" Girly stammered. "But that's what you wanted wasn't it? It's what you've wanted ever since I've arrived."

"That's not in the script." Aunt Lily broke character, snatched the hat off Girly's head and threw it to the ground. "You can't just add things willy-nilly. It's not done. Go back out the gate and let's start again."

The neighbours began clapping wildly. "Bravo, bravo," they shouted in unison. "A command performance, darling. We've seen no better."

Aunt Lily waved her hand at them. "Not now, I'll tell you when to clap." The applause abruptly ceased.

"I'm not going to be part of this." Girly crossed her arms and prepared herself for her aunt's response.

"You're not going to be a part of this? I get out of my death bed and you're not going to be part of this?" Aunt Lily shook her head. "It takes all kinds."

Girly stepped toward her aunt. They were toe to toe. "You're not on your death bed."

"Well, not now. I'm in my yard entertaining the neighbours."
She turned and waved. "Which I might add, was going
rather well until you botched things up."

"You would like me to participate in your little," Girly
waved her hands in the air, "whatever this is?"

"If you would be so kind."

The only thing Girly could think of was a poem she had
memorized for one of her mother's many fundraisers.
It might have been one of Shakespeare's but she didn't
remember. She pinned her shoulders back and looked past
her aunt.

Crabbed age and youth cannot live together:
Youth is full of pleasance, age is full of care;
Youth like summer morn, age like winter weather;
Youth like summer brave, age like winter bare.
Youth is full of sport, age's breath is short;
Youth is nimble, age is lame;
Youth is hot and bold, age is weak and cold;
Youth is wild, and age is tame.
Age, I do abhor thee; youth, I do adore thee;
O, my love, my love is young!
Age, I do defy thee: O, sweet shepherd, hie thee,
For me thinks thou stay'st too long.

Aunt Lily stared; her jaw seemed unhinged. Girly had never
had anyone look at her that way. It was if her aunt had seen
all her worst parts at once and was rendered speechless.
After a slow breath Aunt Lily regained her composure, and
to Girly's relief, continued as if the poem had been part of
the performance. "Where ignorance is bliss, 'tis folly to be
wise." Aunt Lily raised an eyebrow and waited.

Girly tried to think of another poem or at least a line from
a poem that could follow her aunt's but nothing came to
mind.

Aunt Lily lost what little patience she possessed. "I'm
dying, you rude child. Just like you wished for in that poem
of yours." She sucked in her nostrils. "Anyone of standing

79

knows that and yet you recite that poem as if brandishing a blade. You might as well dig my grave while you're at it."

"She's not from around here," The Thief said.

"If she were, she'd know how much I suffer. Day and night I lie awake writhing in agony, my joints stiffen and rigor mortis sets in. I'm a tired old woman. But when I die," Aunt Lily continued, her eyes narrow slits, "I'm sure my kind niece will wear my dresses to the market—maybe even all of them at the same time."

"And I'm sure she will look as lovely as she does today."

At this, Aunt Lily scowled. "And the worm has turned." Her lips tightened until they almost disappeared. "I've never expected much from you, Lothario, but defending her, after what she's just said, that's scraping the bottom of the barrel."

Girly wished the ground would open and swallow her whole. Her imaginary walk with Daphne now felt childish. Pretending to be admired by others, dismissing the hired help. She let out a loud sob; she was the hired help. It all seemed so silly now. Even her poem. What kind of person wished an old woman a speedier death? And she had wished it in front of the neighbours. At least they had thought it was part of some kind of performance, but the Thief, he knew the truth.

"I don't want to be a part of this anymore." Aunt Lily's lips trembled. "Girly Maid, fetch me a glass of water and don't dawdle."

When Girly turned to leave, the Thief caught hold of her arm. "May I see you again?" he asked.

"Why? I'm sure you can find better ways of occupying your time."

"You think so do you?" He chuckled. "But I still want to see you."

"Why? What reason would you have for seeing me?"

"You're refreshing."

Chapter Sixteen

GIRLY TRUDGED up the stairs to her room. The thought of cool sheets and a good night's sleep appealed to her. She just wanted to get the fiasco between The Thief and Aunt Lily out of her mind. If she could, she would take up drinking.

As she pulled on her nightdress, Girly couldn't help but consider her mother. She closed her eyes and imagined the quiet rap on her door, her mother slipping into her room with a brush in hand. The two sitting on the edge of the bed while Girly's mother combed and braided her hair. Sometimes they sat quietly listening to the stillness; but there were others when they talked about the day. Girly wanted to feel the weight of the brush on her scalp, how the bristles dug in. To smell the scent of her mother's perfume. The edge of Girly's bed at home showed the woman's dedication. It was permanently indented by her rather round bottom.

But what Girly missed most of all is what her mother would whisper before slipping out of her room. "You are a wonder to me." The words stilled her heart. "Not every wonder is the star of Bethlehem you know. Some are just gifts that should have never been ours."

These fragments of her old life lapped into the reality of

her new one. She questioned if her mother had any idea what she was being subjected to. Did she care? Did she know who her daughter was becoming? A guttersnipe. So much of her life no longer made sense. But there had to be an answer somewhere. Something that would piece the puzzle of her existence together.

The letters, of course. Girly squinted in the dark towards the highboy. She had promised Harriet she would read at least two of them, but she had put it off until the end of the day. She was afraid she might be disappointed. She didn't think she could bear to be let down again. Yet the letters called her from where they were tucked away. It was as if they wanted to tell her their secrets. By habit, Girly reached for a lamp on the bedside table, but then she remembered this was Forget, not Toronto; there were no electric lamps here. And if Aunt Lily had anything to do with it there wouldn't be any anytime soon: she saw it as a dubious invention, some carnival gimmick.

With a sigh Girly lit a candle and retrieved the next letter in the stack, she would save the third for tomorrow. The envelope read *open me in seven days*. Seven days had long since passed. She looked at it with trepidation; it couldn't make her predicament any worse. With care she opened the envelope, as if this act of respect would somehow make the contents more promising.

> My dear one,
>
> You must have so many questions, but I'm not sure I have the answers. It's been many years since I have seen your aunt, my sister. She was quite different then. Bitterness hadn't festered in her so. As a child, I would sit on her knee and she would take me to the wild places of her imagination, and they were wild. Dragons and monsters of every shape and colour. Together we conquered them all. Despite our age difference, we were quite a team. You see, she was already nine when I was born. A young girl, ready to take on the world.
>
> The year of my tenth birthday Lily was engaged. I can remember

how happy she was. It was a side I had never seen in her before. She even made her own wedding dress. At the time I thought it was the most beautiful dress I'd seen. It was creamy satin covered with dotted swiss tulle and Brussels lace. Wax orange blossom lined the seam where the tulle met the lace and curled around one of the sleeves. I used to sneak into Lily's closet just to smell the blossoms.

My parents did not approve of the match or the marriage, but Lily had her heart set on him. She barricaded herself in her room, saying she wouldn't come out unless they yielded. My father said she could starve. My mother said the house hadn't been so peaceful for years. It was a standoff. But in the end Lily didn't starve and Father didn't yield. Lily's love died when he was thrown from his horse. I think years earlier he had fought in the Red River Rebellion or something. He was Metis.

After his death Lily said she would have no other. She'd disappear for days. No one ever knew where she went and she never spoke of it. In time, her wandering stopped, and she dedicated her life to taking care of our parents. I don't think it made her happy, but she was content. As content as Lily can be. And I'm sure by now you have discovered that being content can border on insanity.

Oh, but I do miss sitting on her knee. Her eyes would snap as she told her wild stories and tales of secret loves. It helped shape me.

I trust this will help you have a better understanding of her. Parts of her past are quite tragic. Be patient with her. And hold my love close.

Always in my thoughts,

Your loving mother

Girly read the letter twice before snuffing out the candle. In the dark she touched the words on the page. She could feel what her mother had written and, for the first time since coming to Forget, her mother was with her, making an invisible indentation on the bed. Girly reached for the spot and began to cry.

Chapter Seventeen

SWEET PEA;

Your father and I are probably on the island now. He wants to see for himself the totem poles Emily Carr painted. We thought travelling might make our separation from you bearable. In theory perhaps, but in reality I think it is highly unlikely.

I think explaining a bit of our family history might help put things into perspective for you. Your grandfather was one of the founding members of Forget. He was there before the railway, before roads, stores or any form of modern comfort. Back then the place was called Uytdewilligen. Almost impossible to remember, so when anyone was asked what this new settlement was called or how it was spelled, the response was usually forget. It stuck.

Being a founder meant your grandfather was instrumental in how much of the town was laid out. Our home, the one Lily lives in now, was one of the first to be built. It was quite grand in its time. Not a tar paper shack as so many around it were back then. Your grandmother insisted on that. But as the town grew and prospered the grand homes became much grander. They were no longer built on the east side of Main Street. They were built on the west side of Grand Avenue. Your grandfather refused to move or rebuild no matter how your grandmother pleaded. I think as Lily aged, and became who she is, even your grandmother realized the east side of Main Street was a better fit.

I'm not sure how to explain the naming of the streets but I will do my best. There used to be a family by the name of Smith. I'm not sure if they're still there. They came to Forget shortly after your grandfather. Mr. Smith was almost insufferable; his wife was even worse. They wanted the town to have a system based on class. I suppose it might resemble something feudal. Your grandfather disagreed. The Smiths firmly planted west of Grand Avenue, began putting up sign posts to identify new streets. The first was 'Am I My Brother's Keeper?' Your grandfather responded by 'Love they neighbour as they self.' It was all downhill from there. Finally, when your grandfather put up the marker 'Roland Smith, le Peteur,' he didn't do it because he had any admiration for Roland. He did it as a sign of defiance. He hoped it would burn the tongues of the Grand Avenue residents every time they said it.

When I married, your grandfather gave the bulk of his wealth to me. He had family money as well as the investments he made in Forget. The properties in Forget became Lily's upon the death of both our parents. It might surprise you that Lily owns much of Main Street. She owns the livery and the grocers as well as the feed mill. I think she still might own the bakery on Grand Avenue but I'm not sure. Half a dozen houses east of Main Street are hers as well. They are all managed by the banker.

This might explain her standing in the community. Anger with her is often limited, or maybe contained is a better word.

I hope this helps, my darling. Only six week left. I pray we can all survive it.

All my love,

Your Mother.

Chapter Eighteen

GIRLY WAS still mulling over her mother's words as she and Aunt Lily were walking home the following Sunday. *Just six week left* she kept repeating to herself, the words were strangely liberating. She couldn't imagine Aunt Lily could do or say anything to take it away.

"I've been raising poultry since I was a child," said Aunt Lily in a voice that carried a moustache at its edges. "Not just any kind of poultry mind you, only the foreign ones with the best of pedigrees."

"I didn't know poultry had pedigrees."

"There's a lot you don't know."

As they walked, Aunt Lily went through her chickens' lineage and many accomplishments and inventions. "You know the hen that scratches twice before she pecks?"

Girly nodded, although she was unaware of the pecking rituals of Aunt Lily's chickens.

"Her name is Sofia and all her scratching isn't just for show. She is sending messages to her fellow fowl. I haven't quite deciphered them yet, but I'm close."

Girly remembered what her mother had said about Aunt Lily being eccentric, and she smiled.

"You know the spotted hen that stands next to her, almost as if she is keeping guard?"

Again, Girly nodded.

"Well, that one took three days to hatch. I was about to give up on her, but then there she was, full of surprises. Did you know she can tell when the weather is going to turn?"

"No."

"She can. She runs around in circles madly flapping her wings. Once she flapped so hard she passed out. It flooded that night. Now the neighbours come over just to have a look. That's how they know if they need to head for higher ground." Aunt Lily paused and waited. Girly wasn't sure for what, until she was hit in the shin with the cane. "I have enlightened you with some of the most amazing marvels of our time, and you say nothing!"

Girly flinched as the cane waved through the air, but she wasn't sure how she was supposed to marvel at the marvels. She folded her hands and did her best to look reverent.

Upon reaching their gated yard, Aunt Lily turned and faced her niece. "Your generation has a lot to learn about grandeur. If you can't see it out of your bedroom window, then it's unlikely you will see it at all." She stepped through the gate and bent to smell a rose. "At least Girly Gardener hasn't given all my roses away. Where is she anyway?"

Girly shrugged.

Aunt Lily pulled a weed. "Look at that! Inefficiency will be the ruin of me."

When the old woman straightened, she seemed to spy something out of the corner of her eye. There amongst her roses were two of her prize-laying hens, motionless. Aunt Lily's hands came to her breast as she fell to her knees. "That's what Sofia was trying to tell me yesterday. But I ignored her. I thought she was exaggerating. Even laughed at her. How could a hen know about an assassination? I ask you that. How?" She reached a weak hand towards her niece. "My heart pills, get me my heart pills."

Girly looked down at her aunt writhing at her feet. "You don't have any heart pills."

Aunt Lily frowned. "Get me something that looks like a pill."

When Girly returned, she handed Aunt Lily a clove of garlic and a glass of water. Aunt Lily was delighted. "Good, now you're thinking. Can't be too safe. Keep my heart strong and chase away whatever evil lurks nearby." Her eyes narrowed. "Evil always seems attracted to dead chickens."

After chewing and swallowing her garlic, Aunt Lily crawled to her fallen hens. She kissed their combs and held their limp bodies on her lap. "We leave the house for a couple of hours and see what happens? Senseless violence."

"I don't see any signs of violence. I think they may have just toppled over."

"Hand me my cane," Aunt Lily snapped. Taking her cane, she whacked her niece in the shin. "Just because you can't see it doesn't mean it's not there."

Girly rubbed her shin. "I didn't realize you had such an unhealthy attachment to your poultry."

"Yes, unusual I know, but touching all the same."

It wasn't until Girly had almost finished plucking the second of Aunt Lily's fervently mourned hens one began to stir. It opened its eyes and clucked.

Aunt Lily flew out of the kitchen when she heard it. "It's a miracle. A miracle!" Sweeping the naked bird up in her arms, she twirled it in the air. The hen burped.

"Oh my," said Girly. "I didn't know chickens could do that."

Aunt Lily stopped short and wrinkled her nose in disgust. "Mine usually don't." Her brow furrowed and she looked towards the Fords'. "Those two have done it again. How many times do I have to tell them?" Setting the chicken down, she stormed out the gate and to the neighbours'.

Girly wanted to warn the Fords, to tell them to pack a bag and run for the hills. She couldn't see any good coming from this. On the Ford's doorstep she could hear the sisters invite her aunt in for tea. They said they were delighted to see her on a non-picketing day. Once Aunt Lily had stepped inside the Ford's house though, and the door was closed, the only thing Girly could do was wait. She could only imagine what was happening within the confines of that home; her only hope was the Fords would make it out with all their limbs properly attached.

A breeze stirred and Girly turned her head. She was sure she had heard her father, his voice on a puff of wind. "Gunga Din, come look." Girly squatted amongst her aunt's roses. She watched as an ant dragged a dead earthworm along the path. "Why do you call me Gunga Din?" she asked. "Did you want a boy?"

The breeze shifted. "No, never a boy."

"Then why?"

"You are more than they think you are."

Emma, Ella and Aunt Lily came clambering out of the Ford's house. There was a headlong dash back to Aunt Lily's. "Get behind me, Satans," Aunt Lily yelled, but the Fords paid her no heed. The three arrived at the gate simultaneously and squeezed through the opening. Aunt Lily tried to jostle the sisters out of the way with her cane, the Ford's, hair flying, pushed past her and reached the chickens first. "The poor dears," Ella knelt down to examine the birds. The foul were nestled on the ground side by side clucking at one another.

"They're so misguided. Must be the company they keep." Emma glanced at Aunt Lily and then at Girly.

"It's not the company they keep," snapped Aunt Lily. "You left your cellar door ajar again and my girls got into whatever intoxicating concoction you're brewing down there. They're drunk."

"I have to agree," said Girly somewhat offended. "I've done nothing to influence my aunt's poultry."

Emma raised an eyebrow, "To the best of your knowledge."

"It's not our alcohol," said Ella. "It would be unbecoming

for us to brew things in our cellar. It may even be illegal. We're not sure. We haven't been arrested yet."

"No," said Emma. "Thank the Lord. Neither of us looks good in stripes."

"That's why Emma and I tend to think of it as accidentally fermented berries."

"Yes, Ella's right. Alcohol and drunk are such harsh words. Almost like judgments. It's not very Christian to judge. I would rather say your hens have a bit more cluck in their cackle."

"Call it what you like, they're as drunk as a priest at communion!" Aunt Lily thumped her cane on the ground.

"Aunt Lily is right." Girly stood beside her aunt. She never thought they would be united in anything, yet here they were battling the Fords.

"Oh, those old gals were just having a good time, letting their feathers down," said Ella. "They can't be worried about egg production all the time."

"Quite right, Sister. Besides, there is no finer day than Sunday to be free and let the wind blow through your feathers."

"Free or not, they are naked," Aunt Lily squawked, widening her eyes until it seemed they would pop. "Their feathers have been plucked. It may seem fine to you to see my hens lollygagging about like the whores of Babylon, but it is not fine with me! Unlike you, I am respected in this community. I set the standard.

"If the common people see I allow my chickens not only to drink but also to flaunt their indiscretions, what would they think? There would be drunkenness everywhere. Horses, cows, pigs and God knows what else. The town would be lost!"

Emma stared, perplexed. "How would one salvage a shameless chicken?" she asked, putting a finger to her chin.

"Quite right," said Ella. "The virtue of poultry has never been discussed in any of our committee meetings."

"Quite a dilemma."

"Quite a dilemma indeed."

It was a situation the Fords had never anticipated. "Oh, Ella, are you thinking what I'm thinking?"

"Maybe. I was thinking how nice it would be if Grandma were still alive."

"Because she'd know what to do?"

"No, it would just be nice."

Emma smiled and patted her sister's arm. "I was thinking about the chickens, dear."

"What about them?"

"Perhaps we could find something for them in our knitting."

Soon, the hens were sporting the finest clothing an orphan could wish. One was resplendent in bright red suspenders with a blue sweater and black knitted skirt, while the other modeled a red and white ensemble. Aunt Lily was uncharacteristically pleased. She held her hands over her heart and flushed with pride. The pride lasted all the way to the next Sunday.

Chapter Nineteen

AUNT LILY and Girly arrived at church together and took residence in Aunt Lily's usual haunt, the back pew. The organist was already pounding on the keyboard like an unhinged lunatic. Aunt Lily said she must be plotting revenge on her husband. As the church filled, Aunt Lily called to different members of the congregation. She started with the grocer's wife. "Isn't that the same hat you wear every Sunday?"

The grocer's wife went about greeting other members of the congregation and gave no consideration to Aunt Lily. Girly grabbed her aunt's arm. "Do you have to do that?"

"What?"

"Yell at people."

"Do you think the grocer's wife is going to come over here and talk to me? I don't think so. How else am I going to tell her that hat is unflattering?"

Girly wasn't sure how to respond. When she was with her parents, church was always a tranquil place. But with her aunt, church and tranquility seemed to be stark opposites, even enemies. Girly did her best to contain her frustration; she drew a deep breath. But when her aunt climbed up on the pew beside her it was too much. "Get down from there."

Aunt Lily frowned at her niece. "What else do you want me to do? I've been forbidden to go behind the pulpit."

Girly tugged on the hem of her aunt's dress. "You're making a scene."

"I'm not the one making a scene. You are."

It wasn't until one of Forget's more upstanding families—the banker, his new bride and their eleven-pound, premature baby—strolled into the church their attention shifted. Aunt Lily eyed up the banker's wife as if she were her next meal. Girly tightened her grip on the hem of Aunt Lily's dress. If her aunt didn't yield, she didn't care if she pulled so hard she ripped the dress at the seam.

The grocer's wife waddled over to examine the babe. "He has his father's hands," she cooed over the wailing infant.

The banker's wife smiled at each comment. She pulled the babe closer to smell his hair and whisper in his ear. The better part of the congregation touched or kissed the baby, as though it were a ritual of acceptance.

Then, by chance, a small Tucker brushed the babe's porcelain hand. The small boy was climbing over pews to get to where his family were already seated. There was an audible gasp throughout the building.

"What is it?" asked Girly.

"It's an unspoken rule. The unwashed woods, don't touch the washed bricks. Poverty has become a disease of circumstance. The bankers will take it as a bad omen." Aunt Lily smiled. "Isn't life grand?"

The minister came in through a side door and took his place behind the pulpit. He stared at Aunt Lily until she climbed down from the pew and took her seat. Once seated, she pursed her lips as if she had always been prim and proper and would certainly not do anything untoward. When the service started Aunt Lily eyes widened. She looked like a kid in school who knew all the answers. The minister did his best to avoid her eager attention. It must have been the only sermon Aunt Lily didn't sleep through. Girly found it disconcerting. She could feel her aunt coil beside her like a spring waiting to explode.

The usual hymns and scripture readings were given up as sacrifices on the altar, to what Girly hoped was a forgiving God. And when the time came, the minister called forward the banker's family. He held up the banker's baby for all to admire. "Here is the newest member of the congregation," said the minister. "Isn't he a handsome boy?"

Aunt Lily stood so fast Girly was afraid she would launch herself through the air. "Girly says she's seen better dressed chickens. She should know, she's from Toronto." Aunt Lily looked down at her niece and smiled as if she had done her some kind of favour.

If she could have, Girly would have become a chameleon and melted into the pew, but as it was, her only option was to blush and shrink down into her seat.

All around her there was a well-blended mixture of chuckles and guffaws, but the oddest response came from the Ford sisters. "Amen to that," said Emma. "But you can't expect a newborn to have the fashion sense of a fully grown hen."

"That's right," Ella agreed. "It is really an unfair comparison."

Chapter Twenty

IT WAS several days before Aunt Lily's finely dressed poultry expired. It was a drawn out event, involving a candlelit prayer vigil. Girly was relieved when it was over, although she never told her aunt.

"We have to wait three days before we can bury them," said Aunt Lily as she tried to place pennies on their eyes. "Just like a Christian funeral."

"Where will we put them until then?"

"In the icebox."

"I don't think there is room, unless we throw something out."

Aunt Lily thought for a moment. "For humans three days may be required but for chickens things are entirely different. They can't count."

Girly had never been to a wake for chickens. It was quite an experience; one she thought she might write Daphne about, but then decided against it. She didn't think she'd believe her. Aunt Lily even wore widow's weeds and a weeping vail. Girly thought it must have belonged to her Grandmother as the outfit had to be from the last century.

"Don't you think they're impeccably dressed?" said Aunt Lily, looking at the two hens lying in roasters. She bustled around fluffing their dresses and powdering their small cheeks. "It gives one reason to reflect."

"Reflect on what?" Girly asked.

"On dressing impeccably, you ninny! Now run tell Girly Cook to stay out of the kitchen. I don't want her getting any ideas."

The morning took on a life of its own. Besides having to go upstairs to change several times, Girly was given many strange tasks. One was to ask the minister to toll the bell once for each hen. The minister groaned before giving his response. "Miss Lily sent you?"

"Yes."

"And this is not some kind of prank?"

"No."

"Well, you can tell your aunt that it will be a cold day in hell before I toll the church bell for a couple of dead chickens."

"She's not in a very good mood. Are you sure that is what you want to say?"

Scratching his chin the minister reflected. "Yes," he finally said.

When Girly told Aunt Lily what the minister had said, the old woman shook her head and clicked her tongue. "The man has no compassion."

To compensate, Aunt Lily had Girly Cook stand on the back porch and bang a large pot. The response was marginal, but to Girly's surprise the Fords and the Tuckers attended. As they gathered around the roasters, Emma sniffed. "They were so young and beautiful."

"Yes, it was quite unexpected," returned Ella. "We were thinking of writing them into our wills."

"That's right, Ella. They seemed like part of the family. Why just the other night I said, 'Sister, what do you suppose we should knit those young birds for Christmas?'"

"How true."

"Sadly," Ella sniffed, "I've already ordered the wool."

Aunt Lily nodded, lifted her veil and wiped her nose on the edge of the tablecloth.

Ella touched Aunt Lily on the shoulder. "Be strong. As the saying goes, there are many hens in the barnyard."

"Oh, that's not how the saying goes, Sister."

"It's not?"

"No, if my memory serves me right, it's something about fish in the sea. There are many fish in the sea."

"I don't think that is very fitting, Ella."

"Why not?"

"In the sea, chickens would drown. The saying would have to go something like, many dead chickens in the sea."

"That's not very comforting is it? I wish I had never brought it up."

"That's okay," sobbed Aunt Lily. "I didn't expect any better from the two of you."

The Tuckers didn't say much. Three younger boys, Girly had yet to meet, joined the ranks of their brothers. Alexander slung the youngest on his hip while two others hugged his legs as if they were tree trunks. For the most part, the Tuckers stayed near the edges of the room. Only when Mean Dog Joe darted out to snatch food from the table was there movement.

Aunt Lily smiled and invited them to fill their pockets. But the invitation was ignored. Girly wondered if they boys were waiting for her aunt to pelt them with cookies.

"No one else is coming." Aunt Lily's tone was sharp. "Apparently in this town greatness isn't recognized."

A small Tucker in threadbare pants tied at the waist with twine, unwrapped himself from Alexander's leg and sidled up beside Aunt Lily. He tugged on her sleeve.

"What do you want, dear?" she asked, as sweetly as she could.

The boy pointed at the roaster as he rested his chin or her knee.

Yes," encouraged Aunt Lily.

The boy hesitated.

Aunt Lily reached down and stroked his hair. "Now's not the day to be frightened, son. Ask for whatever you want."

"They do look lovely, Miss Lily."

"That they do."

"Pa say there ain't no finer looking chickens."

"That's true."

The boy leaned into her and twisted her sleeve between his fingers.

"Well?"

"I am awful hungry."

"And?"

"When are we going to eat those chickens in the pretty pink dresses?"

Aunt Lily gasped and cracked him with her cane.

Chapter Twenty-one

BREEZY SPRING days turned into smouldering summer nights and to Girly's relief Aunt Lily rarely wept openly for the chickens anymore. It had dwindled down to just the occasional whimper. As for Forget, it braced itself for its annual Sunday School Picnic. Girly Maid, with a picnic shopping list in hand, headed for the market. When she rounded Main Street she heard cries of, "We're one in the eyes of God." It was the woods calling over to the bricks. The bricks, for their part, turned their backs on the woods. Girly knew, after reading her mother's last letter, they were probably praying it wasn't true.

The picnic took place on a hill in Forget's oldest churchyard; the only yard that ventured east of Main Street. Shooting stars and tiger lilies dotted its deceptively steep slope while lady slippers hid in the shade of the willows and poplars that defined its borders. The church had long ago burnt down but the outhouse still stood at attention. Leaning mind you, but attention all the same. It was the street the churchyard occupied that Girly found ironic. *No Rest for the Wicked*. It didn't trouble the Townspeople though. They spread over the hillside like a colourful quilt.

That day Aunt Lily seemed to be particularly lucid. Girly

stood beside her while her aunt perused her surroundings. The way the old woman tapped her finger on her chin made Girly nervous. It was as if she was surmising what havoc she could inflict on her fellow citizens. Aunt Lily's eyes twinkled, so Girly assumed she surmised much.

Her first victim was the grocer's wife. A watermelon had been placed on the edge of the grocer's picnic blanket. Aunt Lily gave it a sharp poke with her cane as she passed by. The melon, at first, wobbled harmlessly down the hill but as the slope increased the melon began to roll as if it had been shot out of a canon. The grocer's wife was in hot pursuit, the watermelon plummeting down the hill toward a cluster of Grand Avenue ladies daintily sipping tea.

Aunt Lily was in her element. She clicked her tongue as if the descending watermelon was a great mishap. Girly was horrified. She tugged on her aunt's arm but the old woman planted her heels like the roots of a tree. If she couldn't drag her aunt away, Girly knew she had to make the best of the situation; it might make up for her thespian faux pas.

"Lucky for you I am here," Aunt Lily said as she yanked her arm away from her niece and addressed the grocer. "A natural-born eunuch such as yourself needs instructing." She pursed her lips as if giving the present situation careful thought. "I think she's calling for you but I'm not sure. Her voice has always sounded like the shriek of a dying cat. It grates on one, you know."

"Well, maybe not a dying cat," countered Girly. "Just a suffering one."

The grocer was unresponsive. His attention was on the watermelon. It careened down the hill as if it didn't have a care in the world. His wife cursed as she ran after it. Mothers shrieked and covered their children's ears. And just before the melon reached its target, the grocer's wife hurled herself upon it. As Girly watched she was sure time slowed. The watermelon never stood a chance.

"I'm assuming she was never a dancer," Aunt Lily

interjected. "Does she give herself to you with such abandon?"

The thought seemed to frighten the grocer. His hands began to tremble and blotches formed on his cheeks.

"Don't frighten the man," Girly said.

After collecting her wayward watermelon, the grocer's wife began the long ascent back to her picnic blanket. Her neatly pinned bun was now loose and her hair fanned wildly around her face. Grass stains adorned her skirt where her knees had hit the ground, and the veins in her neck pulsed.

"I would say she looks somewhat like a harlot," Aunt Lily said to the grocer. "A bit heavy on the rouge."

"That's not rouge!" stammered the grocer. "She is red from the chase."

"He's right." Girly said. "If he wasn't, with all that flailing and perspiration she'd be more of a mess then she is now." She smiled at the grocer, sure that he would appreciate her support. But the look he gave her was one of contempt, as if he thought she was in league with her aunt.

"That's a relief." Aunt Lily let out a sigh as if she had been holding her breath. "She would have made an ugly harlot. Would have died of starvation, and then who would have stopped the watermelon?"

When the grocer's wife was within earshot Aunt Lily called to her. "Your disposition isn't very sunny, and I daresay not suitable for a Sunday picnic." Her words were sing-songy, as if meant as encouragement. "And your husband is right. You make a terrible looking harlot."

The grocer's wife didn't seem to be in an encouraging mood, and taking her watermelon in both hands she raised it above her head and flung it through the air towards the spot where Aunt Lily had stood. But it was to no avail; Aunt Lily had already slipped into the crowd.

"That, my dear," she whispered to Girly, "was cheap entertainment."

Girly felt the blood drain from her face. She was a part

of it. She was part of the humiliation of the Grocer's Wife. Although she didn't care for the woman, she didn't need the bricks to know it. They judged the woods enough. Now they knew she was one of them.

Chapter Twenty-two

A GROUP of women gathered around the grocer's wife. Girly could hear their scolding tongues from where she stood. So did Aunt Lily, who kept smiling and waving at them. Girly wanted to get her aunt as far away as possible. At least then they could be the watchers and not the observed.

The trick, for Girly, was to try to make it feel like Aunt Lily's idea. "Where would you like to sit?"

Aunt Lily wrinkled her nose. "I'm not sure." She looked around. "How about up there under that elm tree? It looks nice, lots of shade."

The spot seemed perfect to Girly. It was the furthest point from the grocer's wife. As she lugged her aunt's handbag, picnic basket and quilt, while avoiding ant hills, Aunt Lily used her cane to swat at small children who happened to get too close.

"This is a Sunday school picnic," Girly reminded her.

"And you know what they say, suffer the little children."

Girly was sure her aunt was taking something out of context but was not in the mood to argue with her. A small cluster of older women had already taken refuge under the tree. They were seated liked an aged harem on an Aladdin's carpet of mix-matched throws and quilts. The Fords yoo-hooed at Aunt Lily as she crested the hill. Emma pointed to a spot where Girly could lay their quilt.

The ladies sat interspersed among plates of sandwiches, pint sealers of preserves, sweets and quart jars of lemonade. As Girly slipped into the knot, she nodded at Emma and Ella.

Harriet Simpson squeezed her arm, "Nice to see you're still alive," she whispered. Girly smiled. The two women sitting on the edge looked away as Girly took her place.

"I saw the commotion," Emma took a flask from her garter, poured a good jot into a quart of lemonade before passing the quart to her sister.

"Yes," said Ella. "Will that woman ever learn? Each year she places her watermelon on the edge of her picnic blanket and each year Miss Lily pokes it with her cane."

Aunt Lily scrunched her shoulders. "Except this year I called her a harlot."

"Will wonders never cease," said the sisters.

Not everyone seemed to think it was a wonder. Harriet Simpson snorted as she plucked a blade of grass and waved it through the air. "She causes havoc every year. Then she comes and joins us under the elm tree."

When Girly first arrived in Forget she had tried to see the town as anyone outside the town limits would expect. But that had been a mistake; this town was a world unto itself and she had been duped again. The morning's ordeal was another example of her naiveté as she tried to make the best out of, unbeknownst to her, an orchestrated situation. Strange was a tradition here, even a celebration, like Christmas. Girly glared at her aunt. She hoped the old crone would sit on one of the bee-infested wild flowers she had noticed speckling the hill top.

Emma picked up a plate of sandwiches and passed it to Girly. "Best have something to eat; can't enjoy the lemonade on an empty stomach.

Girly considered the selection—egg salad or ham and cheese—not a vast assortment. The fresh-baked buns though, with their golden crust, made Girly's mouth water. She envisioned burying her nose in their soft interior. An act that would probably be encouraged in a place like Forget, but she restrained herself. Unable to choose, Girly closed her eyes and plucked a sandwich off the plate before passing the plate on to Harriet.

Aunt Lily didn't join the others on the blanket, instead she stood in front of the group and tapped her cane on a small rock. Looking up at her, Girly thought her aunt looked taller than before. It was as if she were taking on the persona of a chiseled Greek deity, jutting her chin at an awkward angle to show off her magnificence.

"Order, order, I now call to order The Sunshine Circle," Aunt Lily said through her nose. "All rise to recite the pledge."

Girly almost choked on her sandwich. As Girly Historian she had heard her aunt talk incessantly about The Sunshine Circle. Aunt Lily had attended it for years and had a long list of reasons why each member was going to hell. She vowed she didn't discuss the list in public though; it might create hard feelings. Girly wondered what her aunt considered to be public. She couldn't think of any good coming from this meeting.

Aunt Lily tapped her cane harder. "On your feet."

"Is that necessary?" asked Harriet. "Emma's got a bad hip. Ella has bursitis. Widow Jenkins gets the vapours with any sudden movement and the duped Organist is likely dehydrated from all that weeping and carrying on."

The clutch of women nodded in agreement and rubbed their hips, knees, shoulders or brow, depending on the location of their infirmity.

Aunt Lily rolled her eyes. "Honest, I have never seen a more pitiful bunch. Can we at least try making it through the pledge without someone passing out or dying?"

Emma raised her hand, "But we are allowed to have seizures aren't we? They can't be helped."

That seemed to rattle Aunt Lily, causing an unheard-of capitulation. "Alright, I'll allow seizures but nothing else."

The group placed their hands on their hearts. They began to recite some hodgepodge pledge. Girly wasn't sure if they each had written their own or if it was the lack of being in unison that made it completely incoherent. Whatever it was, they seemed rather delighted with themselves. Emma wiped away a tear.

"Well, lets' get straight to business." Aunt Lily reached over and picked up her handbag from amongst the paraphernalia on the quilts. She fished out a notebook and pencil. "Who's secretary this week?"

Ella put up her hand and Aunt Lily passed her the book and pencil. "Now for attendance. If you're present say yea, if you're absent say nay." Aunt Lily surveyed the group. "All are present and accounted for."

Ella wrote something into her notebook

"The first order of business," Aunt Lily continued, "concerns knitting socks for soldiers. I know most of the boys are home now but I still think our work is timely. All agreed?"

Harriet cleared her throat and raised her hand. "What I think would be timely is if someone else chaired the meeting."

"Not this again." Aunt Lily threw her head back. "It was decided at the beginning of the war that the one who supplied the most soldiers with socks got to chair the meetings. And I supplied the most soldiers."

"Yes. But you only knit for one legged ones."

"Mind your tongue, Harriet Simpson. Are you denying their sacrifice?" Aunt Lily tapped her cane on a rock with every word. "A soldier is a soldier and who are you to say any different?" Aunt Lily's eyes were wide as if she were daring Harriet to make a response. "Besides," she continued, "my niece has come up with a marvellous idea." She rose on her toes. "Girly raise your hand so everyone knows who you are."

There were seven of them including Aunt Lily and Girly was pretty sure everyone knew who she was. Besides she was the only one not taking swigs from the quart of lemonade and complaining about her deteriorating health. She let out a breath and raised her hand.

"Nice to meet you dear," Emma said reaching over her for an egg salad sandwich.

"We've already met."

"Oh, I don't think so. That was a different Girly."

"Enough with the introductions," Aunt Lily interrupted. "Let's get back to business. As I was saying, my niece had a marvellous idea. She wept into the soldier's sock I was teaching her to knit. Can you imagine? Weeping into each individual sock. I've seen her do it with my own eyes. It's a very touching tribute. One we should consider making."

"I nominate the organist," said Emma, "That woman cries more than any other woman I know,"

"Do we have any seconder?"

"I second the motion." Ella turned to one of the women sitting at the edge of the blanket and smiled.

The Organist of course; Girly was sure she recognized the bony woman but hadn't been able to place her.

"She's an inspiration to us all," Ella continued. "Our own resident sock-weeper."

"All in favour?" asked Aunt Lily.

The ladies raised their hands. Girly scratched her nose. She didn't want Aunt Lily to single her out. A non-committal scratch could be interpreted either way.

"Any dare to oppose?"

Girly stopped scratching.

"Next order of business. Anything from the floor or shall I say quits?" Aunt Lily scanned the group. The Organist's hand shot in the air. "Shall we move on?" Aunt Lily asked.

"I think you need to recognize the Organist." Harriet pursed her lips and rose to her knees. "She's not waving her arm in the air for the good of her health."

"Of course I recognize the Organist; she been living in Forget her entire life." Aunt Lily leaned towards Harriet. "I can even pick her out in a crowd." She surveyed the group of women and pointed. "See there she is. I'm not senile."

"Then let her speak."

"Then let her speak," Aunt Lily mimicked Harriet before she grabbed the notebook out of Ella's hand and flipped through the pages. "Look she spoke three months ago and I think that was quite enough." She jabbed the page with her finger.

Harriet rose to her feet, her hands firmly on her hips.

"Alright," Aunt Lily turned and gave the Organist a cold smile. "What would you like to add?"

"Well," the Organist cleared her throat. "I've been thinking."

"That doesn't sound promising," Aunt Lily said under her breath.

"Give her a chance," snapped Harriet.

"I've been thinking," The Organist fidgeted with the edge of a lace hanky. "That maybe we should put aside our knitting needles for a change and concentrate on the missing in action."

"You mean your husband?" asked Aunt Lily.

"Well, yes."

Aunt Lily waved her cane wildly in the air. "You bring this up every chance you get. Your husband was not in the army. He did not fight in the war. He ran off with Dead Hillary."

"Technically that does make him missing," interjected Emma.

"And I'm sure he is seeing lots of action," added Ella.

"That doesn't count." Aunt Lily's nostrils flared. "For all I know he's down at the horseshoe pits with a well-endowed blonde."

The organist's lip quivered and she dabbed her eyes with the corner of her hanky.

"Or maybe a redhead. Who knows with that man's libido."

The organist stood, burst into tears and ran straight for the grocer's wife.

"Meeting adjourned," Aunt Lily called after her.

The Fords smiled. "It never feels like Sunday until the organist weeps," they said in unison. "It's become a religious experience."

Aunt Lily straightened her dress. "They depend on me."

Girly sat somewhat bewildered. She didn't think there was much Sunday School in this picnic. Her aunt was twittering around like some little flesh eating bird, taking her turn drinking from a quart of fortified lemonade might have been a contributing factor though. There were women at the base of the hill, who Girly was sure were forming a lynch mob. She had never attended any of her mother's ladies aid high society meetings. Now she wished she had: if they were anything like The Sunshine Circle, they would be bizarre. She could imagine her mother's friends facing off as Aunt Lily and Harriet Simpson did, except their battle cry would be pinkies up. What was even more frightening was that Girly overheard Harriet Simpson say to the Fords that Aunt Lily was having a slow year.

"Watch this," Aunt Lily said, pointing to the base of the hill. Girly rose and joined her aunt on the crest of the hill. She couldn't make out what her aunt was pointing at.

"That's Bessie Hilmar talking to the minister. Her five-year-old boy is standing over there on that boulder."

Girly wasn't sure how impressed she should be by a boy standing on a boulder.

"Lottie Smith's younger brother palmed him a silver dollar," continued Aunt Lily. "There is something afoot."

"Maybe he was just making a donation to the church."

"Not the minister, you ninny, the boy."

"You saw that from here? Lottie's brother giving him a silver dollar?" Girly found the whole situation somewhat doubtful.

Aunt Lily leaned forward and smiled. "No, I saw him do it at the annual watermelon roll. Just you watch."

The boy stood surveying the crowd. His hands were placed firmly on his hips, his feet apart. Girly had to admit he looked formidable for a five-year-old. Then out of the blue he threw himself upon an unsuspecting bystander; and not just any unsuspecting bystander either. Bessie's son had attacked Wilber Sykes, a fifty-five-year-old disabled dwarf. Amazingly, Wilber didn't topple over, partly due to the fact he was on crutches, giving four points of contact. Bessie ran to Wilber's aid, closely followed by Doc Dippel, the town doctor. Wilber was whisked into the shade and bombarded with smelling salts.

"Oh," Aunt Lily shrieked, "I wish I would have thought of that. How many boys can say they've fought a crippled midget? Not many, I wager. 'Tis a proud moment! This picnic has the makings of being the best one ever."

If there were words that could have provided an adequate response to her aunt's proclamation Girly could not find them. She and Aunt Lily had very different ideas of what made for a good picnic. She decided it might be best if she stayed out of her aunt's line of sight.

Delighted, Aunt Lily began to survey the crowd more thoroughly. "After a display like that I don't want to overlook even the smallest detail," she said. "You never know what might cause the biggest scandal." The old woman fussed and tut-tutted as she examined every situation, every pairing. "Is that who I think it is?" Aunt Lily asked when her attention caught on a couple at the bottom of the hill.

Harriet Simpson joined Aunt Lily, shading her eyes with her hand. "Who do you think it is?"

"That's what I just asked."

"No it isn't."

"Yes it is. I should know what I just asked because I was the one who asked it!"

"What was it that you just asked then?"

"How am I supposed to remember?"

"Did I ever tell you you're the most irritating woman I have ever met?"

"Not today." The comment seemed to agree with Aunt Lily as if someone had told her she were particularly attractive or charming. Her head bobbed slightly before she once again scanned the hillside, and once again she caught on a couple at the bottom of the hill. This time, though, Aunt Lily directed her question to her niece. "Is that who I think it is?"

Girly nodded.

The Thief was at the base of the hill with Lottie Smith.

The women around Aunt Lily began to talk of the rumours surrounding the couple. One said they were to marry. Another claimed they were distant cousins renewing childhood bonds. Still another asserted he delivered laundry. The last comment they discarded.

"Well," Harriet Simpson proclaimed, "he could put his shoes under my bed anytime."

"With countless others," Aunt Lily muttered, and taking the list from her handbag, she wrote down one more reason why Harriet Simpson was going to hell. Harriet Simpson, for her part, hissed and put a pox on Aunt Lily and her cats. The two then ignored one another as if their own actions were the only ones of true consequence.

A trumpet sounded. Aunt Lily returned her list to her handbag and rubbed her hands together. "It's time for the annual pie auction," she announced and then turned to her companions. "Too bad the organist isn't still here. She might find her husband among the buyers. He so loves the smell of fresh young things."

The other women twittered at the inappropriateness of the statement, but in the end, most nodded in agreement. Harriet Simpson neither twittered nor nodded. "There could be a more delicate way of putting things, Miss Lily," she said, her tone somewhat harsh and indignant.

"I'm getting old," scoffed Aunt Lily. "I have no time for namby-pamby delicacies. And if you had taken the time to look in the mirror recently you would realize you don't either."

Harriet Simpson narrowed her eyes and Aunt Lily offered to get her a compact mirror and a pair of spectacles. Mrs. Simpson didn't even acknowledge the offer.

"I thought not," Aunt Lily said. "There are some things best left unnoticed." Aunt Lily smiled as if dismissing the other, turned, and shouted to her niece. "You better go see if anybody wants you. Pickings are slim since the war, but remember, miracles do happen." Then she added in a loud whisper, "Just don't tell anyone Girly Cook made your pie. She is getting quite a reputation around town."

Girly made no response. It was only that morning Aunt Lily informed her of the pie auction and that Girly was to be a participant. The whole conversation seemed insignificant and had slipped Girly's mind. Now that it was time for the actual event she felt leery. Who knew what a pie auction in Forget would entail. Reluctantly, she took the pie, which Girly Cook had picked up at the bakery the day before, and trudged down the hill towards the spot where Wilber Sykes had been blindsided. Emma and Ella got up and joined her, bringing their own brandy-soaked pies. "Nothing like a little encouragement to tempt a buyer," said Emma smelling her pastry.

"True sister. When you get to our age," Ella nudged Girly, "you get to know these little tricks."

Girly smiled. She really didn't know what to say. Emma and Ella were unlike anyone she had met. For that matter, most of the people in Forget were. Her misgivings about the auction grew. It wasn't the first pie auction she had attended, but it was the only one where two old spinsters were competing with young, unmarried women.

When they reached the bottom of the hill, Emma eyed the waiting girls suspiciously. "Look at them," she said to her sister. "They think we are too old. Not youthful enough."

"How sad," responded Ella. "They have yet to realize they are only a hair's breadth away from being us."

112

"A hare's breath," yelled Emma at the crowd. "Did you hear me? A hare's breath."

The girls all took a step back. Emma shook her head, "I can't believe after all these years of auctions they still only see the wrinkles in our skin." Stepping forward, she cleared her throat. "If any of you think you have more life in your bones than I, I challenge you to a leg-wrestling match."

Images of Emma easing herself to the ground, shots of lemonade to fortify her wonky hip, filled Girly's mind. She could see Emma's skirt flying, showing what long ago had been forgotten. It would have caused quite a commotion. It was like an ancient David challenging a youthful Goliath. The girls, standing across from Girly, broke out in nervous laughter.

"Taunt me if you like," Emma countered. "I will be victorious."

The laughter ceased, but not a soul came forward.

"That's because of last year," Ella whispered to Girly, quite triumphantly.

"What happened last year?" Girly asked.

"Emma was leg-wrestling a girl when your aunt thumped the poor young thing in the head with her cane. Knocked her out cold."

"Why would she do that?"

"Everyone knows it's very bad form to wrestle a Communist, especially an old one."

"Oh," said Girly. Moving away from the sisters, she placed her pie on the table. The other young girls nodded as she approached, but that was their only acknowledgment. Girly wondered what they thought of her and the company she kept.

The pie table was covered with a white lace tablecloth and had more pies than Girly cared to count. In disappointment, she surveyed the table. Her pie was rather plain when compared with the others. Apple just didn't sound as magnificent as rhubarb marmalade watermelon twist. And the pie crusts were an art form all on their own. A variety of colours, some with pinched edges and carefully cut out images of fruit or flowers, while others were topped with a crust of intricately weaved lattice. If Girly had known the variety she would have ordered something a little extra special from the bakery.

Emma and Ella wisely held on to their own pies, winking at all the young men who had gathered for the auction. "After you eat this," Ella shouted, "you won't care how old we are."

Emma hiked up her skirt and the flask in her garter glinted in the sun. Wilber, who was lingering in the shade and somewhat incoherent from the infamous attack, hollered, "You'll never take me alive." Bessy Helmer doused him with another round of smelling salts. And the auctioneer raised his gavel and called the bidding to commence.

"Gather round and set your peepers on this beaut." The auctioneer, tilted the pie for the crowd to see. "It's only a little black around the edges." He glanced down at the girl who was responsible for the offering. The over-done crust was in contrast to her pale, freckled complexion. Her thin arms and legs were more bone than flesh. "But," the auctioneer continued, "you should never judge a pie by its crust. Who will start the bidding? Who'll give me fifty cents?"

A sea of young men, the bricks in bowlers and the woods in newsboy-caps, shuffled their feet, no one raised their hand. The auctioneer leaned over and smelt the pie as if it were still streaming. He smacked his lips. "It's time, boys, pony up."

A red faced wood in cuffed trousers and rolled up shirt sleeves rummaged around in his pocket for loose change. "Two bits," he stammered as he looked at the girl and pulled out a coin covered in lint. The auctioneer came to life, speaking so fast Girly had to close her eyes and concentrate just to understand him. She wondered if the boy bidding were just as lost as she was.

"Who'll give me fifty cents? Fifty cents, now a dollar. One dollar bid, now two, now two, who will give me two? Sold one dollar."

Emma and Ella squealed with delight.

"The auctioneer is off to another sluggish start; isn't that wonderful?" Ella clapped Girly on the back.

"How true," said Emma. "But now the ball is rolling it's all downhill from here."

"Amen to that, sister. Just you wait and see, Girly." Ella paused and looked Girly up and down. "Whichever Girly you are, just you wait and see. Pies will start to disappear and those pasty-faced boys will panic. Mayhem will ensue. It will be a sin to be left without a pie and a girl to eat it with."

Emma scrunched her face. "The shame will be unfathomable."

The women were right. Girly watched the crowd transform. A bashful bunch of bachelors, not wanting to commit, rocked back on their heels and refused to make eye contact with the auctioneer. The woods had their hands thrust deep in their pockets, discreetly counting coins, while the bricks casually joked as if money had never been a concern to them. But as the pies began to disappear the posture changed and hesitant hands lost their inhabitations. Pies left the auctioneer's hand almost as fast as he could hold them up. Even Emma and Ella's pies sold with ease.

As the pies disappeared, Girly's chest tightened. In the end, it was only her's and Lottie's left. Lottie had tenderly tied a crisp yellow ribbon around her pie plate, not to have it confused with any ordinary pie. She pulled back her shoulders, proudly showing off her wares as the auctioneer raised her pie and commenced bidding.

"Now we have a pie," said the auctioneer, "that comes from one of Forget's finest families."

Lottie stepped forward and curtsied.

The auctioneer nodded towards her. "And I am sure the

pie will be as delightful as the girl who brought it. Now let's start the bidding."

The auctioneer didn't have to say another word. Bids were called from the crowd. As the bids rose, shouts and insults accompanied them. It was as if that pie was the only thing left to feed the starving multitudes. Even the men who had already bought pies bid on it. Lottie widened her eyes in mock surprise while Girly's tightened in disbelief. Of all the pies to buy, The Thief in his sacque suit bought Lottie's. Girly shook her head; the fool's attire was more reminiscent of Rosedale than a church picnic in Forget. All around her there were cheers of celebration and three fist fights.

By the time Girly's pie reached the platform there were few buyers left. Most had vanished into the shade to enjoy their spoils.

The auctioneer raised Girly's pie and addressed the crowd. "We have one last pie. The name of the girl who brought it is unimportant. What is important is that she is Miss Lily's niece. I suggest the buyer step lightly." The men laughed.

Girly ignored the auctioneer and studied what was left of the crowd. There were a few stragglers. Most were woods with bricks peppered between them. Some were on crutches or had a disfigurement they seemed to be trying to hide. One young man had an eye patch; another had an empty sleeve tucked into his jacket pocket. Others stared on with an empty, vacant look. The Great War had taken a horrible toll. Aunt Lily didn't talk to any of the Girlys about it. She said you didn't have to stir up heartache to know it's there. And now here it was staring back at Girly. The broken faces before her weakened her knees. She didn't know what she would say to such a wounded man.

Girly hoped The Thief would realize his mistake and reappear from the shadows to buy her pie. How easily she would've forgiven him. Poor Lottie left in the trees with nothing to comfort her but her wares. How sad for her, she would have said. However, The Thief didn't reappear and Girly resigned herself to the fact Lottie had won.

Before the auctioneer had called for the first bid, the pie was sold. Wilber bought it. Wilber had been semi-conscious since the attack, and as he struggled to regain his faculties, his arm inadvertently rocketed into the air. This seemed to please the entire crowd. They cheered and clapped with wholehearted approval. It was as if a miracle had taken place. The auctioneer immediately ended the bidding.

Aunt Lily called to her niece from her perch at the top of the hill. "How many girls can say they've ever had one of their pies purchased by a crippled midget? None in the town of Forget, except you. Maybe it's your boyish figure. You need to learn not to take anything for granted."

Girly retrieved her pie from the auctioneer and trudged towards where Wilber was reclining in the shade. His eyes fluttered in her direction and Girly was sure he went a deeper shade of pale. Taking a seat beside him on the grass, Girly didn't even bother to cut a slice of pie. She took the fork she had picked up from the pie table and drove it into the middle. Out of everything she had been subjugated to since coming to Forget, this had to be the worst.

Wilber was propped up against a tree. His body almost crumpled into itself. "How are you feeling?" asked Girly.

A finger on Wilber's right hand moved slightly. Girly knelt down beside him, he was worse off than she thought. She didn't know what to do. Forgetinans had already began to gather around; they had such expectation in their faces; as would loved ones at a wedding. Girly closed her eyes and took a deep breath.

"Maybe a little sustenance will help," said Bessie Hilmar.

Girly wanted to tell her that maybe he should just stay away from five-year-old boys but before she got the chance the tightening crowd echoed Bessie's endorsement.

With a tight grip on the fork Girly began to feed Wilber. He moaned and drooled, it made pie eating more than a culinary experience. She thought she was killing him and was relieved when Dr. Dippel pushed his way through the crowd.

With his hands on his knees the doctor leaned forward. His fedora pushed back to reveal a patch of coarse grey hair that matched his unmanaged eyebrows. "Give him another forkful and I'll take his pulse."

Girly could feel her face redden. He was no help.

Around her she'd heard comments. "Aren't they cute?" "How darling!" "Would you have ever imagined?" On Wilber's cheek there was still a tiny handprint embedded in his skin. Girly was humiliated but this time without the help of Aunt Lily. Apparently now she had the ability to do it all on her own.

Later Girly ran into The Thief and his beautiful Lottie. Lottie was winding the crisp yellow ribbon around her fingers. Girly thought it would look better around her throat. Lottie smiled. Girly groaned. It was no wonder The Thief had bought her pie. Standing in such close proximity, Girly realized how beautiful Lottie was.

Lottie flipped her ribbon at Girly's face. "I was glad to see that someone so suitable bought your pie. The town has been so worried that Wilber is more inclined to admire males than females. Perhaps you have proved them wrong."

"Now, now. Be nice," said The Thief.

Girly bit her lip.

The Thief wisely changed the topic. "I see your Aunt is enjoying herself," he began. "I do hope the day hasn't been too trying for you."

"I'm fine."

"Yes, I can see that." Then he added, "Tucker's Pond is also fine this time of year. Perhaps you will think of it tomorrow."

"I hadn't realized we were talking about Tucker's Pond," Lottie snapped.

Girly wanted to tell Miss Lottie there were many things she had never realized, but she was distracted when Aunt Lily pelted her with a handful of pinecones. As she turned to leave, The Thief grabbed her arm, "Have you ever thought of Tucker's Pond?"

Girly rolled her eyes. She had never been to Tucker's Pond and therefore had no reason to give it a thought. Tugging her arm out of his grasp she gave him no answer but instead headed up the hill to tend to Aunt Lily.

Chapter Twenty-Three

EVEN THOUGH she was exhausted, Girly couldn't fall asleep. While a light breeze slipped through the open window and teased the curtain hem, she waited for the day's events to come to an end. Surely something more would happen. Sleep couldn't be the only predictable thing. The hall clocked ticked; the crickets chirped in response, but nothing more. Slipping out of bed, Girly retrieved the fourth letter from the highboy. She thought, being a full moon, she might be able to read by its gentle light. Girly squinted and twisted her letter to try to catch the beams but reading proved impossible. Frustrated, Girly lit a candle and risked her aunt seeing the faint glow beneath Girly's door.

Buttercup,

I remember the first time your father visited Forget. I watched for his reaction. Whether it was through my own self-preservation or embarrassment, I'm not sure, but I didn't explain to him where I came from. It is almost impossible to describe Forget without coming across ridiculous. An issue of a penny dreadful would depict it best. Surprisingly, your father took it in stride; he offered me his arm and we strolled down the centre of Main Street and Grand Avenue, neither wanting to acknowledge the dichotomy.

My parents welcomed him as if he were a refreshing breeze. My father would sit on the front veranda swing with him, reluctant to say a word. It was as if there was too much to say and neither knew where to start.

At first, I thought he delighted in my sister. They spent many an hour debating societal ills. Soon he discovered he could not win a debate through the application of logic. It took suspension of reality to be the victor, something your father was really never good at.

A few days before our wedding, your father's parents arrived. My parents greeted them at the railway station in hopes of lessening the shock. It was an exercise in futility. The shock of the place was evident as they touched everything with gloved hands. I think their eyebrows were permanently raised the week they were in Forget. It must have felt like being transported to bedlam for them. Your paternal grandmother hardly spoke any English back then, and I don't think there was anyone in Forget who spoke French, although your aunt tried. She said anyone with half a brain could speak gibberish. The effort did not endear her to your father's family.

Despite the obvious difference between our upbringing and our families, the nuptials went ahead as planned. I wore my grandmother's dress and carried a bouquet of wildflowers your aunt gathered. The service passed without incident but the dance was another story. The Ford sisters plied my new mother-in-law with elixir. If you are not already aware their elixir is highly intoxicating. An hour into the dance and your extremely reserved French grandmother was not only singing but translating in her limited broken English some of the foulest ditties ever sung about Marie Antoinette. Your father was mortified but the residents of Forget, at least those east of Main Street, clapped wildly and encouraged her to do the can-can. The dance ended soon after that. When your father walked downtown the next day all whom he met sung to him their own versions of his mother's song.

Our honeymoon was in Europe, where your father and I had a second wedding; that's the only one he mentions when asked. Our first wedding is reminiscent of a bad dream, at least to your father. I would have expected nothing less.

You must question why would we sent you to such a place. A place your father would just as soon scrub from the map. Well, it's complicated to say. If your father had his druthers we wouldn't have. It was only under Lily's threat to come to Toronto and ingratiate herself upon our rather closed society that he relented. Sending you to stay with your aunt is the least of the two evils. But sending you away, some days seems to be the hardest decision we have had to make and for it I ask for your understanding.

Your sorrowful Mother.

Chapter Twenty-four

THE MORNING after the picnic, Girly sat in her bedclothes, on the edge of the window seat. She yawned and stretched herself awake, somewhat mesmerized by the clouds. They hung low, almost taunting the ground to come and join them. The sun peaked through this playful charade, making them look like Neapolitan ice-cream. She clapped her hand at the sheer joy of such splendour.

The early morning light broke through the clouds, washed over her; she felt naked. Her mother's letter was still clutched in her hand. She couldn't think of it now. The words lay in a jumble on top of the bitter-sweet memory of the previous day. She didn't want to re-read it but she didn't want to put it back in the envelope either. Holding it seemed to be enough.

And despite the myriad of questions spinning through her head about her parents' strange compliance with Aunt Lily's request, there were other things occupying her attention today. Girly couldn't get thoughts of The Thief out of her mind, thoughts that had come to her in the night and refused to leave. They were like a lingering dream. If she breathed deeply enough she was sure she could smell him. How could he so fully occupy her attention? She hardly knew him. Besides a few brief encounters they were virtually strangers. The strong attraction she felt was something akin to the whispers she heard the kitchen maid trade with the delivery boy by the back gate, or something she glimpsed in the copy of *Madame Bovary* that was stashed in the bottom of Daphne's mother's closet. The book, that when she and Daphne were almost caught reading it, they pretended they were trying on shoes.

She knew she had better be careful or that Thief would steal more than roses.

Girly closed her eyes and tried to remember all the good things from the day before. The smell of fresh bread and preserves, the sound of children laughing, Wilber's full recovery. Aunt Lily and the embarrassment she caused faded away as if it had been an aberration. After all, she didn't badger Girly any more than anyone else, and Girly decided if the town could survive the old woman's antics, so could she. Her mother was right; better here than in Toronto. She sighed once more and hugged her legs. The Thief. For one fleeting moment she had diverted his attention from Lottie Smith—that was a great thing.

Running her fingers down the length of her hair, she got up and looked at her face in the mirror. She wondered if she was beautiful. She hoped so. There was no answer in the mirror. How does one know if one is beautiful? Girly never had the confidence to be exactly sure. Some days she saw nothing in her reflection, but other days she was pleased with it.

Girly knew what her mother would say. That beauty was not skin deep; that's what she always said. She could hear the words as plainly as if they stood side by side. *Superficial beauty only lasts a brief window of time, after that beauty comes from within.* The very thought frustrated Girly. Right now all she cared about was between the pages of *Madame Bovary*.

She dressed quickly and put up her hair in a lazy bun. She glanced once more into the mirror and wrinkled her nose. She would have to seek her answer elsewhere. But if she didn't like the answer she received, she'd ask Ella and Emma. After spending the afternoon with them at the Sunday School Picnic, Girly knew by two in the afternoon they'd have had enough brandy to tell her she was an elephant, if that's what she wanted.

Aunt Lily was usually up and barking by this time, but that morning she was unusually quiet. Girly held her breath and listened. Nothing, not a sound. No coughs or sputters. Not even a *What the hell do you think you're doing?*

Girly tiptoed down the hall and stood motionless outside her aunt's bedroom. Nothing. It was as if her aunt didn't exist. The house was cool and Girly stood shivering.

Aunt Lily was dramatic in all that she did, pushing everything beyond what most would tolerate. She couldn't even sleep without putting on a performance. It was like living with a vaudeville act. But the house was deadly silent, an eerie feeling hung in the air.

Girly gently pushed her aunt's bedroom door open and peeked inside. Aunt Lily sat at her dressing table, motionless. There was even uncertainty as to whether or not she was breathing. Her hair remained half done. She could've been putting it up or perhaps taking it down. The hairbrush hung limply in one hand. The other clutched the locket she always wore close to her throat. Then she trembled.

"I must be worth something," she wept. "Something. The way you kiss me and hold me close. You love me. I know you do."

Through the gap Girly scanned the room. There was no one there. Someone could be hiding under the bed but she doubted it. The room had only one occupant. Girly left her aunt alone to her thoughts. She turned and tiptoed to the stairs before she sank onto the top step. She could see her aunt's room down the hall and heard half of a muffled conversation. It was the first time she had intruded into Aunt Lily's private world, and she hoped she'd never have reason to again. Even her mother's letters hadn't made Girly feel so intrusive, as if she were combing through someone's most intimate secrets; as if she had broken a trust.

Aunt Lily guarded her soft and tender places so well they seemed to disappear. Girly sat perplexed, wondering how much they might have been alike—her aunt being so old and she so very young.

Chapter Twenty-five

AUNT LILY eventually came bounding out of her room as if that morning were just like any other. Girly watched her for a long time. Her aunt's hair was in a tidy roll, and her face was clean and fresh. Any evidence of her morning's ordeal had gone. Her soft and tender parts were neatly tucked away, out of the reach of prying eyes and comforting hands. She quickly surveyed the room.

"Well," she said, "this is in much better shape than the library. Have you seen the library lately? You'd be lucky to make it out alive. I want you to give it a thorough going over today. I don't care if that is all you accomplish. I want it done."

"Yes, Aunt Lily."

"I shouldn't have to tell you these things," she added before dropping her eyes and slipping into the kitchen to bother Girly Cook for her breakfast.

Aunt Lily didn't have a library, den, or any of the fine places she boasted about, but when she wanted to be alone, she sent her niece to clean them. It would've been unlike her to give Girly a day off; Girly doubted Aunt Lily could've lived with her conscience if she had. But it seemed that, in

Aunt Lily's mind, if she could send her niece to do some imaginary task, then she could rest at ease.

Girly ran through the gate, untying her apron and dropping it to the ground as she went. She knew her aunt watched her from behind the lace curtains, she imagined her knuckles were white from her tight grip on her cane. They both would have a day of freedom. Girly alone with her daydreams and Aunt Lily with her reality.

Racing past the Ford's, Girly crossed the street to the Harrisburg's. She imagined Mrs. Harrisburg wandering from room to room, as she did at Aunt Lily's house, hardly leaving a ripple in her wake. Girly supposed everything she did was done in silence. The secretive Mrs. Harrisburg was a fascination to her.

She darted down Beggars Can't be Choosers and Love Thy Neighbour as Thyself. Racing under the boughs that framed the empty meadow, she whispered good morning to all the fairies that might be hiding among the leaves. This Boy is Ignorance and This Girl is Want hardly registered. Then she came to an abrupt stop. The dust from the path rose around her shoes. She now had the foreboding task of passing the grocer. Girly wasn't sure how the grocer and his wife felt about Aunt Lily—and herself for that matter—since the picnic, but she was convinced she would soon find out. It seemed all of her relative's intriguing ways were inevitably attributed to her. But to be honest, Girly was aware that since coming to Forget she was compiling some intriguing ways of her own.

Girly hid behind a bush that flanked the corner of the store while she gathered her resolve. The grocer was sweeping the wooden walk. Girly wasn't even sure the bristles of the broom made contact with every stroke. His wife sat by the door briskly rocking herself in the shade of the dutiful organist. The organist's spidery fingers were interlocked in pensive consideration.

The grocer's wife seemed in high form. "I should never have married him you know," she said loud enough for

Girly to hear. "My mother was against it. She said I would have to endure him. That when he came for me, I'd have to close my eyes and think of England."

The organist nodded. "Mothers are usually right."

"I could have had a shop on the other side of the street. Those buildings taunt me every day with their fancy archways and coloured glass. I could have been somebody."

"I think we all wanted to live on the other side of the street."

"But I actually had a chance. And as for this marriage," the grocer's wife glared at her husband, "I can't close my eyes and think of England forever."

The ladies' chat came to an abrupt end when they saw Girly emerge from her hiding place. They snorted and pursed their lips in unison. A rare talent, Girly thought.

Girly tucked her chin close to her chest as she walked past the trio. "You poor man," she muttered.

The grocer, without looking up, nodded and kept sweeping. Out of the corner of her eye Girly could see the grocer's wife stiffen and the organist's spidery fingers unweave themselves and sink deeply into the grocer's wife's meaty shoulder.

"That girl has got a little bit of Dead Hilary in her," the organist said. "Bold as brass and common as dirt."

"I agree," said the grocer's wife. "But dirt is so much more appealing."

Chapter Twenty-six

GIRLY'S TRAVELS eventually wove their way to the edge of Tucker's property. The entrance stood on one end of Grand Avenue and Main Street and the rail yard on the other. The two faced off like bookends to an endless argument. Planted at the head of the Tucker's drive were chipped pillars with broken hinges, which whispered now, but at one time they would have shouted as they ushered in an arrival to the Tucker's territory. The gate that had once been clasped within the rusty hinges was not to be seen.

The drive itself wound in such a way that the estate couldn't be seen through the trees. Such a place of peaceful beauty. Girly Historian had heard stories of how it had once been an honour to dine with the Tuckers, a mark of status and wealth, but not anymore.

The Tuckers, in years past, had been pillars of the community. They had walked with pride down Forget's narrow streets, the townspeople elbowing each other for a better look or a simple handshake. To be known by a Tucker meant that God himself must have smiled on you. It had been good for the family back then, until Mr. Tucker died.

Mrs. Tucker was comforted and consoled in the kindest of fashions, and while well-meaning friends lined their pockets with her misfortune, she never had the fortitude to stop them.

Soon everything had either disappeared or been sold. The only thing left for Mrs. Tucker's young son was the house and the pond. Greatness he could ill afford. The young Tucker began to drink, and in some twisted minds that became the reason for his family's fall from favour.

The town was convinced the young Tucker wouldn't have expended the energy to take his next breath if he had been given a choice. When he married Widow Wilson, everyone thought it was because the widow already had children, Tucker being too lazy to accomplish the task. To the town's surprise and disappointment, however, that was the only thing Tucker excelled at. The Tuckers and the Wilson's became so well- blended it was impossible to distinguish one from the other. It was as if they were trying to take over the world through procreation. It would have taken all the prayers in Forget to save even one of their angry souls. That is, if anyone in Forget prayed for the Tuckers.

Old man Tucker smiled and nodded as if they were old friends when Girly passed the house. His wife stood beside him rubbing her back. There would soon be another Tucker. The very thought exhausted Girly.

"Morning," said Girly.

"Mornin'. How's your aunt this fine morning'?" Tucker asked.

"As good as can be expected."

"Nice to hear."

Old man Tucker nodded as Girly continued on her way. It had been the longest conversation she had ever had with him.

The pond was just beyond the edge of the house, hidden in a maze of trees. As Girly approached, she heard laughter and playful taunts. Thrashing around in the cool water were the bare shoulders of several white, gleaming boys. The finest belonged to The Thief. His hair was matted and hung strangely over his eyes.

When Girly appeared through the trees, their gazes met. "Come join us," he playfully invited, pointing to a tree where she could hang her clothes. "I promise you it won't offend anyone, including myself."

The boys, sombre-faced, placed their hands on their hearts and shook their heads. They looked sincere except for an uncontrolled glint in their eyes.

Girly shook her head. "Your offer is tempting, I assure you, but I don't think it would be proper."

"You're letting your modesty get the best of you. Can't truly enjoy life if you're always thinking." The Thief laughed and dove under the water. When he reappeared it was near some bulrushes where he could make a safe departure.

The Tuckers, not as aware of their situation, came directly out to greet Girly. Their thin undergarments clung indiscriminately to their clean white bodies. She blushed for them, but they, in their naivety, seemed oblivious to her reaction.

"Good to see you, Miss," Alexander offered his hand. "The Niece of the Chicken lady." He said it as if it were a grand title.

Girly took his hand and did a little curtsy.

The other Tuckers filed by her, each taking her hand. Some shook it, some kissed it; Mean Dog Joe nipped it.

When The Thief reappeared, he was fully dressed and quite different. His clothes were relaxed and suited his mood. His eyes, still partly hidden by his hair, were remarkably blue. Most striking of all was that he seemed to belong. And not just at the pond, but to the Tuckers. Although Girly hadn't seen him associate with the family beyond the borders of the pond.

"I see you have met the boys," he said before he sent them into the bush to retrieve their clothing.

Girly nodded. "They do most of my aunt's gardening. Although they usually come by when I'm on an errand or before I get up."

"And they attend your chickens' funerals."

"Yes." Girly was somewhat taken aback. She knew her aunt's activities were common knowledge to the woods but to the bricks, she didn't think they'd be bothered with such things.

The Thief grimaced. "The chickens' funeral. A sad occasion, I am sure. I should have sent flowers, or at least grain." Then he reached over and lifted her chin with his finger. "If my horse should take to drinking," he said, "I'll know where to turn."

Girly made a face.

"My God, you're intriguing."

The boys darted out of the bush, hollering and slapping each other on the back.

Girly found the image striking: the blue pond behind them, the darker sky above, and the patchwork of sand and grass at their feet. Everything about the place was carefree.

The Thief turned and offered Girly his arm. "May I?"

"Most certainly."

He led her to a flat marbled rock, large enough for two to sit. It looked like the fossil of a dragon's head, with dips and divots marring its surface. Girly was sure it had to be sculpted, hand hewn. With as much grace as she could, she hoisted herself up into one of the hollowed out eye sockets. The Thief took its counterpart. As for the boys, they all clumped together by one of the long-ago fire-breathing nostrils.

"This is her first trip to the pond, boys. How can we make it memorable?" The Thief asked.

"Toss her in," was the first response.

"If we do that she won't come back," said The Thief.

There was a short silence. Then almost in unison all the Tuckers responded, "Toss her in."

The Thief laughed while Girly sat stunned.

"What would your father say?" he asked. "Remember, she is the Niece of the Chicken Lady."

There was a lull, intermingled with sounds of shifting bodies and hushed whispers. Alexander the Great stood to make their response. "Out of our respect for the great Miss Lily, we will not toss her in."

Girly smiled.

"Instead," he continued, "we will just splash her."

Girly snorted.

"That won't do," said The Thief. "There'll be no greeting involving water. In polite society, young ladies aren't treated that way."

"But this ain't polite society," Napoleon Bonaparte reminded him.

"No," said The Thief, "it isn't, but we're not a bunch of barbarians either."

"What's a barbarian?" asked Mean Dog Joe.

"Someone who would toss the Chicken Lady's niece into the pond."

"Oh," said the boys.

Chapter Twenty-seven

IN THE end, Girly found the Tuckers equally as adventurous and divine as they were rough and unrefined. They sat before her as if painted by a grand master. A portrait from an ancient court, a shadow of who they might become. Napoleon sat with a hand half submerged under the placket of his shirt, scratching what Girly hoped was a bug bite. Leonardo mindlessly drew in the dirt with a stick. Peering over Romulus' shoulder, William encouraged a black bug to scurry away as Romulus prepared to squash it with a small stone. Socrates and Alexander sat side by side. Socrates tapped his finger on his chin and Alexander smiled knowingly. While Joseph, in his brightly coloured shirt, sat in amongst his jumble of brothers seemingly oblivious.

Napoleon finished scratching and sauntered up to her in a way that promised mischief. "Are you brave?"

Eyeing Napoleon, Girly hesitated before she responded. Admitting she was brave might put her into a perilous situation. She may be asked to stand barefoot in an ant hill or steal honey from a wild hive. She traced the hollow eye of the dragon stone with the tip of a finger and took a chance. "I am," she said, hoping that if the boys got carried away, The Thief would bring them to heel. She turned to

The Thief for reassurance but his smile led her to believe he was enjoying the challenge too much.

"You don't look very brave." His gaze dropped to Girly's hands. "You've probably never even had a blister." Girly slipped her hands under her thighs. Napoleon leaned over and whispered into Romulus's ear. They both nodded and looked at her with doubt. Girly's courage melted away.

The would-be Bonaparte leaned in so close she saw the edges of the blue in his eyes were laced in green. "This might frighten you." The words slid though his lips with an ease that raised the hair on the back of her neck. "Make you wish you were never born."

Girly shook her head, and her voice caught at the back of her throat. "I live with Miss Lily. Nothing can frighten me."

There was a twitch in the corner of Napoleon's mouth. "We'll see. When the sliver moon's out tonight we'll see how brave you are then."

In the sunlight Girly found bravery hard enough to hold on to; under the light of a sliver moon she was sure it would be impossible. Even so, she sat on her dragon rock with as much dignity as she could muster, hollow though that dignity might be.

"Don't say I didn't warn you." Napoleon seemed to stretch up past his full height and he looked down his nose. Hands behind his back he paced the length of the boulder in a well-worn path. His brothers crouched in front of him, as if waiting for manna to fall. Girly could only assume these boulder talks were a common occurrence. She felt as if she were in a back country church service.

When Napoleon reached the tip of the dragon's nose he crouched down and let his voice carry on the breeze. "Let's see how fearless she is. Cause if she isn't fearless she can't be here." He looked back at Girly with the summer sun beating down on her through the poplar leaves. She felt the perspiration beading on her brow, the back of her dress sticking to her skin. "See if she'll sneak out with us tonight."

The colour left Girly's face, she could feel it, and she was sure the boys were aware.

"And if she does, this is what will happen." Napoleon crouched lower. "On a slip of a moon, like the one we'll have tonight, Ma says strange things lurk. They can't help themselves when the moon hides its face. It's like they know they ain't going to get caught."

Romulus pelted Girly with the stone he had threatened the bug with. "Have you ever looked into a faceless moon?"

Girly shook her head and rubbed the spot where the stone struck. She had never been pelted with rocks before and was of the mind to leave but wondered what The Thief might think of her if she did. She knew her aunt would ridicule her, being chased off by a simple stone. Keeping one eye on Romulus, Girly resolved to stay.

Napoleon's lips twitched. "On those nights, I feel kind of itchy and toss under my covers. Well, one night earlier this spring, I couldn't stand it any longer. *Alexander,* I whispered.'

"'*Yeah,*' he whispered back.'

"Ya think tonight might be a good night for prowling?'

"I hear Alexander sniff the air. 'As good as any I suppose. Where do you want to prowl?'

"'Out in the woods.'

"'Why would you want to do that?'

"'No real reason, except I think I can hear the Cat Lady calling.'

"'Gawd, Napoleon, you always think you can hear the Cat Lady calling. She's been dead since before you were born.'

"'I know, but I just want to make sure.'

Napoleon scratched his bug bite. "I've always had a fascination with the Cat Lady. As soon as I was old enough to make sense out of the story, it's all I wanted to talk about. '*But why did she die?*' I asked my mother as she peeled potatoes."

"'Because her heart was broken.'

"How did it break?'

"Honestly, Napoleon. We have gone over this time and time again.'

"How did it break, Ma?'

"Ma, set down her paring knife and looked at me. "I will tell you once more but that's it.'

"I nodded.

"'The cat lady came to Forget as a young bride with her groom. They were from a faraway place, somewhere people are meant to be together, as if they were tied that way at birth. Her groom was strong and hard working. His hands were wide and scarred from labour on the land. His wife was lovely and mysterious. So lovely, in fact, few dared to look at her. It was as if they were viewing something sacred. It might have been the magic in her blood that made folks feel that way. Magic blood can change a woman.'

"I asked Ma if she had magic in her blood. She ran her hand through her uncombed hair like she does when someone knocks on the door unexpectedly and asked if it looked like she had magic in her blood. I said no, not even if I squint my eyes.

"'That's the way magic is. No one is ever really certain; neither was her husband. He was worried someone might whisk her away. That's why he moved here, so he could hide her deep in the woods. It was only when a stranger happened by, or someone made deliveries, that people heard tales of a remarkable woman.

"'For years people wondered about her. She was the town's greatest mystery. Then her husband left one morning, never to return. No one knows what happened to him. His wife was at a loss. She gathered her cats, locked the door, bolted the windows and waited for him to come home.

"'When Henry Henry, the iceman, came to make his delivery, he heard her cats crying inside the house. He broke down the door, but all he found was a skeleton and one, half-eaten eye. Since then, when the moon is but a sliver, folks say you can see a one-eyed woman, shrouded in a long black cloak, calling, "Here kitty, kitty. Here kitty, kitty.'"

"What a horrible story." Girly gasped the words more than spoke them.

Napoleon puffed up. "The best stories are. That's why we're going looking for her tonight. You'll be the first one through her old door. See how brave you are then."

Before Girly could respond a shotgun blast sounded, causing the boys to jump to their feet and begin to disappear into the woods. Alexander stopped and turned. "Don't worry," he said. "That's just Pa calling us for lunch."

The Thief smiled. "Your Pa is very inventive. You should be proud." They were the first words he had spoken since the Tuckers started questioning Girly on her bravery.

Alexander drew a line in the sand with his toe. "I am proud," he said.

For an instant Girly saw something ancient in the boy's eyes, as if the true Alexander the Great were peering from behind them. His mother had named him well.

Chapter Twenty-eight

As the boys disappeared, Girly felt The Thief's attention rest on her. Her skin grew hot and prickly. It was the first time since she'd met The Thief they were truly alone. No one spying on them from behind lace curtains, no one throwing a ball on the street, no Lottie and her marvellous pie. Girly awkwardly played with her dress, trying to think of something to say.

"There are more of them," he said, interrupting her thoughts. "At least three, too young to come to the pond."

"Who?"

"The Tuckers."

"That poor woman."

"Don't feel sorry for her; she's happy. The whole family is. Her pride has helped build those boys. At night, she reads to them about their namesakes and tells them about the greatness they have come from and how great they'll be one day."

"What about their father? I heard he was a bit of a drunk."

"He is a bit of a lot of things." The Thief looked at his feet and mumbled. "At one time our families were close."

Girly felt as if her question had picked at an old scab. Yet despite the uncomfortable conversation she pressed on, compelled. "But not anymore?"

"Not anymore."

"Since they fell from greatness?"

The Thief continued to look at his feet as if she had never spoken. An uneasy silence slithered between them.

"Do you have magic in your veins?" she finally asked.

"No, I'm afraid no fire stirs my blood."

"Oh."

"Do you?"

"Just my Aunt Lily's kind, if you can call her charmed. I think it's only the Tuckers who think she's somehow enchanted."

"What about your parents? Do they live close by?"

Girly said nothing. It wasn't something she wanted to discuss. The thought of her parents didn't belong in a place like this. She changed the subject. "Why do you come here? This is certainly not indicative of your social standing."

"Indicative? I'm impressed."

"As historian my aunt makes me read the dictionary."

"It must be riveting."

"Answer the question."

He smiled and raised his eyebrows. "Do you think Lottie would ever come to a place like this?"

"No."

"Well, there's your answer." Turning, he stared at her for some time before unclipping her hair and letting it fall slowly over her shoulders. He ran his hand down its length and said those words: "My God, you're beautiful." And she believed him.

Chapter Twenty-nine

AUNT LILY was nattering about the library when Girly returned. A group of churchwomen had been by earlier with a list of evil things — things that could bring disaster on any God-fearing home. On this list, there were a number of evil books.

The whole neighbourhood had become obsessed with the *Damnable List of Evil Things*. Ella was burning Emma's things and Emma was burning Ella's things. The grocer's wife was burning the grocer's things and the grocer was handing them to her.

Aunt Lily was beside herself. "I'm sure we are harbouring something foul, besides you," she said, looking her niece up and down. "Apparently, it is now illegal to burn people. Believe me, I asked. Instead, they gave me this damned list and said I was supposed to stick to it, not go off on some tangent. Me going off on a tangent! Never heard of anything so ridiculous in my life." She thrust the list in Girly's face. "See these many evils?" she screamed. "They are the reason I can't sleep at night — that I get angry and sometimes lose my temper! I can't live in a house where such evil dwells! If something doesn't change, dire consequences will befall this house. You mark my words. Dire consequences." At that she shuffled backwards towards the davenport, looking over her shoulder as she went. When it was in close proximity she recoiled her hand and dramatically fainted.

Girly pried the list from her aunt's hand. "We aren't harbouring any foul things," she said.

Her aunt wasn't assured. She sat up and rolled her eyes before flopping back down to her previous position. Aunt Lily was on a witch hunt, and until she found her witch, in the form of a book, she wouldn't be satisfied.

Girly searched the house. There was nothing. No sin to be found. Aunt Lily was right, disaster had struck, there was nothing to burn. The old woman wept bitterly as Girly told her. "I can't find anything on the list. We're safe, nothing can harm us."

"You're wrong. Evil has deceived you. Don't give up so easily." She grabbed Girly by the shoulders and pulled her close. "Shall I ask Girly Cook to give it a go? She may be incompetent, but that is her strong suit. That child has a nose for anything vile. Have you tasted her cooking?"

Shaking her head, Girly dismissed her aunt's suggestion. "I'll give it one more try," she said, getting up and leaving the room.

After a time, Girly dug up a book titled *The Art of Birdwatching*. She sat down by her aunt and stroked the back of her hand. "If you just change one letter in the *'watching'* you have *'The Art of Birdwitching.'*"

The book had a remarkable effect. Aunt Lily seemed to regain her health. "That's as evil as evil can get," she crowed. "Build a fire and let's burn it."

Aunt Lily told the neighbours about the evils of birdwatching and how just one careless letter could make the difference between eternal life and eternal damnation. She was convinced it should be added to the damnable list and sent Girly to the church to tell the minister.

The minister found Aunt Lily's discovery strange, to say the least, and wasn't sure it should be added to the list. He said she would have to prove that there was evil in birdwatching.

When Girly returned home and repeated his comments, Aunt Lily was furious. "How does that idiotic fool expect me to oblige? He has such unreasonable expectations. I've burned the damned book! I'm not a witch! I can't read ashes! Did you tell the idiot that?" Then she paused. "I know his game," she said. "He's trying to trick me. Does he think I'll fall for that? The oldest trick in the book — make me read something from the ashes of a burned book. The witch test."

"I've never heard of that trick."

"How could you? It's one of the oldest tricks in the book, and most of the oldest tricks have been forgotten." Aunt Lily rummaged around for a bit of paper and scribbled down a few barely legible words. "Say this to him," she said thrusting the note at Girly.

"It says, *You're a damned idiot!*"

"Well, I know that I wrote it, you fool. Go tell him."

"I will not tell him that!"

"Hmm, maybe you're right." Aunt Lily snatched the paper from her hand and added a few strokes from her pen before giving it back. "That's better," she said. "Stronger and more to the point."

"It says, *You're still a damned idiot*. May you burn in hell."

"Much better, isn't it?" she said, seemingly proud of her death-defying accomplishment. "Now take it to the minister. He'll appreciate you for your honesty." Her voice was wistful as if she was asking Girly to do something kind. "Then say, *God bless you* when you're done, so he doesn't put a curse on us."

Girly rolled her eyes. "Great advice from a would-be witch."

Aunt Lily blanched. "Who told you I could be a witch?"

"You did."

"Oh, I was trying to keep it a secret. That damned minister. Now I've failed the second test. He'll pay for that. Take the fool the note."

"I will do no such thing. If you want him to have that note, you'll have to take it yourself."

Aunt Lily hesitated for a moment, grabbed her cane, put on her shawl, and tucked a small package under her arm. She walked briskly out the door. "Light the lantern and follow me," she yelled over her shoulder, "It's black as pitch out here."

Girly followed her aunt with some trepidation. The only upshot to their late night trek was when the Tuckers came to call, she wouldn't be home. They would have to search for the cat lady on their own.

Chapter Thirty

AUNT LILY, her shawl wrapped around her, mumbled something to ward off evil. She stopped near the gate, where the chickens were buried, made a hasty cross and kissed the tips of her fingers.

"You're not Catholic," Girly said. "There is no need to carry on so."

Aunt Lily pulled hard on her shawl. "The hens were!" she cried. "But I doubt even a prayer from a dead chicken would save me now."

Her first stop was the Fords. It was half past six and more than likely Emma and Ella had turned in as soon as the supper dishes were dried. Aunt Lily rapped on their door anyway. They seemed dazed at first but sharpened quickly when she insisted that they give her a bottle of their elixir.

"Elixir," said Emma. "It's been years."

"Yes," answered Aunt Lily.

"If you need elixir there must be something awful brewing," said Ella. She quickly produced a dusty brown bottle. With a funnel she filled it with her home-distilled brandy. She winked at Girly. "In one bottle its spirits, in another its elixir. Will you be needing anything else, Miss Lily?"

"No, just the elixir."

"Well, while we're up we might as well decant a batch for ourselves, Emma." Ella rubbed her hands together. "For the good of our health." The sisters bid them goodnight and began funnelling brandy into dusty brown bottles.

Aunt Lily seemed to gain momentum after leaving the Fords', and before she reached the end of their walk she had taken a long drink of elixir. She passed the bottle to Girly, but Girly declined, insisting one of them had to be sober.

Aunt Lily waved her hand at her before pausing momentarily at the Harrisburg's. She again crossed herself. "If anyone is cursed it's that poor woman," she said.

By the time they reached the church, Aunt Lily had finished her bottle and tossed it casually behind her. It was impossible for Girly to even guess what her aunt would do next, let alone what the minister's response might be. Girly wondered if he was up to the challenge. The minister had grown quite gaunt and tired since his marriage. It was rumoured his young, vigorous wife had high expectations of his weak, old body.

The church was deserted. The minister had apparently already retired to the parsonage. Aunt Lily sighed but continued her trek. "He will be relieved to see me. It will give him leave from his marital duties."

The minister's young wife answered the door and greeted Aunt Lily with an uncertain smile. "George," she called. "There is someone here to see you."

Her husband trudged to the door and quietly peered around its edge.

"Test this!" Aunt Lily yelled as she flung open her arms. Her package fell to the ground and she teetered as she bent to pick it up.

The minister raised his eyebrows and shrugged, as if he wasn't quite sure of what she meant.

Aunt Lily leaned over and shoved the note into his shirt

pocket. She put one bony finger in the air. "It's from the girl," she said as she staggered away.

When Girly caught up with Aunt Lily at the end of the walk, she was exasperated. "Why would you do that?"

"What did I do?"

"You gave the minister that awful note."

"He is only upset with you, dear, not me."

"That's only because you said I wrote it."

"It's not my fault that man believes everything he's told."

Girly threw her hands in the air and screamed. "You are hard enough to manage without elixir. Now you're just impossible."

It was getting dark and Girly implored Aunt Lily to return home, but the old woman ignored her. "There is nothing more you can accomplish tonight."

"That's what you think," Aunt Lily said, continuing on her way.

Girly followed her, not sure what else to do. She was unfamiliar with anywhere west of Grand Avenue at night and didn't want to be separated. The next home they stopped at was down a street Girly hadn't been on before. It was large, somewhat reminiscent of Rosedale, though it was hard to see just how large as the moon shed little light. Back home Girly wouldn't have thought twice about approaching the place; she would have marched in the front door. But now she knew she wouldn't be welcome. She was on the wrong side of Grand Avenue, on the street named I Shall Not Want. Aunt Lily pounded on the door several times before there was a response. The door opened to expose a tall, robust man fingering his moustache. It was the banker.

He greeted them formally as if they had come to do business. Aunt Lily burped elixir. "I need to speak to the missus."

"My wife is away visiting family."

"Come now," said Aunt Lily. "You don't expect me to believe that."

"I don't care what you believe," the banker said moving to shut the door.

Aunt Lily jammed her cane between the door and its frame. "I've known you since you were a little boy, and you're no better a liar now than you were then, Rupert Montgomery Beaumont. Besides, if you don't get your wife right now I'll strip naked, right here on your front porch."

"That has never been my name."

"And pray tell why is that important now? I've been calling you Rupert Montgomery Beaumont for the last thirty."

The banker raised an eyebrow and Aunt Lily raised one back as she undid the top button of her blouse.

"That will not be necessary," he finally said. "I'll go get her."

As the banker retreated into the house, Aunt Lily smiled. "You only have to do something like that once and you kind of get a reputation."

The banker's wife seemed taken aback by Aunt Lily's forwardness, and she stood stiffly in the doorway, her arms folded in front of her. She gave no greeting, formal or otherwise.

Aunt Lily came directly to the point. "I have come on behalf of the chickens. I'm sure you have heard of their passing?"

The banker's wife tightened her lips.

"Well," Aunt Lily continued, "I think the girls would have wanted your boy to have their things." Aunt Lily took the package and handed it to her. The banker's wife's arms remained folded.

"Really," Aunt Lily said, "I'm not a witch; I don't care what the minister says. Do you think a witch would care if your ugly boy has nice things?"

At that, the banker's wife unfolded her arms, but it was not to receive the package; it was to slam the door. Aunt Lily tucked the package back under her arm, stuck one bony finger in the air and yelled something about ugly children not deserving nice things from chickens.

It was well into the night by the time Girly and Aunt Lily had retraced their steps home. Aunt Lily's strength had left her and she was dependent on her niece for support. Girly assured her no one believed she was a witch and everything would be better in the morning. Aunt Lily moaned. "I hope you're right," she said. "I hope you're right."

Chapter Thirty-one

IN THE morning, most of the effects of the elixir had worn off. Girly helped make Aunt Lily comfortable on the davenport in the sitting room. She drew the curtains and brought her a cup of tea. She didn't know what to say to her aunt. Nothing could have prepared her for the previous evening's events. Girly wondered if she should comfort or scold. She didn't have to decide; the Fords came over. As Girly hung their sweaters on the hooks in the hall, the sisters nattered at her. "We need to discuss with you your aunt's sinister events of last night," said Ella.

"Quite right," said Emma. "News of it has passed from house to house and is now known throughout Forget."

"And the surrounding county."

Girly let out a long breath. That's all she needed—another scandal. "I'll put the kettle on." It was going to be a long morning.

Aunt Lily held her head as the Fords broke the news. The two sisters took turns in the telling. "The banker's wife is enraged you paid her a visit," said Emma.

"Yes, quite violated," Ella continued as she poured her sister and herself a cup of tea. "In fact she had her porch not only scrubbed but repainted this morning. Said she wouldn't step out of the house until it was done."

"She thinks in your drunkenness you showed a lack of regard for her son's reputation. She is really quite grieved."

"Apparently the woman is daft," Ella scowled. "Not being able to tell the difference between a perfectly harmless elixir and the demon alcohol."

"Yes, Sister and I were taken aback as well." Emma reached out and patted Aunt Lily on the arm. "We've decided we really don't like that woman."

Ella nodded in agreement, picked up an oatmeal cookie and dipped it into her tea. "Her biggest complaint, though, was not that you compared her son to a chicken. She probably knew there was truth in that. No, what upset her most was all the talk of witches. She even went to the minister with her concern."

"I heard he tried to console her," Emma said, taking her sister's cookie and biting into it. "Explained that you are unpredictable; always have been. Even told her to go home and rest. He was sure she'd be more understanding then."

Ella picked up another cookie, this time being careful to keep it out of reach of her sister. "But the banker's wife felt the insult had been too great and the minister was avoiding the matter. She said if he didn't deal with you, this very morning, she and her husband, with their large contributions, would leave the church."

"The minister agreed to look into the matter."

Aunt Lily listened quietly as the Fords related the morning's events. She seemed to not exactly remember what had happened the night before but, all the same, was relieved she was still alive. "After all," she said, "how many can say they've taken the witch test and lived?"

"Not many," answered the Fords. "Not many at all."

Girly thumped her head with the palm of her hand.

The minister arrived soon after the Fords left. He handed

his hat to Girly. "I won't be staying long enough for tea," he called.

"I don't remember asking you to tea," Aunt Lily barked from the sitting room.

"You're right, Miss Lily. It was wrong of me to expect you to be hospitable."

"Apology accepted."

The minister appeared in the doorway, his hands folded behind his back. "Miss Lily," he began, "what were you drinking last night?"

"Elixir."

"From the Fords?"

"Yes."

"That's a dangerous brew."

"It was a dangerous evening."

"Miss Lily, you are getting too old for elixir."

"And you're getting too old for sex."

The minister paused and put his hands in his pockets. "You have the whole town talking about witches and ridiculous tests. What possessed you to come up with such an idea?"

"It was not my idea; it was yours! Just ask Girly."

Girly fumbled with the minister's hat. All she wanted to be was a fly on the wall. She didn't want to be drawn into Aunt Lily's escapade.

Aunt Lily narrowed her eyes at the minister before continuing. "You're the one who wanted me to read from the ashes of a burnt book! You're the one who wanted me to take the witch test."

"I'm afraid you misunderstood me. I've thought you were many things, but I have never thought you were a witch."

Aunt Lily smiled coyly. "Is that because I give clothing to the ugly children?"

"No," said the minister sternly. "And I would advise you to stay away from the banker's wife."

"And her ugly baby?"

The minister grit his teeth, "And her ugly baby."

Chapter Thirty-two

AFTER AUNT Lily had dealt with the minister and the Fords, she sat on the davenport and began to knit a sock for a man with an undersized foot.

"It's truly an unappreciated segment of the population, the tippy-toe soldier." The ball of grey yarn rolled in her lap as her knitting needles knit and purled. "I should be napping. Lazarus took to his grave for far less. Yet here I sit once again thinking of others." As Aunt Lily continued her commiseration, Girly slipped out of the sitting room and up the stairs. Her aunt didn't even seem to notice.

Unsure of how long it would take her aunt to finish her act of benevolence, Girly took the chair from the hall and braced it under her bedroom doorknob. It was her only way to ensure privacy, as Aunt Lily guarded the keys to every door in the house as if they were another appendage. Opening the top drawer of the highboy, Girly reached for the bundle of letters. The soft yellow ribbon that bound them was missing and the bundle lay in a sloppy pile at the bottom of the drawer. Girly was sure she had retied it the last time she took them out. She searched for the ribbon. It wasn't in the drawer. Nor was it under the bed or by the window seat. It wasn't until she swept her hand under the highboy she found it. "Aunt Lily!" she said.

There were so many things Girly had put up with since coming to live with her aunt. But this topped them all. She'd mistakenly thought her room was hers alone—not to be intruded upon or invaded without invitation. She felt violated.

Picking up the dishevelled stack, she counted the envelopes. There were still eight but the eight felt different. They were no longer her little secrets. With a heavy hand she carried them to her usual reading spot. The bed squeaked a complaint as she flopped down on it.

The first four letters in the stack were as she had left them, as were the rest in the bundle. All, that is, except the fifth— the one she was to read next. The swells in the envelope flap showed it had been steamed opened and resealed. The prospect of delving into the next one felt less inviting, like eating unsavory leftovers.

Reopening it, Girly examined its contents. It was now a crossed letter. Girly had heard her mother talking about them. It was a practice from her great grandparent's time, to save on both postage and paper. Aunt Lily had taken her mother's letter, turned it ninety degrees, and written over top of it. By the looks of it, Girly knew it would take a practiced eye to read such a thing. Even so, she was determined to decipher it. She started with her mother's.

> My Little One,
>
> I trust you sleep well in my old bed. It used to be one of my favorite places on earth. In the morning, I imagine, the sun will shine its dapple rays through the window and call you to a new day. The birds singing through the screen. Days that won't end. I hope it's glorious but considering who my sister is, I won't hold my breath.
>
> I suspect your father and I are still travelling. His silence being my only company. I don't think he will ever forgive himself, or me for that matter, for sending you away. All your life a day hasn't

gone by that we haven't seen your face, heard your voice. And now the prospect of that not happening makes life sour in my mouth. I could go on and on about how much I will miss you but it will only make this letter impossible to write and our parting impossible to bear.

Instead I'll write of the characters that populated my childhood. It's been some time since I've had the pleasure of their company but a monthly underground newsletter from Main-Street keeps me apprised of the goings-on. Vive La Forgetta. It's comprised of who Harriet Simpsons has placed poxes on and who should receive them in the future. Henry Henry's road reports. Wilber Sykes musings of fashion. A sommelier commentary of their cellar by Ella and Emma. And Lily's up dated list on who is going to hell. The list accompanies the obituaries. I'm not sure who sends the newsletter but if I had to hazard a guess I would say it must be the grocer. His way of letting me know if Lily had set anything alight.

So where to begin? The individuals that I remember most readily could have stepped out of one of these old nursery rhymes. The ones that delight small children as they bring warnings of the perils of life. Do you remember reciting them for your father and me? Your hands clasped neatly in front of you as you rocked back and forth on the heels of you shoes. The memory is so vivid in my mind's eye that I can almost reach out and touch it.

Lily has to be Mary, Mary quite contrary; the contemptuous Bloody Mary to some of her fellow citizens. Especially to Jack Sprat, could eat no fat and whose wife could eat no lean (the grocer and his wife). The grocer's wife and Lily have always been adversaries. For the two women it was hate at first sight. Even as a child I can remember them squaring off on Main Street/Grand Avenue. Men would lay wagers; children would be herded away to more suitable entertainment. Nothing ever came of their stand-offs except cold stares and harmless mudslinging. Mudslinging in the summer, in the winter they usually peppered each other with bits of ice. I suppose they're too old for that sort of behaviour now, more's the pity. When I became of age and was particularly frustrated with my sister, I looked forward to the grocer's wife beaning her with a well-placed ice chuck.

The fact the grocer runs the store on Lily's behalf doesn't help. I think Lily sees the hostilities as part of the financial arrangement. No matter what Lily does, Jack Sprat and his entourage of one have to serve her at the counter. It must strike a bitter cord. A cord that I think your aunt strives at striking often. The three will not be shed of each other this side of the grave.

Emma, obviously Tuesday's child, is full of grace, and Ell, is Friday's child, loving and giving. Which is a godsend, considering how they keep the peace. I've always marvelled at their simplicity. They take everything at face value and never consider an ulterior motive. It's probably why they have lived so long. Even in my earliest recollections Ella and Emma were old. According to Lily they were born old and their house has always been yellow. The colour of their house irritated your aunt. She claimed the colour wasn't keeping with their communist teaching.

Don't think less of them if I tell you the brandy the Fords brew in their cellar isn't really brandy. They seem to think brandy sounds more refined and sets them apart from anything brewed in some backwoods still. Their elixir isn't really elixir either. It just happens to be whatever concoction they pour into a brown bottle. For some reason they think the brown of a bottle makes its contents medicinal. There is no one in town that will dispute that dubious fact. At least no one east of Main Street.

I suppose Harriet Simpson should be the next candidate for my pen. She is the Poor Jenny is a Weeping of the bunch. Not because she is prone to tears; from what I gather from the newsletter that title lands squarely on the organist's shoulders. No, for Harriet, it has had to do with her long string of beaus, not that any of them were aware they were on said string. And they all were rather shocked when she turned down the proposals they weren't aware they made. Hence Harriet's current position.

And then there is the infamous Tuckers. That brood can't be missed. Viva La Forgetta has spent reams of paper concerning them. They are What are Folks Made of — loving a spot and fighting a lot. The boys — snips and snails and puppy dog-tails. Tucker — slippers that flop and bald-headed tops. Widow Wilson — reels and jeels and old spinning wheels. If ever a family sprung straight from the soil, it is the Tuckers. They hold the most peculiar ideals that seems to seep from the marrow of their bones. Even when life has been more than a little unfair. I'm sure you have heard how many on the west side of Grand Avenue lined their pockets with the Tucker's misfortune. I suppose it was the easiest way to accumulate wealth. Although I don't know how they could look at themselves in the mirror afterwards.

In spite of all their hardships though, the Tuckers are faithful to my sister, in ways that would make God himself scratch his head. Tending to her needs and being vigilant in her defence. I read in one newsletter how they sat outside her house in a downpour just to report back to her on the behaviour of her chickens. Their logic eludes me, as do most things in Forget.

My reminiscing, for now, has come to an end. Your father is pacing the hall. I hope it helps you to understand the place in which I spent my childhood. Keep me in your thoughts, for you are always in mine.

Loving you always,

Your Mother

Girly could see all the characters just as her mother had described them. The sketches in her nursery book fit each and every one. Things made a little better sense now. The uneasy relationship between the grocer and Aunt Lily, the Tuckers change in circumstance, and poor Harriet Simpson and her lack of a brute of a husband. Forget intermingled comedy with tragedy in a way that made it impossible to predict.

Girly closed her eyes on tears. Whether it was the strain of reading the letters or living in Forget at this point she couldn't tell. She had to refocus, a crossed letter held more difficulties then she imagined. Her mother's spidery hand lay beneath the thick letters of Aunt Lily's contribution, like veins beneath muscle, the one almost obscuring the other. All the things her mother had written, Girly stitched together in what seemed to be a situation devoid of reason, even the newsletter. But, even in that, Girly had an unwilling hand.

One of the many tasks Aunt Lily assigned her, was to deliver a letter sealed in two envelopes. Aunt Lily said that was to make sure Girly couldn't hold it up to the light. Her instructions were for Girly Gardener to give the letter to the man with a pipe. Girly hated the thought of going downtown as the gardener. It was the most ridicules get-up; the only consolation was she was sure no one would recognize her.

The man was to be found at dusk leaning against a post in front of the Chinese laundry. He was the same man Harriet Simpson spoke to the day Girly arrived. The one that said Girly wouldn't need much of a coffin. He touched the tip of his nose with his forefinger when Girly handed him the letter. She lifted her veil and did likewise. It was like a secret handshake. There was no doubt in her mind now that he must have been an agent for Vive La Forgetta. Why else the clandestine meeting place and the handoff of an unmarked envelope? Not that a pole in front of the laundry was particularly clandestine, but it felt like it at the time. She rubbed her eyes; when she was able to refocus, Girly began to read the second letter.

> Dear Girly Maid, Girly Gardener, Girly Cook, Girly Butler, Girly Historian, and any other Girly who has yet to be named:
>
> I was looking for mice when I stumbled across a strange bundle of letters. "What's this?" I said only to myself, for as far as I could tell there were no mice within earshot. "Secret letters."
>
> The ribbon that fastened them fell away with ease, as if it were begging me to read what was inside. I felt obligated, for who would offend such an accommodating fastener? As I perused the content, I noticed several discrepancies. First of all, your mother has no idea what goes on in this town. Have you heard anyone mention her? Ask about her health? No. She is as forgettable as

she is memorable. An aberration. Prim and proper stick figure; if boredom doesn't kill her, I don't think anything can.

Furthermore, the Fords weren't born old. Never heard of anything so ridiculous. Why would I claim such a thing? How some memories can become so fabricated I'll never know. We are not a band of nursery characters to be played with at will. The Tuckers are more than what a pen can put to paper. They are impossible to understand, let alone define. Why would she spend her time writing such nonsense? I'm certainly not going to waste any more of my time reading it. It is nothing more than the blatherings of an inferior woman. Let me repeat myself.

Girly rolled her eyes. When her aunt wrote she was going to repeat herself, that was exactly what she did. She rewrote everything that Girly had already read, including the greeting. And when her aunt had finished repeating herself, she reiterated the whole thing again before she signed off.

Yours (I would write lovingly but why?)

Aunt Lily

Girly refolded the letter and put it back into the envelope. She couldn't hear the sound of click-click-clicking knitting needles from the sitting room but assumed Aunt Lily was still working on a sock for a tippy-toe soldier. With a sigh she sank deeper into the bed. Forget and her aunt would be the death of her, she was sure. How to make sense of such non-sense?

Chapter Thirty-three

BEFORE LEAVING her room, Girly dressed as Girly Historian. If she was going to confront her aunt regarding her mother's letters, she wanted to do so in the most intimidating attire she had. She descended the stairs in a stately manner—head high and shoulders back.

Aunt Lily watched her from the bottom step with a look of disbelief. "What's wrong with you?"

Girly stopped mid-stair. "Nothing." She worried her entrance wasn't having the desired effect.

"You look like you're in a constipated funeral procession." Aunt Lily waved her hand at her before turning and disappearing into the sitting room.

"Damn her," Girly said under her breath. She quickly dismissed any thought of a majestic entrance and sped after her. "I have something to say to you."

"Do you?"

"Yes I do."

"Well, it must be something important; you're so distracted you haven't scratched your neck. Not even once."

The awareness of how itchy she was flooded Girly. There wasn't a place she didn't want to scratch. "I'm not itchy," she lied.

"Who are you trying to convince? Me or you?"

The comment made Girly even more flustered. She could hardly articulate what she wanted to say, but then the words flew from her mouth almost of their own accord. "You read my letters, and—"

"And what?"

"And...and...I'm furious with you."

Aunt Lily crossed the room and seated herself on the davenport. "Tell me, how long have you been here?"

"I don't know, a little more than a month."

"And can you remember a time when you haven't been mad at me?"

This was not the way Girly had imagined the conversation going. Even so, she couldn't remember a day that she hadn't been angry enough to pull out her hair or, to be truthful, her aunt's hair. Frustration seemed to be her most constant companion. "That's not the point."

"No, that's not your point. It's my point."

"This is getting us nowhere." Girly took a deep breath. There was no way of getting through to her aunt. "Just don't go into my room again."

"What if there's a fire?"

"What are you talking about?"

"Well, if there's a fire, don't you want me to come get you?"

"Why do I even bother?" Girly turned and headed back up to her room. She scratched all the way.

Chapter Thirty-four

GIRLY HAD barely slammed her bedroom door when Aunt Lily called for her. She stood with her back against the door as she tried to catch her breath. Would she ever be able to deal with that woman?

Aunt Lily bellowed again.

"Who do you want?" Girly called back.

"Girly Historian."

When Girly re-entered the sitting room, her aunt acted as if it was the first time she had seen her that day. The words they'd had a few moments earlier were of no consequence.

"Do I need the typewriter?" Girly Historian asked, still fuming inside.

"Yes, dear."

Girly lugged the typewriter over to a small side table and pulled up a chair.

Aunt Lily told her she was relieved the elixir had done its job. "Now I am cleared of all witch allegations."

Girly scratched her neck. "You want me to type that?"

"Of course, what else would I want you to type? Future generations need to know how quickly things can run amuck; a peaceful town like Forget turning on me with such ease. Maybe this way, it won't happen again."

"You're the only one who accused anyone of anything."

"Well, there's no use pointing fingers now, is there? It only makes you sound petty. How sad. Do you want to be known as the pettiest person in Forget? I think not. Besides, petty people have a reputation of being small-minded, and nobody ever wants to hear from a small-minded, historian. They have such little heads, it's all rather off-putting. Now go fetch Girly Gardener. There are some weeds she should be tending to."

Girly Historian stood up from her typing. She almost ran out of the room, relieved not just to be getting away from her aunt, but to be getting out of the black dress. She had been wearing it longer than usual and was now convinced she would be thoroughly chafed.

"Look at you," Aunt Lily called after her. "The head of a turtle and the shoulders of a bull, looks like every historian I have ever met."

By mid-afternoon Aunt Lily was over the elixir's lingering effects. She was sitting at her post watching Girly Gardener tend the grounds. Girly was weeding the hens' grave when a small pebble struck her on the forehead. She looked up to see Mean Dog Joe beaming down at her.

"I've come to ask you to the pond. Lothario Bill said he would like to see you again."

Girly wiped her hands on her skirt and glanced back to the window where Aunt Lily was loudly rapping. "I think she wants us to come inside," she said.

Mean Dog Joe looked hesitant. "I'd rather not, considering she's a witch now."

"Oh, don't worry about that, apparently she's passed the witch test."

"Passed it because she is or because she ain't?"

"Who knows?"

Mean Dog Joe reluctantly followed Girly into the house. As they entered the sitting room Aunt Lily called him to her. Mean Dog Joe inched his way across the room, but he evidently miscalculated her reach, and soon her bony fingers were wrapped firmly around his jaw. "This one is healthy enough," she said, as she turned his face from side to side.

"Healthy enough for what?" Girly asked.

"To travel."

"Travel?"

"Yes travel. You know how long I have desired to travel. How I've ached to walk the plains of Africa."

"I've never heard you talk about Africa."

Aunt Lily frowned and turned to Mean Dog Joe. "Tell me, boy, how long did it take for you to get here, and what route did you come by?"

Mean Dog Joe twisted his jaw free and stared at her.

"Speak, child, I long to go to your homeland. I long to go to Africa."

"I live in Africa?"

"You most certainly do."

"But Ma always says we live at Tuckers Pond."

"Tuckers pond is Swahili for Africa."

"Wait till I tell my pa!" Mean Dog Joe yelled as he turned and ran out of the house.

"You lied to him," Girly said.

"You can't lie to a pygmy."

"Aunt Lily, he's not a pygmy, he's a Tucker. Blond and blue-eyed, no more African than I am."

"No less African than you are either. Have you ever thought of that? Besides, Tucker, pygmy, there's really no difference. That little trout has helped me make up my mind. We are leaving in the morning for the greatest adventure ever. We're going all the way to Africa — to Tuckers Pond."

Chapter Thirty-five

IT WAS already dark when Girly slipped away to the pond. Aunt Lily thought she was in her room, reading about Africa and its indigenous peoples, of which Aunt Lily said there were at least nine. She had also warned Girly to be leery of wayward pygmies and birdwatching. Girly rolled her eyes and thanked her aunt for her concern. Aunt Lily smiled and insisted she mustn't mistake it for anything sincere.

It was a beautiful evening. Girly kicked a pebble down the street and made cat noises until the dogs barked with venomous intent. She sang to the stars and danced on the tail of a moonbeam. In spite of Aunt Lily, she was beginning to think she might like living in Forget.

As promised, the Thief was waiting for her by the pond. He seemed anxious. "Didn't Joe give you my message? I was about to leave."

"Yes he did, but Aunt Lily had other things she wanted me to tend to. I was reading about Africa."

"Africa?"

"Yes, Aunt Lily decided that Tucker's Pond is in Africa, and all the Tuckers are pygmies. She plans to be their missionary."

"But just last night she was trying to prove she wasn't a witch."

"I know, I'm not sure which I would rather her be—a missionary or a witch; they're both quite exhausting."

The Thief put his hand on her shoulder and laughed. "You'll survive."

"I suppose."

The Thief looked up at the moon. "It amazes me," he said, "that you and I can sleep under the same moon, live in the same town, go to the same church, and I still don't know anything about you."

"I'm not in love with Wilber."

"I know."

"Well, what else would you like to know?"

The Thief stepped toward her, grinned, and raised an eyebrow.

Girly blushed, her breath became short and shallow. "I think I should go."

"Don't go, all I really need to know is this." He brought his mouth gently down on hers.

Later, when Girly crept back into the house, Aunt Lily was waiting for her in the sitting room. She didn't yell or curse. She seemed distracted, and Girly assumed she hadn't been missed.

"I have a letter I want to read you," said her aunt.

Girly took the chair next to a basket of needlework.

Aunt Lily snapped open the page and began to read.

> *Dear Myself,*
>
> *If you remember, my niece has come to live with me. I know I write of her all the time, but I also realize you are getting older and tend to forget. I think the girl is happier now because I don't hear her crying as often in the night. To my surprise, I have even begun to enjoy her company. I hope she feels likewise.*

Aunt Lily dropped the letter and looked directly at Girly. "I'm aware of who you're seeing, and it troubles me," she said. "I want more for you."

Girly sat dumbfounded. She wanted to explain but didn't get the opportunity.

Aunt Lily stood and bent over her niece, in both hands she cupped the girl's face. Then she turned and went upstairs to bed.

Girly was left in the sitting room, gazing after her. "I don't know that woman."

Chapter Thirty-six

PREPARING TO be a missionary in Africa wasn't a simple task, especially with Aunt Lily doing the preparation. Girly was given a whole new persona for the task. Girly Lackey, an all-encompassing name that would alleviate the need for any future Girlies.

Girly Lackey told Aunt Lily Tucker's Pond wasn't in Africa, and she needn't carry on as if they were going on safari, but Aunt Lily just grunted and said Girly Lackey was young and didn't know anything.

"Africa is a long way. We couldn't get there in just one day.

"You silly girl. I suppose you still think the world is flat?" Aunt Lily yelled. "I have gone on many expeditions and have travelled great distances and when you're as experienced as I am, you take shortcuts. We'll go through Greenland."

Girly Lackey gave up her argument.

Aunt Lily had borrowed a dried up milk cow from a nearby farm. She accosted the farmer as he took it to market. She insisted she only need the cow for a few days and if he would allow her such a grand gesture she would take him off the list of people going to hell.

She told Girly a cow was like a camel, only more humble. She was of the mind that she couldn't enter the wilds of

Africa in the same manner as a commoner. Girly cringed at the scheme Aunt Lily had devised. "All the great missionaries, such as Archibald Herrick the Third, made grand entrances, and I'm going to surpass them all," she said.

"Archibald Herrick the Third! There is no such person."

"Shut up."

Planning Aunt Lily's memorable arrival took some time. "I think I shall appear just before twilight. Then the sun will be at my back and will shine radiantly about me, enveloping me in a holy halo." Aunt Lily's brows knitted. "If the masses see me riding a humble milk cow surrounded by a God-like aura, even the hardest heathen heart will break down and weep."

"Or laugh," mumbled Girly Lackey.

When Girly stepped on to the veranda she saw that the cow was wandering around the yard, already washed and curried. The Tuckers must have been there earlier. They had used blueing to whiten its whites and the yellow ribbon that had bound her letters was tied around the tuft at the end of its tail. Girly could feel her cheek muscles tighten. "Aunt Lily," she yelled, "I asked you to leave my letters alone."

"I did," Aunt Lily called through the screen door.

"Then why is my ribbon tied to the cow's tail?"

"You never said not to touch the ribbon," Aunt Lily said as she joined Girly on the veranda. She rubbed her gloved hands together.

Girly gave up, there was no use arguing. "Are you sure you want to do this?"

"Why wouldn't I?"

"It could be dangerous."

Aunt Lily waved her hand through the air. "Pishposh. That cow has been around so long it's almost dead. Besides the farmer's kids have been riding it for years."

It was laborious maneuvering the bony cow into place. Aunt Lily wanted to mount the cow using the front step; the beast wanted to eat her precious flowers. Girly Lackey spent much of the afternoon twisting and driving the ornery cow into a position that would please the most uncommon missionary. Aunt Lily waved her hand and directed Girly in hallowed terms. "Hark now, child, the way is hither," bellowed Aunt Lily from the front step. Her tone still lacked the gentleness that matched the meaning of her words. "I'm beckoning you! Cans't thou hear me beckon?"

"I hear you beckon, Aunt Lily."

"I don't think so. I thinketh thou needest a healing."

"I don't need a healing."

"Come close and I will heal thee with my cane."

Ignoring the love Girly Lackey had for the great missionaries, such as Archibald Herrick the Third, she kindly asked her aunt if she had ever considered missionaries were more often burned at the stake than witches. Aunt Lily stood quietly for a moment and contemplated. It had not occurred to her.

Girly Lackey laboured to lift Aunt Lily from the step onto the cow. As she heaved the old woman, this way and that, she envisioned Aunt Lily flying right over the top and landing in a heap on the other side. It was a relief when Aunt Lily was finally seated, without a horrific incident. Girly heaved a sigh of relief. But it wasn't done; Aunt Lily now insisted on being wrapped in fine netting. It wouldn't have bothered Girly Lackey to perform this simple task, if it had been simple. She had to wrap not only Aunt Lily but the cow.

This was to prevent an attack from the tsetse fly. "I'm not sure what a tsetse fly is, but I am more than convinced it's deadly," said Aunt Lily.

Girly Lackey was left hopelessly unprotected. "One of us needs to die a romantic African death, and I'm far too old for it to be truly romantic," Aunt Lily said. "Just think how many hearts would be turned at the sight of your limp, decaying body, lying lifeless on the ground?" Aunt Lily leaned towards Girly Lackey, squeezing her eyes together. Girly Lackey wiped her aunt's eyes before Aunt Lily continued. "It will be the only time I can say I'm truly proud of you."

Aunt Lily sat erectly on the cow as if she were the Queen of Sheba about to view her royal subjects. She asked Girly Lackey to christen her with a half-empty bottle of elixir she had borrowed from the Fords.

Girly looked at the bottle she had picked up from the veranda. "People don't christen other people this way. They only christen ships."

"How would you know? Have you seen anyone christen a ship?"

"No."

"Well, there you have it. Now just do as I ask."

Girly Lackey rolled her eyes but relented, and to bring peace to an already horrid day she christened her aunt. After several hard blows, though, Girly Lackey gave up. The bottle refused to shatter. Although Aunt Lily didn't lose consciousness, she did bob and weave for some time. Girly Lackey was fearful she might have seriously injured her. In time, Aunt Lily found her voice and made an unholy utterance. "What in the hell did you do that for?"

"You asked me to," Girly Lackey answered, wondering if the blows had damaged her memory.

"I asked you to christen me like the damned minister does a newborn baby. Could you do that? No. Just a few drops of elixir on my blessed forehead, you imbecile. That's all I wanted. Have you seen the minister belt a newborn baby with a bottle of booze?"

Girly Lackey had to concede she had never seen the minister do such a horrendous thing. "I misunderstood. It isn't very often you make a sane request."

The cow began to bellow miserably. Aunt Lily nudged the cow forward with her bony knees. The cow didn't move. Aunt Lily had even less patience after the christening. When the humble beast didn't move after two or three quiet nudges, Aunt Lily began to flail around like a drowning rat. She yelled obscenities to both heaven and hell. Her outrageous behaviour only managed to entangle her in the netting and make her look quite hideous. It took Girly Lackey some time to straighten her out again.

Strangely, the cow quietened and commenced chewing her cud. She seemed to be enjoying Aunt Lily's wild antics. The cow's eyes rolled back in her head, and she appeared to be smiling.

"Should we name the cow?" Girly Lackey asked.

"The donkey in the Bible didn't have a name and neither should our cow." Aunt Lily's face brightened. "Unless, that is, we name the cow after the donkey in the Bible. It's rather fitting don't you think?"

Girly nodded.

As soon as Donkey began her perilous trek to Tucker's Pond, she seemed to have misgivings about her situation. The netting prevented her from taking her usual plodding steps. Instead, she was forced to take dainty little steps as if she were a high society cow. Every time Donkey protested, as cows do, Aunt Lily commented on how treacherous the roads were, and how bad the wind was. It was clear Aunt Lily would never admit that any animal, dumb or otherwise, would object to her as a rider. Girly Lackey made sure they took back lanes and seldom used roads. The less attention they attracted the better. She didn't want to be a spectacle. Even so, a few of the more picaresque citizens of Forget seemed to sense they were coming and lined the lanes and alleyways Girly and her Aunt travelled. Some threw flowers while others gave a noble nod.

They eventually arrived at the pond at sunset. Aunt Lily looked like an ancient Egyptian mummy. Her ravels of netting, twisting in the wind, glowed yellow and orange around her slender frame in the sun's fading light. Donkey had an odd gait and was quite unrecognizable. The two of them were woven so tightly together by the netting they looked as if they were half human, half bellowing beast. Which was which, Girly wasn't sure.

The Tuckers unwrapped Aunt Lily as if she were an oversized Christmas present. They clapped at the sight of her. Donkey seemed greatly relieved to be delivered from her awkward predicament. Aunt Lily proceeded to let the boys touch her fair hands. They made her a necklace of pinecones and laid shiny stones at her feet.

The Thief watched for a while. "Why is your aunt tottering to and fro?"

"Oh, I belted her with a bottle of booze."

The Thief closed his eyes. "There are some things about you I'd rather not know."

Aunt Lily stretched and sat down at the base of a large tree. "Build me a fire," she instructed. "It will keep away the man-eating kangaroos."

The boys ran to gather sticks and twigs. When the fire was bright and snapping Aunt Lily began telling the boys a somewhat fabricated life story. "You know I used to be on stage," she said. "My legs were longer then. Could I ever tango! The men lined up just to get close to me, emptying their pockets on whatever I desired. However, I was chaste, not giving up my virtue for even one kiss. It was the death of many a man." She looked directly in the Tuckers' faces. "There is a lesson in here for you boys."

"What? What's the lesson?"

Aunt Lily looked at her nails. "Virtue is not worth death. It is one of the many lessons I came to teach you. As you are well aware, one has to be careful on this continent. Birdwitchers and birdwatchers are very similar indeed. Mortal men like yourselves can easily be tricked into not seeing such evils. That's what I've been sent here to tell you."

"Who sent you here?" asked Alexander.

"The Society for the Prevention of the Perversion of Birdwatchers."

The boys clapped with approval. Girly rolled her eyes. Her aunt, the chicken lady, and has-been-witch was now the Tuckers' very own missionary.

Chapter Thirty-seven

GIRLY LACKEY watched her aunt deliver a life-changing lecture. Animated, Aunt Lily furrowed and unfurrowed her brow like a flag flapping in the wind. "Subterfuge," she said pointing to her forehead. "That's how we beat the Huns. Never let them know what you're thinking." Her brow furrowed again. "I'm concerned." It unfurrowed. "Now I'm surprised. Concerned, surprised, concerned, surprised."

The Thief leaned against a nearby tree. "I see your aunt is in fine form," he said. "Her pretend Africa hasn't changed her a bit."

Girly could almost see her aunt's ears prick at the perceived slight. The old woman rose to her feet and came nose to nose with The Thief. "Pretend, my pretend Africa," Aunt Lily cawed as her fingers curled like claws. "How dare you, after what your family has done."

The Thief stepped into her. "I'm not my family."

"Yet by their acts you have prospered."

In the shadowy light Girly could see The Thief close his hands into fists. She got between them. "He has only come for a swim Aunt Lily," she said.

"You take me for a fool. No one travels all the way to

Africa for a swim. He's up to no good. Perhaps he needs to fill the corners of his pockets."

"What are you talking about?" Girly asked, feeling the whole situation spiraling out of control.

"Ask Girly Historian," she said to Girly before turning back to The Thief. "I can tolerate you anywhere but here. Here you are wearing a dead man's shoes."

Girly looked at The Thief; her gaze dropped to his shoes. She knew it was just a saying but she couldn't help herself. The Thief just shrugged and continued glaring at her aunt; the standoff wasn't going to be bridged. Aunt Lily curled her lip and drew a line in the dirt with the toe of her shoe before turning back towards the Tuckers. "Lothario the birdwitcher," she said.

"Is that the worst you can come up with?" The Thief asked.

Aunt Lily didn't respond; instead she pursed her lips and resumed furrowing her brow and talking about subterfuge. Girly had no idea subterfuge could be such an all-encompassing topic. It lasted well into the evening. When Aunt Lily finally nodded off, Girly let out a sigh of relief.

"Come," The Thief tugged her arm at the elbow. "I have something to show you."

The thought of slipping off in the moonlight with the Thief was something Girly had dreamed about. But after her aunt's comment and the Thief's response, an unease stirred inside her.

"I don't think we should," she said as she took away the stick Mean Dog Joe was about to poke her aunt with. "It will only prove her right."

"We're not going birdwitching."

The Thief tugged again and Girly relented. He led her down a goat path to the water's edge. The moon showed its full face and the scattered clouds trapped its light, making the night almost as bright as a dull day. The Thief pulled a handful of flat stones from his pocket. "See, I'm not leading you astray." He laid the pile by a clump of cattails. "Have you ever skipped stones?"

Girly shook her head. She wanted to ask him what his family had done but didn't have the nerve. On other occasions The Thief and Aunt Lily had been cordial. They would have never been mistaken for close familiars but neither would they have been considered foes. But now Girly didn't know what they were. What was worse, she didn't know where that left her.

With the tip of his finger The Thief brushed a stray lock across her cheek. The touch both startled and endeared The Thief to Girly. The Thief was the one good thing that had happened to her since arriving in Forget, and according to her aunt that was now dubious. Even so, when The Thief stepped closer, and without asking slipped his arm around her, she did not refuse him. He laid a smooth stone in the palm of her hand, bending her fingers until they carefully cradled the stone between the curve of her forefinger and thumb. He drew her hand back; Girly felt light-headed. And when the stone went sailing through the air, he didn't release her. The stone skipped along the water's surface, once, twice, thrice, before it disappeared into the ripples. His breath brushed the side of her neck and he whispered in her ear. "That wasn't that bad, was it?"

She could feel his heart beating through her paisley dress and she trembled. "No," she said. The word straddled Girly's misgivings.

The Thief's hand still cupped around Girly's, "Shall we try again?"

All Girly wanted to do was to slow her breathing and heart rate; they were so loud, she could hardly hear what he was saying. She couldn't answer. It was almost a relief when Aunt Lily's horrified shrieks brought them back to the fire.

The boys had taken the netting and wrapped it around Aunt Lily and the tree she was leaning against. They braced her with sticks and the odd log. Alexander said they were afraid she might topple over.

Now that Aunt Lily was awake, she was plainly horrified. Her gaze moved wildly from face to face. "Burn me at the stake would you? You wretched swine!" She lifted her face toward heaven. "I'm coming, Archibald. I'm not a witch, and to be truthful I'm not much of a missionary either."

The Tuckers stared uneasily, as if wondering how their act of kindness could have been so thoroughly misinterpreted.

Girly Lackey tried to calm her. "They meant no harm; they were just making sure you didn't hurt yourself."

"And you expect me to believe that? I suppose when I turn my back you'll all try to christen me! I knew coming to Africa was a mistake, but no, you wouldn't listen to me. Thought you knew better, didn't you?"

The Thief pulled a jackknife from his pocket, which elicited a shriek from Aunt Lily; he leaned over and cut her free.

Taking a few shuddering breaths, Aunt Lily calmed herself. "I forgive you for trying to take my life," she said to the Tuckers. "I think it's because you were trying to watch birds at night. It's easy for simpletons to get watching and witching confused in the dark. Especially when they can't spell."

"That's not true, Miss Lily," Alexander explained.

But Aunt Lily was steadfast in her belief and ignored any claim to the contrary. "It's time for me to be off. I will never forget you boys, but I must leave for the land of my youth, and return to civilization."

"I'll take you, Miss Lily," The Thief offered.

"That won't be necessary. The only thing I need is the moon. The poor man's lantern." Aunt Lily dramatically turned, called Girly Lackey, and they began their long trek back to town.

Chapter Thirty-eight

SHE WAS aware The Thief watched her as she tried to drag Donkey. He had such a smug look on his face. It made Girly want to smack him. Donkey seemed to have enjoyed her liberty so much she refused to leave the pond. "It will take the loving hands of a missionary to show that cow the way," Aunt Lily insisted.

Donkey disagreed.

"The only explanation I can think of," Aunt Lily tugged hard on the lead, "is that Donkey is not a God-fearing cow."

"How do you make cows fear God?" asked Girly.

"That's a stupid question." Aunt Lily eyed the Thief, who was now sitting by the fire in amongst the Tuckers. "Best leave her here for now, but I don't know if all the subterfuge in the world can save her from that Hun."

After bidding Donkey adieu, Girly and Aunt Lily retraced their steps back to town. Although the moon gave an abundance of light, the odd root or rotted tree trunk impeded their progress. As they passed Tucker's front porch, Aunt Lily complained she'd already grown tired of her journey.

Tucker and a companion rocked by lamplight on the front porch. Aunt Lily turned on her heel judging them both.

Girly recognized the man sitting next to Tucker; he was the one who had delivered her bag and her mother indicated in her last letter that he wrote the road report for *Vive La Forgetta*.

Aunt Lily threw back her shoulders and placed her hands on her hips. "Henry Henry," she bellowed, "get off that step and drive me back to town."

Henry leaned back in his chair and sucked on his pipe. "I'm visiting, Miss Lily, and not of the mind to take you anywhere."

Aunt Lily kicked dirt into the air. "I know things about you H.H., and I'm not afraid to tell them. You may think you are a powerful man but I know what you keep in your pocket."

Henry Henry tapped his pipe on the heel of his boot and rocked uncomfortably in his chair. He examined Aunt Lily before rising to his feet. "Be seeing you, Tucker," he sighed as he stepped off the porch and ambled towards his wagon.

Aunt Lily rubbed her hands triumphantly together. "You can come too, Girly Lackey," she said. "Won't want to abandon you in the woods like some Gretel. You don't even have breadcrumbs."

Tucker followed Henry Henry to the wagon. He picked Girly Lackey up and tossed her in the back. She scrambled to her feet and tried to spy over Henry Henry's shoulder. She wondered what he had in his pocket, but by then Aunt Lily had climbed up beside him and told Girly to avert her eyes. "Young girls shouldn't be so concerned about what a man carries around in his pants," she said.

Girly Lackey sank back in the box, wanting to disappear. She had barely settled when Henry Henry snapped the reins and turned the horses towards town. "Hold on," he yelled. Aunt Lily tightened her grip. An evil smile spread over her face. "I hope we run over someone I don't like."

"That could be almost anyone," Girly Lackey answered back.

"Then our odds are good."

Henry Henry groaned and urged the horses on.

"You're not much of a talker are you H.H.?" Aunt Lily said into the night. "We have a long journey ahead of us, and I would appreciate it if you could be a bit more sociable. Have you ever spent an evening with pygmies?"

Henry Henry grunted and the horses quickened to a trot.

"I'm not just talking about ordinary pygmies! I'm talking about albino pygmies." Aunt Lily paused and waited for a response, but none came. "I expect you haven't," she continued. "Of course, being a missionary, I have. I think I'll write a book."

As abruptly as the trip had begun, it was over—long journey a myth—and they were home. Aunt Lily's feet barely touched the ground before Henry Henry was off. She didn't even have time to utter a rude goodbye. Girly and Aunt Lily stood in the roadway a moment longer watching moonbeam dust stirred up by the wagon wheels.

The fatigue of the day hit Girly as she trudged into the house and made her way up the stairs. She longed to climb in between cool sheets. Outside her bedroom door, Aunt Lily took the hallway chair and handed it to Girly, "You'll be needing this."

Girly could feel herself blush. She wasn't aware her aunt knew how she braced a chair against the door. "Can I ask you a question?" Girly said almost without thinking.

"I suppose."

"What did The Thief's family do?" She closed her eyes as she waited for the response. If The Thief's was one of the families her mother wrote about in her last letter, Girly didn't know how she could face him again.

Aunt Lily laid her hand on Girly's arm. "If I tell you I'll only start to cry." Aunt Lily's hand remained on Girly's arm a moment longer. "But I can tell you about Henry Henry and what he keeps in his pocket."

Girly put down the chair; Aunt Lily saw the gesture as an invitation and sat on it. "Well, he's named after both his father and grandfather. Both were Henrys. They were heroic; men that H.H. could be proud of. It had been a tradition in the old country for the H. men to have the fastest horses. Whenever anyone married, it was the Hs they depended upon. If the young couple could get out of town before anyone could pass them, their happiness was guaranteed. But if they were passed, they were doomed."

"What does he keep in his pocket?"

"You've heard of the cat lady?"

Girly nodded.

Aunt Lily narrowed her eyes and her response made Girly shiver. "He's the man who found her, and in his pocket he keeps her half-eaten eye!"

Girly Lackey shook her head in disbelief.

"You'd be surprised at the things men have bulging in their pockets."

Girly wanted to ask more, but Aunt Lily said she had hurt her liver on her continental journey and needed rest.

"How do you know it's your liver?" Girly Lackey asked.

"All great missionaries hurt their liver at one time or another."

Chapter Thirty-nine

In the morning, Aunt Lily said her liver still hurt and sent Girly Maid over to the Ford's for elixir. The sisters were practicing taking communion. They were wearing black, their gloved hands pulled back their veils when they greeted Girly at the door.

"There is a new young priest in town," Ella explained. "And we are going to the parish to see if we can tempt him."

"Yes, it is the only way we can tell if he is worth his salt," said Emma. Her bright red lip-colour was as much on her teeth as her lips.

"But you attend the same congregation as we do," Girly said, "and it's not Catholic."

"He doesn't know that," said Emma.

Girly couldn't think of a response that would sway the sisters. They seemed too determined. She wondered what that poor young man would think, two stale vixens bent on defiling his reputation, it would be quite an introduction to Forget. Girly almost wished she could be there. Instead she focused on the matter at hand. "Aunt Lily has sent me for elixir."

The sisters looked at each other knowingly before

producing a dusty brown bottle. "We've already mixed it," said Emma. "We thought Miss Lily might need it after she finished her missionaring."

"Yes," Girly said. "She hurt her liver."

"Nothing like elixir to fix a liver."

Girly was pretty sure the Fords lacked something when it came to medical diagnosis but she nodded her thanks and left the Fords to their communion.

Aunt Lily was busy writing her memoirs when Girly Maid returned. She had propped herself up on the davenport in the sitting room with a pen in one hand and an empty glass in the other. "Hurry up and pour," she ordered as soon as Girly Maid entered the room. Then she patted the spot beside her and instructed Girly Maid to sit down. "Don't tell Girly Historian, but I'll do this bit of writing on my own; it's a bit too steamy for her." She carefully looked her niece over. "Have I ever told you about Archibald Herrick the Third?"

"I think I've heard you mention his name."

"He was a great love of mine; the greatest missionary who ever lived. He has inspired me from the grave. I think it was said best in his book, *Archibald: The Boy, The Man, and The Corpse.* He said that a man was a person, and a missionary was a man. What a genius! Can you feel yourself being inspired?"

"No."

Aunt Lily took a long drink of elixir. "It was when I was just a girl. Unlike most girls, my beauty didn't fade. He wanted me to join him, as his partner, on his journey through life. I had so many wanting my hand, I couldn't say yes to him. He was skinny and unattractive, like you, but if I had known he was destined for greatness, things would have been different."

"How would they have been different?"

"I would have made uses of him. Goodness knows what kind of wonders a missionary might come across—wonders that he might send the girl he loves." Aunt Lily took another drink of elixir and primped her dress. "Being a missionary isn't an easy life you know. Have I told you of my trip to Africa?"

"I was there, and it wasn't to Africa, it was to Tucker's Pond."

Aunt Lily grunted and waved her hand in the air. "I think it is time for you to tell Girly Lackey to fetch the cow."

Bringing the cow home was much easier than Girly had anticipated. Donkey was much more agreeable in daylight, and she contentedly ambled behind. When told, Aunt Lily was delighted. "Donkey must have found God in the night, which in itself made our trip to Africa worthwhile." Aunt Lily narrowed her eyes and thought for a moment. "I think we should tell the farmer about Donkey's conversion. Any man would be proud to know that on Judgment Day, his cow will be standing by the pearly gates, mooing his name."

Girly wasn't as eager as her aunt. Donkey seemed content eating the flowers, and Girly was happy to hide in the house. But Aunt Lily insisted, and she complied.

As they wove their way through town, the dried up milk cow in tow, Aunt Lily stopped and talked to anyone who would listen. "Touch the cow and be healed," she shouted. To Girly's surprise, some actually stopped and touched the cow.

"We just got back from Africa last night," Aunt Lily said to the crowd petting the cow. "And it will be a few more days before we know if my niece will die of some unfortunate disease. We can pray it is so. It might make up for the disappointment when Dead Hilary lived." She smiled and looked tenderly at Girly. "It's been a long time since we've had a really good funeral. If she'd put in a little effort, I'm sure we won't be let down."

The crowd nodded and patted Donkey hard on her side. Girly wasn't sure what to make of the situation, but it didn't matter. In the middle of her aunt's unorthodox sermon the grocer's wife lumbered by, and Aunt Lily's audience mindlessly turned and followed her. Aunt Lily snorted and spat. "One trip to Africa and you're forgotten," she said. "I don't know what's become of this town, but I'm going to find out."

They followed the procession to the train station. There were already a number of people gathered there. Aunt Lily spied the crowd and sniffed. "Shows you how much I get out. I thought some of these folks were dead."

People huddled around whispering about some grand event. "It must be some great missionary's return from Africa," Aunt Lily crowed, but this proved not to be the case. The crowd had come to watch the grocer's wife.

The grocer's wife blinked slowly and held her hands demurely in front of her. She didn't speak and acted as if she were quite alone. Aunt Lily poked the man in front of her. "What's going on?"

He shrugged and turned away.

Aunt Lily continued to poke people while Donkey swished her tail impatiently. Every time the tail thwacked some unsuspecting spectator, Aunt Lily turned and said, "You're healed."

Girly stood well back from Aunt Lily and the cow. She could see her aunt was getting frustrated with Donkey's public service; it was interfering with her spying on the grocer's wife. Aunt Lily grabbed Donkey's tail and held it securely in her gloved hand. She waved the crowd back. "There will be no more healing today." Donkey bellowed, but Aunt Lily would not let go of her tail. "In spite of your fervour, Donkey, there are still priorities a cow just doesn't understand. Who do you think you are? A head-thwacker extraordinaire?"

From a distance, Girly could see how her aunt might be entertaining, but close up she was just exhausting.

The grocer's wife was waiting patiently on the platform when the train pulled into the station. She cleared her throat, stepped towards the conductor and loudly inquired, "Perchance, Sir, is there any cargo on board for me?"

"And who is me?"

She swatted him on the arm, "You know who I am. We grew up together."

"Just following protocol; can't be too careful." The conductor checked his list. The crowd leaned forward as he opened the door of one of the freight cars. Aunt Lily began poking people again.

He disappeared into a car only to reappear leading a large hairy thing, the size of a small emaciated horse. The grocer's wife again cleared her throat and again inquired about her cargo, seemingly not willing to believe this could be hers. "I've come to fetch a dog, and not just any dog, mind you. A golden afghan; a dog fit for queens."

The conductor checked his papers and then looked at the creature from the train. "Have you ever seen a golden afghan?" he asked.

"No, but I've imagined that it's gold and fluffy, something I can tuck in the crook of my arm."

He handed the leash to the grocer's wife. "Well I hate to be the bearer of bad news, but there is no doubt about it. Fit for queens or not, this monstrosity is yours."

The grocer's wife stood motionless for a moment as the dog panted beside her. She tried to hand the leash back to the conductor but he refused it, as he had already checked the delivery off his list.

Aunt Lily eyed the whole scene suspiciously. Her nostrils flared, "Why anyone would waste their time coming to see a big ugly dog is beyond me." She raised her voice so it carried above the crowd. "That's just a dog," she said. "I have a healing cow; come get your head thwacked."

No one seemed to be listening; they were too busy watching the grocer's wife trying to look stately as her new dog dragged her down the street.

"Let's go home," said Girly.

Aunt Lily put her hand on Donkey's side. "Let's." All along Beggars Can't be Choosers, Aunt Lily leaned heavily against Donkeys side. "I've never had a friend like you," she said to the cow. "Too bad the farmer is planning to eat you."

"Don't tell her that," Girly said, pulling on the lead.

"You want me to lie to her? We're kindred spirits." Aunt Lily slipped in a yard adjacent to the street, stooped down and began picking a bouquet of flowers: daisies, pansies, and sweet peas.

Girly knew her aunt took liberties but this was far more than a liberty; it was theft. She tugged harder on Donkey's lead but it did nothing to hurry their procession. "Do you know whose yard that is?"

Her aunt stood and examined the yard she was pilfering. The house was smaller than her own but well cared for. White with blue shutters, it seemed a pleasant place. "I think it's the grocer's."

"You think."

"Well it's not like we socialize on purpose."

The quiet peaceful walk that could have been was now, for Girly, a slow dash home. She envisioned the grocer's wife spying Aunt Lily through her window or worse coming down the street and sicking her dog fit for queens on them. "Come on, Donkey, can't you walk any faster?"

Donkey stopped short, chewed her cud and blinked her big brown eyes. Girly tugged harder on the lead, almost losing her balance.

Aunt Lily, oblivious to the panic Girly felt, meandered through the flower bed breaking some blooms off by the stem while pulling others out by the root: monkshood, marigolds, and poppies. Between plucking flowers and shaking the dirt off the roots, she glanced up at the grocer's house, "Did you see that woman make a spectacle of herself today? I would never do anything like that."

Girly wanted to scream.

In time the three adventurers made it back to their yard. Girly tied Donkey to the hitching post at the gate. Aunt Lily leaned against the railing while Donkey munched the flowers she held in her hand. "Give me a minute to catch my breath," she said. "Being a world renowned missionary takes a lot out of a person."

Girly knew her aunt wanted her to sympathise but she couldn't bring herself to, instead she walked past her and into the house. "Would you like Girly Cook to put the kettle on?"

"No," said Aunt Lily. "I think I'll go up for a nap,"

As the afternoon wore on and there were no signs of Aunt Lily rising. Girly went out on the veranda on her own to wait for Henry Henry. It had been arranged that he would fetch Donkey. When he arrived, Girly handed him the cow's lead. "She doesn't like to eat marigolds," she said, "and she's kind of an ambler."

Henry Henry nodded and tied the rope to a ring fastened at the back of the wagon's box. Girly leaned her head against Donkey's. She wanted to tell Henry Henry that Donkey had become a Christian and that there was no longer any need to take her to the butcher. It would be like the Romans throwing believers to the lions. The words lay on her tongue but she swallowed them back.

She closed her eyes and felt Donkey's lashes brush the side of her cheek. "God speed." she whispered in Donkey's ear as Henry Henry climbed onto the wagon's seat and urged the horses forward. "Moo my name too." Being witness to the old cow swaying lackadaisically behind the wagon seemed cruel, considering what was likely waiting for her. Girly watched the once crisp yellow ribbon in Donkey's tail swish back and forth until the cow was out of sight. She wished Aunt Lily was there.

As she walked back into the house Girly checked the clock on the mantel. Aunt Lily should have been up already. Girly went upstairs to check her bed, it hadn't been slept in. Nor was the old woman reclining on the davenport or pelting anyone with cookies from the back porch. Aunt Lily was nowhere to be found. It took a great deal of searching to track her down. Girly finally found her rounding the corner of the chicken coup. Aunt Lily was covered with long golden hairs and looked like something had mauled her.

"Aunt Lily," Girly gasped, bringing her hand to her mouth. "What have you done?

A somewhat dazed look covered Aunt Lily's face. She brushed her hand down the front of her dishevelled dress. "Nothing."

"Are you sure?" Girly leaned over and plucked a long golden hair from her aunt's eyelashes.

"As sure as sure can be," Aunt Lily said, as she skipped into the house.

Aunt Lily was still divesting herself of hair when the minister rapped loudly at the door. After taking his hat, Girly led him into the sitting room. He got straight to the point. "Miss Lily, where were you this afternoon?"

"Napping."

"Napping?" He looked at Girly for conformation. Girly shrugged and slipped into the rocking chair across form the davenport.

"Yes napping," Aunt Lily repeated.

"I don't believe you." He turned towards Girly. "And where were you this afternoon?"

Girly almost fell out of the rocker. "Waiting on my aunt to finish her nap."

"I think this plot was devised by more than one; you were seen."

Girly wanted to ask him what the hell he was talking about but thought better of it. Whatever this misunderstanding was, it had to be connected to the chicken comment Aunt Lily attributed to her in church, Girly was sure of it. Now the minister thought they were in cahoots. Aunt Lily was blinking innocently when the minister grabbed her arm with one hand and Girly with the other. He half led, half dragged them to the window. There on the other side of the white picket fence stood the grocer, and tied to the grocer was the great dog. The dog stood there panting and drooling and looking rather thin.

Aunt Lily pulled her arm free. "I've looked out this window before, haven't I, Girly?"

"She has."

The minister grabbed her arm again, "What do you see?"

"My garden."

"And you?" He shook Girly's arm.

"My aunt's garden." Her heart was beating in her throat. She had never been accused of anything before, let alone grabbed and tossed about by a ruffian. "You're hurting me," she blurted out.

Aunt Lily looked around the minister to her niece, a note of disgust in her voice. "I forgot to tell you, she's made of sugar, I never let her go out in the rain. That being said, she has been known to verbally attack thespians willy-nilly."

Girly narrowed her eyes. "You're going to bring that up now?"

"Now as good as any." She narrowed her eyes back.

The minister ignored their comments and tightened his grip. "I'm losing my patience, ladies. What lays beyond the garden?"

"I see the grocer tied to that ugly dog," said Aunt Lily.

"And why is it ugly?"

"It was born that way, wasn't it Girly?"

Girly had to concede that it was probably born ugly.

"No, he was not born that way! He is ugly because someone shaved him!"

Aunt Lily put her finger to her chin. "Perhaps he had lice."

"No, he didn't have lice!"

"Well, at least now he's something worth seeing, isn't he?"

The minister turned red as he questioned them further, but Aunt Lily insisted she had been napping and Girly just stared at him blankly. He seemed as flustered as when he arrived.

As Aunt Lily pulled the last golden hair from her mouth, she patted the minister on the arm and winked. "Maybe that dog needs to go see the healing cow."

Chapter Forty

IT WAS a relief when Girly finally braced her bedroom door with the hall chair that evening. Aunt Lily locked herself in her own bedroom, weeping about Donkey's demise. She even refused supper. Girly felt tired to the bone. She didn't know what day of the week it was, or the time for that matter; nor did she care. It was dark outside and she was making her escape. Taking her stack of letters in hand she settled on the window seat and lit a candle. She needed to read her mother's words. Something to connect Girly with who she used to be.

The untampered envelope tore easily; she felt the paper rip beneath her fingertips. Maybe the talk with her aunt had made a difference. Maybe she would have some privacy, some secrets.

> Lemon drop,
>
> I'm sure it has crossed your mind, on more than one occasion, that you have a somewhat fabricated idea of your family history. For that I take full responsibility. The family tree we hung in the drawing room reflects your father's family. Mine is rolled up in the far corner of the upstairs linen closet. I didn't think you would ever look for anything in there.

I would hate to give you the impression I was ashamed of where I came from but the longer I lived in Rosedale, the more I hid my past. Then when Lily insisted you come to stay with her or she would pay us a visit, I knew we had no choice. Imagine your aunt in Rosedale; I would never be able to show my face in public again.

It was at one of my many bridge games that the ruse started. My mother painted sunsets on the French Riviera and my father wrote poems to commemorate the emancipation of the butterfly from its cocoon. In truth my mother never held a paint brush and my father had a tin ear when it came to poetry. In spite of this, I assure you, your grandparents were neither grand nor plain. They were splendid. We were splendid, the four of us. I can't say what broke the spell.

After I went away to finishing school things changed. On my visits home Lily became more remote. My life bloomed and hers faded. I know she secretly wrote letters to her dead fiancé. My mother said she used to burn them in the fireplace so her thoughts could mingle with his spirit. The whole notion made me sad for her.

When I brought your father home, she hardly spoke to him. He said it was jealousy; she said she couldn't stomach him. I don't know what it was. At our wedding she turned her back when we said our vows. I never asked her why.

Just before your second birthday I brought you to Forget; Lily was away. Your grandmother sat all night watching you sleep while your grandfather paced behind her. Unfortunately, Lily came home unexpectedly. It didn't go well, and I never returned.

This is my sad story to tell. I'm glad I've finally put pen to paper. In truth I pray that at least one of us can look upon Lily's declining years with fondness. She deserves that much.

I trust I have given you more answers than questions. Think of me often, as I think of you.

Always,

Your Mother

Girly looked out the window but saw nothing but the reflection of her face in the candle light. She couldn't imagine her family falling apart as her mother's did. The very thought of such a thing brought about a feeling of vulnerability she had never felt before. Even when her parents sent her away, her anger didn't squelch the need for them. What squelched her mother's need for her only sister? Surely it couldn't have been an unknown misunderstanding. Girly brought her knees to her chest. She felt more alone than before, and instead of answers, her mother had only given her more questions.

Chapter Forty-one

GIRLY COOK rose to Aunt Lily fluttering about the kitchen. "There will be two coming for tea this morning," she said. "You'll have to go to the bakery to buy some fresh dainties."

"I bought fresh dainties yesterday."

"That's yesterday's dainties. We didn't have anyone over for tea yesterday. Company expects today's dainties." Aunt Lily put her hands on Girly's cheeks. "There are so many things you need to learn as a cook."

Girly wanted to tell her aunt that this wasn't Rosedale and day old pastries wouldn't hurt her social standing. But considering what she read the night before, thought better of it. "Why are you making such a fuss? It's only tea."

"Only tea! Only tea! How can you say such a thing? Tea is the essence of a civilized society."

Girly Cook took an apron from the hook on the back of the cellar door and put it on. If tea was the essence of a civilized society, she questioned why they sold tea in Forget.

"Make sure you set out the best china," her aunt continued, "you know the matching set, the ones that aren't glued together." Aunt Lily surveyed the kitchen as if she were an inspector of some grand hotel. "And tell Girly Maid to iron a clean tablecloth, without burning down the house."

"Is there any other way to iron a tablecloth?" Girly Cook muttered.

Wilber Sykes was the first of the two guests to arrive. He appeared leery, and made a maneuver on his crutches that would have impressed the Flying Wallendas as he swept past Girly when she offered him her hand at the door. "I have come to see Miss Lily," he said.

"Yes," Aunt Lily called from the sitting room. "We are going to make a plan for how to exact revenge on Bessie Hilmar's son. Can you imagine that boy thinking he can get away with what he did? Attacking a perfectly good midget at a Sunday school picnic. The gall of some six year olds."

Wilber nodded. "That's right." He turned his head as he hobbled, not seeming to want to let Girly out his line of sight. "I want to make it clear that I'm not here as your, or any of the other Girlys', love interest."

Girly smiled. "Thank you for being so upfront."

"It's the least I can do," Wilber said, the muscles in his face tightening, "for the girl who tried to force feed me her love."

"I didn't force feed you."

"Really? Then what would you call it?"

Girly wanted to say she was being kind but considering he was semi-conscious at the time, he probably had a skewed interpretation of her actions. Despite Wilber's misgivings, she escorted him into the sitting room.

When he was within swatting distance, Aunt Lily knocked his crutch with her cane. "What did you expect?" she asked in a somewhat hushed voice. "Buying pastry from a volatile virgin at a pie auction; it's all the makings of a scandal."

The Thief was the next to arrive. "I'll welcome him myself," Aunt Lily said; pushing past Girly, she opened the door and waved him in. "Come in, come in and make yourself at home." The Thief stepped nervously over the threshold.

"What are you afraid of?"

"Not afraid, Miss Lily, leery."

Aunt Lily frowned before spritzing him all over with perfume. "That's not what I expected you to be wearing, it's so disappointing, but I can't change the verse now."

The Thief coughed and sputtered as he stepped out of the cloud. Although it was The Thief who'd been sprayed, it was Wilber who nearly fainted. Girly had to half drag, half carry him to an armchair.

"A deadly allergy," he wheezed.

"Oh, not again." Aunt Lily slammed the perfume bottle down on the mantel. "Every time your tongue swells a little, Wilber, you act like it's the end of the world. I swear if you wreck my tea party I'll never forgive you."

"My tongue's not swollen."

"Good, then there shouldn't be a problem."

Wilber sank deeper into the arm chair, his face as white as it had been after the infamous attack. Girly Maid wiped his brow with a wet cloth while Aunt Lily leaned over him and pinched his cheek. "We'll get some colour in you yet," the old woman said as her efforts brought tears to Wilber's eyes.

"Stop that," Girly said, slapping her aunt's hand away. "I think you've done enough damage for one morning."

Straightening, Aunt Lily walked to the table where the tea had been arranged. She examined the cups with an air of indifference. "That's enough lying around Wilber. Come sit for tea. You'll get no more attention carrying on that way; I should know."

"I've not come for tea. I've come to seek vengeance." Wilber's voice was a faint whisper.

"Plans have changed. I think both you and Lothario Bill here need a little culture—a poetry reading to be precise." Aunt Lily pulled a folded piece of paper from the sleeve of her dress. "Coincidentally, I have written such a poem for this very occasion. It is called, *The Small Man and The Man of Significant Aroma*."

"I don't think this is a good idea," said Girly Maid, realizing what her aunt was about to do. The Thief and Wilber looked uncomfortably at one another.

Aunt Lily held her up hand to silence them. After a pause, she pursed her lips into an almost perfect heart and began to recite her poem.

> If I were small, not big at all, who should my love be?
>
> Should he smell sweet as roses, be old as Moses or sing diddle dum de?
>
> I search high and low, but where should I go? From the ground or to the top of a tree,
>
> But then I saw a red dress upon him and smelling a smell that could kill me.
>
> And what do you know his name was Lothario, a name that did suit me
>
> In spite of my height he gave my heart flight and I bounced him right here on my knee.

There was no applause as she refolded the paper and returned it the sleeve of her dress. "What the poem lacks in length, it makes up for with passion," she said, looking from Wilber to The Thief, a hopeful smile on her lips.

Girly could feel the silence, every tick of the mantel clock was almost jarring, but she wasn't sure she wanted to bridge it. The poem was preposterous. How her aunt could have written such a thing, let alone recite it, she'd never know. Yet she felt she had to do something, as the strain of the stillness was almost unbearable. "Aunt Lily," she finally said, "I'm not sure your matchmaking services are needed right now; why not pour the tea?"

Seeming somewhat dumbfounded from the lack of response, Aunt Lily appeared not to have heard her niece. She walked over to Wilber. "Don't you think Lothario has pretty hair?"

Wilber wheezed that he did.

"Well, that's something." Aunt Lily squeezed his shoulder and let out a long breath. "Now if Lothario Bill would only admit he was a hermaphrodite the whole town will be happy."

Chapter Forty-two

"**Every season** has its joyous celebrations," Aunt Lily told Girly, "and for the summer solstice, we have the Moonlight Dance. Some think it's a lower form of entertainment. It's even been scandalized in the Regina paper. If I remember correctly, the article quoted me as saying: *At the dance there is drinking and smoking and dancing too close with thy neighbour's wife. But not coveting. That doesn't happen until closer to Christmas, at the annual revival.*" Aunt Lily narrowed her eyes and folded her hands in her lap. "But no matter how base it is, it doesn't stop the folks from Forget from going. There is no form of entertainment too low for them."

The town was full of happy preparation. People had been tapping their toes for days. Even the grocer's thin face sported a smile. He winked at Girly Maid when she came into the market. She looked down at what she was wearing. The buttons on her blouse were done up, her apron neatly tied, although the maid's cap bulged in its tiny lace pocket. It must have been an anomaly. She stepped back out the store and re-entered; when she did he winked again.

"Careful," the grocer's wife said as she dusted a shelf of canned goods, "you're going to pull a muscle."

"Are you talking to me?" asked Girly.

"No, I'm talking to my dolt of a husband."

Girly Maid looked down at her shopping list, perusing its contents, but when she looked up again there was the grocer leaning on a broom, winking. His wife was right; he was going to pull a muscle. He reminded Girly Maid of the automaton in the fortune telling machine. She had seen it outside United Cigar Store at Sunnyside Beach. It was obvious winking was something the grocer wasn't in the habit of doing, as the wink was almost mechanical in its execution. Girly Maid was so flustered that she left without filling her order. Aunt Lily was furious.

"How can you be defeated by a little winking? He does that every year. The thought of a little libation makes him lose his mind; everyone else ignores him."

Girly Maid looked at the list in her hand. "Do you want me to try again?"

"No, I'll send Girly Gardener. In that getup it's more libel he'll take her for a wicker man than anything else. If she comes home unsinged it will be a miracle."

She hated going downtown as Girly Gardener; it was humiliating. Since coming to live with her aunt she hadn't refused any of her aunt's requests when it came to her attire. Girly thought of doing that now, just refuse, but then she thought of her mother's advice: *as long as you do as she asks you'll fare well, but remember to do as she asks even if you think her logic is a bit muddled. It will keep her calm and make your stay bearable.* How difficult would the woman be to live with if Girly showed she had a mind of her own? She suspected impossible.

Pulling the injured trolley was even more difficult in her rubber boots and the improvised bee-keeper hat. The traction on the boots was non-existent and the netting on the hat obscured her vision. She ran into at least three trees, or at least she thought they were trees; she apologized just in case. The grocer didn't wink when she entered the market but he didn't toss lit matches at her either, which was a relief. He just stood there and gawked, his jaw unhinged.

The grocer's wife told Girly she never looked better. Girly couldn't think of a worse shopping debacle.

When her mortification was complete, it was a relief to slip up to her room. She didn't even bother bracing her bedroom door with a chair. What was the use? Girly threw her beekeeping hat to the floor and flopped down on the bed. She didn't want to think about what just happened, praying with every step in those damnable rubber boots The Thief didn't see her. At least she was pretty sure he hadn't seen her, but with the netting obstructing her vison, she couldn't be entirely sure. She closed her eyes and let out a long sigh. There had to be something to distract her, something to take her way from it all. Her eyes snapped open—the Moonlight Dance! It must be something extraordinary to cause such a stir, at least for those who lived east of Main Street.

Girly sat up, she didn't know what to wear. Reaching under her pillow she pulled out the Eaton's catalogue she had pilfered from the sitting room. It was out of season but she didn't care; there had to be something within its pages that would trump anything in the high boy. Why her mother had the upstairs maid buy her traveling apparel, Girly would never understand. Esther and Girly had never been fond of one another and the clothes Esther picked only mirrored their mutual distain. There wasn't an ounce of celebration in any of them.

Dead Hilary's dress wasn't even a consideration and Aunt Lily refused to let her charge anything at Deauvilles, the fancy dress shop on Grand Avenue. Closing her eyes, she envisioned the sea-foam frock that was displayed in the store front window. Its beaded fringes spiralled down it like a cascading waterfall. If she bobbed her hair, Girly was sure she would look divine—a real flapper, even Daphne would be jealous. Every time Girly Cook went to the bakery she stopped in front of Deauvilles to admire it. She promised her aunt if she were allowed to buy it, she would forgive her of anything, even the poem. Aunt Lily only laughed and said families never forgive.

Girly lay back down on her bed and flipped through the catalogue. Satin dresses with accordion pleats, modish frocks made of some kind of artificial silk tricolette, and still others of silk crêpe de Chine. In Toronto, Girly would have never dreamed of perusing the pages of a sales catalogue; but this was not Toronto, and these dresses were now something only to be dreamed of. She closed the catalogue and stared at the ceiling. Cinderella must have felt the same way, she thought, but unlike Cinderella, she didn't have a fairy godmother.

"Can I come in?" Aunt Lily asked as she opened the door. "I think I may have a solution to your problem."

"And what problem is that?" said Girly propping herself up on an elbow.

"Well I know how tempting it might be to go to the dance as one of the Girlies, but I don't think it would be a good idea. Girly Maid falls apart at a simple wink and Girly Cook is so fixated on dainties I'm afraid people might find her odd."

Aunt Lily walked over and unlocked the closet. It was empty except for one item, a dress. "Since you didn't get bitten by the tsetse fly, you owe me this one small sacrifice." Aunt Lily took a satin dress out of the closet. "I never got the opportunity to wear this," she said, running a finger across the fine stitching. "But I imagined wearing it." She held the cream coloured dress close and swayed back and forth.

"How old is it?" asked Girly getting up to get a closer look.

"I made it when your mother was about nine or ten." Aunt Lily held the dress next to Girly. "It might need some taking in or letting out, but I think it will suit your purposes fine."

"What are these lumps on the sleeves?"

Aunt Lily pulled the dress back. "They're not lumps they're orange blossoms."

Girly's mother was in her forties and Girly couldn't imagine wearing anything even close to her age. She wrinkled her nose as she looked it, "isn't it out of fashion?"

"Oh, that really doesn't matter, any man worth his salt will only notice your face."

Girly groaned. Aunt Lily took the garment, hung it back up and slammed the door. "Find your own dress then," she said as she relocked the closet and left the room.

Girly flopped back down on the bed; her aunt could be so difficult. They were getting along, in their own way, and the old woman had to ruin it. She ruined everything. Girly propped herself up on her elbows. "Why would I wear a dress she made when my mother was little — one my aunt didn't even wear herself? It's ridiculous."

She had such a hard time trying to understand that woman. If it weren't for her mother's letters, none of it would make sense. Thinking back to what her mother had written, Girly's eyes widened. "Wax orange blossoms, the ones my mother went into the closet to smell. It's Aunt Lily's wedding dress!"

The days that followed the great frock rejection were quite uncomfortable. Girly didn't know how to broach the subject to her aunt; should she apologise for being insensitive regarding the dress and risk having to wear it as recompense, or pretend she had no idea why her aunt had taken offence? Girly Maid slipped into the sitting room and sat down on the davenport. "Can I knit a sock?"

Aunt Lily didn't look up from her clacking knitting needles. "Oh, I don't think just one sock will be adequate for the Moonlight Ball do you?"

It was the Ford sisters who rescued Girly from her dress dilemma. Emma came over with a formal written invitation for tea. She handed it to Girly at the door as if Girly was being summoned to see the Queen. "Your presence is required," Emma said bowing slightly at the waist.

Girly curtsied in return, "I would be honoured." It was the first time Girly had been invited into the Ford's inner sanctum. She had stood on the front step, waited in their porch but never had she set foot in their living space. The sisters' house was a mosaic. One wall was dedicated to wallpaper. Its entire length was covered with mismatched pages rescued from a sample book. There were bolts of fabric and paper strewn throughout the sitting room. Girly picked her way over to a comfortable chair.

After the sisters settled, they told her they had called her over for a special reason. Somehow, however, in the midst of pouring tea, they were sidetracked and began telling her tales of their childhood—the summer of Emma's terrible rash.

"It was so distasteful the doctor wouldn't even touch it," Emma began.

"That's true, it was bright red and raised. If the boys had been blind they could have read your body like Braille," Ella said.

"I wore a daisy print dress that summer; it was very fashionable. Ella used to say *Twirl, rash girl, twirl*. What a wonderful time."

"As I recall, one day you twirled until you passed out, remember? Mother wouldn't let you twirl after that."

"Oh yes, Mother was a stickler for rules, but do you recall what Father said?"

"Yes, Father was always a bit blunt in his view of things."

"That's right, Father said, *Mother, let the girl twirl. She can't lose her virtue twirling*. Good advice, some of the best Father ever gave."

"That was the same summer Grandma used her teeth to communicate with aliens. I think that's how you got your rash."

"That explains why I never liked Grandma."

Girly told the Fords that although she liked hearing stories about rashes and twirling she had to get back to Aunt Lily. "Why did you need to see me?" she asked.

"It was on a night when we had drunk enough elixir to

see into the future," Emma began. "We saw a tall, naked orphan girl."

"A very significant vision," Ella chimed in.

"Yes, orphans aren't usually tall."

Ella looked askance at her sister. "Well, upon realizing its importance, we began to sew. The elixir only stimulated our creative abilities."

Emma reached down and picked up a package wrapped in brown paper and tied with string from under her chair. "Then we sat on our porch and waited."

"We faithfully sat."

"Yes, more so than some wives."

"But after several months of never seeing a tall, naked orphan girl casually strolling down the street, bending down periodically to pick daisies, we've given up."

"We've decided to give the dress to you."

"My dear," said Ella, "Emma and I realize that you may not be an orphan, but this is hoping that someday you will be."

Emma handed Girly the package. As Girly untied the string the Fords leaned forward, they were practically on top of her by the time she had the package unwrapped. Inside the brown paper was a lilac coloured dress that could have rivaled the sea-foam dress in Deauvilles' front window. It wasn't quite a flapper dress, with fringes, beads and spangles, but its shape resembled one, somewhat loose but closely following the curves of the body. She brushed the watered silk against her cheek. It had been so long since she had worn anything so fine. The Fords clapped as they watched her.

Girly wasn't sure how she was going to explain to her aunt that she would rather wear the dress made by the Fords. She tried to slip into the house and up to her room undetected, but before she reached the stairs Aunt Lily accosted her with a pair of knitting needles. "What's in the package?"

Looking down at the package she held, Girly shrugged. "Just a dress the Fords made for a tall, naked orphan girl."

Aunt Lily pointed her needles at the parcel; it felt like a threat and Girly took off the brown paper wrapping and held up the lilac dress.

"Well," Aunt Lily shook her head as she examined the dress, "it's nothing compared to my timeless creation, but what can you expect from two Communists?"

Chapter Forty-three

THE MOONLIGHT Dance was more than Girly expected. As she mounted the steps she had to check to see if her shoes were made of glass. Pots of blooming petunias lined the path leading to the hall. In the cool evening air, they smelled divine. Large crepe paper flowers with tulle bow leaves surrounded the double door entrance. A rainbow of streamers twisted and tied, fell in loops from the ceiling. Girly had been to dances in Rosedale before, with its purchased paraphernalia, but there was a special feel when it was done by the community. Henry Henry had been by earlier, gathering the flower pots from donor's doorsteps. The Ford sisters had made all the crepe paper fauna, as they did every year, and Miss Poppy, the school marm, had arranged a group of young volunteers to put up the decorations. All the effort made it somewhat bewitching. Girly sat on the front steps and enjoyed a cool breeze.

"Evenin," said Tucker.

"Evening," said Girly.

Tucker's brood following him like a row of ducks chanting some limerick about a man from Nantucket. The lot of them were barefoot, their Sunday shoes tied at the laces and slung over their shoulders.

"For old shoes, they hold quite a shine," said Girly.

With a proud grunt Tucker nodded. "There is no use in shining shoes," he said, "if you are just going to get them dirty walking to a dance." He turned and examined the clutch behind him. "Ain't that right, boys?"

The boys nodded without skipping a word of their rhyme. They passed Girly on the step as they tossed their shoes in a pile outside the hall door before disappearing into the building.

"How's your aunt been keeping?" asked the Widow Wilson as she eased herself down beside Girly. The tent of a dress she was wearing rippled at the belly.

It was the first time Girly heard the widow speak and was surprised at the pitch of her voice. If she closed her eyes, she'd have sworn it was a man. "She's well. Right now she's in the kitchen arguing with Harriet Simpson about what time the midnight lunch should be held."

"Uh, nothing good will come of that." The widow lifted one foot then the other so Tucker could slip on her shoes and do up her buckles.

"We can always hope." Tucker bent down to put on his footwear. "We can always hope."

Girly wasn't sure what he was hoping for, a good outcome or a row. She wasn't even sure if she'd be able to tell the difference. As Tucker finished tying his shoe, the grocer's wife showed up arm and arm with the organist. The grocer was left to trot behind, his eye twitching uncontrollably. His wife was right he had hurt himself. The two women charged up the steps oblivious to who might be in the way. Girly and Widow Wilson had to stand so not to be trodden.

"Some things never change," Widow Wilson said holding her belly, "but you can't make a silk purse out of a sow's ear."

Girly smiled. "At least they have beautiful matching brooches."

"Pearls before swine," Widow Wilson said as she followed her husband into the hall.

As the crowd inside grew, it began to drown out the sound of the crickets. Folks were laughing and enjoying one another's company as if they hadn't seen each other for years. Girly sat on the step and listened. If she let herself, she could be part of it, but somehow it felt like she might be betraying her old life—what she thought she was in Rosedale.

The Fords came meandering towards the hall singing. Girly wondered if the two ever had a care in the world. *If you were the only girl in the world, and I were the only boy, nothing else would matter in the world today, we would go on loving the same old way.* Their old voices scratched at the words, but the way they sauntered Girly knew they felt every syllable. Catching sight of Girly, the ladies stopped their joyous rendition and began clapping. "Just like the orphan we envisioned," said Emma.

"Her eyes were redder," said Ella, "but just the same, you look lovely."

Girly stood and curtsied.

"What Girly are you tonight?" asked Emma.

"I'm not sure."

"Well never you mind, at my age I get confused all the time. Some mornings I have to ask my sister which sister I am, Ella or Emma. She always says Emma, Ella wouldn't ask such a daft question."

Ella patted her sister's arm. "Give us a pose, Girly; let's see if that dress can pass muster."

Girly looked at the Fords blankly, she wasn't sure what to do.

"Pretend you're standing in a strong wind and it's all you can do to keep from being blown away," Emma said.

"Oh, that's a good one, Sister. I would've had her digging potatoes in the rain."

"She can do that too." Emma flapped her hands. "This is so exciting."

For a moment Girly wondered if the dress was worth it, but considering this was Forget and it was a request made by the Fords, she closed her eyes leaned into the gale force, grabbed her pretend shovel and began to dig.

The sisters were still examining Girly and her fabulous dress when Harriet Simpson and Henry Henry came rushing towards them. Henry Henry tipped his cap as a greeting to the Fords and Girly. Harriet giggled and slipped her arm into his. Girly could have sworn that she saw Henry Henry's skin crawl. A more retiring man Girly couldn't have imagined; save his bulk, he could have happily abided between two sheets of blank paper. Henry Henry propelled himself forward, taking the stairs two at a time as if he were trying to shake Harriet off. "Henry Henry," she screeched digging in her claws and stumbling up the steps behind him.

Emma nudged Girly in the ribs. "I don't think Harriet's told Henry Henry he's her new beau."

"It's a hard subject to broach," said Ella.

In amongst the clamour Wilber Sykes huffed and laboured past Girly. She had never seen a man on crutches move with such skill. The Ford sisters watched in disbelief. "It's as if what happened at the picnic didn't matter," Emma said, clicking her tongue.

"How true, sister, how very true. Don't be too broken-hearted, child," Ella reached out and touched Girly's cheek. "There are more dwarfs out there, surely even one you can love as your very own."

"Thank you for your concern." Inside Girly burned. She wanted to beat Bessy Helmer's son for his infamous attack.

"Don't mention it, dear," said Ella. "There is so much to be concerned about when it comes to you."

"That's what Aunt Lily says," Girly said, feeling her cheeks redden. She knew the sisters meant well, but sometimes she wished they would keep their thoughts to themselves.

As Girly stepped into the hall, she was struck with a waft of wonderful aromas. The ladies from the Sunshine Club were busy in the kitchen, cooking the midnight lunch. She had heard every year they tried to outdo the last. Everyone had requested their favourites and the ladies had kindly obliged.

The Fords follow Girly into the hall. "There's our punch table." Emma tapped Girly on the shoulder and pointed to a table covered with a white linen cloth nestled in the corner. "We must take up our station."

Picking up where they left off in their ditty, the sisters laced their arms together and skipped across the floor; their voices barely audible above the mingling crowd. *A garden of Eden, just made for two, with nothing to mar our joy. I would say such wonderful things to you, there would be such wonderful things to do, if you were the only girl in the world, and I were the only boy.* The sisters took up their positions behind the punch table; each suspiciously surveyed the crowd before hiking up their skirts to reveal their garters.

"If they were in the Resistance they'd be shot. They couldn't be discreet if they wanted to."

Girly turned and looked at her aunt. She hadn't noticed her sneak up; she'd have to push tacks into the bottoms of Aunt Lily's shoes. "I thought you were in the kitchen."

"I was asked to leave; can you believe that?"

Every bone in Girly's body wanted to say yes but instead, she did her best to look shocked.

Aunt Lily turned back to the Fords just as Ella pulled out a brown bottle from her garter and dumped its contents into a bowl marked *For Medicinal Purposes*.

"That one's always thinking of our health," Aunt Lily said.

Emma was not as successful in her attempt, as a bit of lace from her garter seemed to have caught on the flask's spout. Her effort to free it was unsuccessful. Girly watched her approach the grocer for assistance, pointing to the flask's unfortunate dilemma; he ceased his winking and collapsed into a nearby chair. Ella rushed him a glass of medicinal punch.

Aunt Lily rubbed the palms of her hands together. "Those two can't do anything without me." She began weaving her way towards them, yoo-hooing through the throng, Girly only steps behind. As they reached Emma, Harriet Simpson was already bracing herself. She wrenched the flask so hard from Emma's garter, that both women nearly lost their balance.

Aunt Lily was appalled. "I yoo-hooed first; that means I had dibs."

Girly let out heavy sigh. "Does it matter?"

"Of course it does. It's not every day an opportunity arises to yank a Ford."

As ruffled as Aunt Lily was, Emma was not. She smoothed her dress, sauntered up to the bowl marked For All Other Purposes and emptied her flask. Harriet Simpson was the first to partake of the concoction.

"That's one more reason why you're going to hell, Harriet Simpson," Aunt Lily raged. "When we get home, Girly, remind me to write it in my book."

"No need," Harriet said dumping her punch back into the bowl. "I got the signs confused." She turned to Ella and had her glass refilled.

In amongst the racket Wilber pushed past Girly and sidled up to the punch table.

"Excuse me," said Girly almost losing her balance.

"You're excused," said Wilber seemingly indifferent to his actions.

"She must have farted," said Emma looking down at Wilber and waving her hand in front of her face.

"No that was me," said Aunt Lily.

Girly closed her eyes; she felt as if she had stepped into Victor Hugo's Feast of Fools. The Fords with their wayward garters, the grocer with his uncontrollable winking, and Harriet Simpson's misguided love affair. Somehow it had all become commonplace to Girly. She would be bored if she awoke in Rosedale with only the society pages for entertainment. For the first time since coming to Forget, Girly wondered if she would still fit in at home. If Rosedale still was home. Besides her parents, Girly wasn't sure she wanted what she had. What frightened her most was Daphne; Girly wasn't sure she would like Daphne anymore, or that Daphne would like her.

"Come for a glass?" Ella asked Wilber as she looked sympathetically at Girly. "Or to break a heart?"

Girly rolled her eyes.

"For a glass," Wilber leaned against the table.

"Better drink fast," said Emma handing Wilber a glass of *For All Other Purposes*. "Bessie Hilmar's son just walked through the door."

The group turned in unison. For Girly it felt the same as it did at the Sunday School picnic when the grocer's wife flung herself on the watermelon; everything was in slow motion. Wilber used a crutch to nudge anyone in his line of sight. Bessy Hilmar's son stood on his tiptoes as he tossed a silver dollar in the air. The Ford's looked from Wilber to the Hilmar boy; Aunt Lily cackled as she rubbed the palms of her hands together. Any thoughts of a pleasant evening evaporated from Wilber's face. Girly thought he looked like he just came down with the Black Death. He downed his glass and shot underneath the skirted table like a rabbit into a hole.

"Oh, your aunt will be so disappointed," said Emma. "It will never be the best Moonlight Dance ever now."

Girly didn't want to admit it but she was glad Wilber was under the table. Hopefully now no one would call him her love interest and force them to eat the midnight lunch together. But she thought if she had a chance she'd dance with that Hilmar boy and trod on his toes.

"Don't worry, we'll take care of him," Emma said to Girly, giving Wilber a little wave. "By the end of the evening, he'll have had the time of his life."

"That's right, Sister, since we were unable to tempt the new priest, we think he will do nicely."

"The one you were practicing communion for?" Girly asked.

"That very one," Ella said. "That priest's an odd duck. When we went to the church for confession he was out switching the wooden grave markers. Said he wanted to see which families knew where their loved ones were buried."

"He timed me," Emma eyes widened. "Said I put things right in remarkable time."

"Although some of the crosses were upside down."

"That's true, but the dead don't mind."

Wilber peeked from beneath the table skirt, the sisters hiked up their hems to just above their knees. "We can't show you any more, Wilber, and still attend church on Sunday."

Girly was starting to change her mind about Wilber's predicament. Being stuck under the table and plied with a nefarious concoction, could prove more unfortunate than the picnic. She lifted the skirt of the table and wished him luck.

"He doesn't need it," said Emma. "We have been tempting men since before you were born, and now, at our age, we are really good at it."

Leaving Wilber to the Fords, Girly made for the far corner where her aunt was circling the banker's wife and her premature baby. She didn't know why, but for some reason she was drawn to whatever commotion her aunt was causing. Whether it was to limit the havoc, or just curiosity, Girly couldn't say. Whatever it was, though, she wasn't the only one heading in that direction. The grocer's wife and organist with their matching brooches were just ahead of Girly.

Aunt Lily walked past the baby and poked him with a curled finger. "I told you not to look at ugly people when you were pregnant, but did you listen to me? Now look at him. Can't do much about it now. Well, does he talk at least?"

"No," said the tight-lipped banker's wife and she pulled her son closer.

"The chickens could, but then again poultry are known

for their good looks and intelligence. What is your family known for?"

The grocer's wife and organist swooped in and stood between Aunt Lily and the banker's wife. Girly was sure if the grocer's wife had horns she would have lowered them. A curious following began to fill in all the empty spaces around the women.

"Let's get some air," Girly said, taking Aunt Lily by the arm.

"That's a good idea," said the grocer's wife. "It's a little stuffy in here."

Aunt Lily looked from Girly to the grocer's wife. Girly could hardly breathe while she waited for her aunt to decide.

"Don't need air, already got some." Aunt Lily picked a hair from the front of her dress. "But I think I might have a shot of elixir, though, considering the riffraff they let into this place."

They all turned to the grocer's wife and waited. The woman just stood there twisting her lips back and forth. Girly expected more, something diabolical to match her fiendish nature. She wanted to say, 'Is that all you can come up with? A little lip maneuvering? Sometimes you're so disappointing.' But Girly didn't say anything. Instead she ushered her aunt through the expectant crowd.

Walking her aunt past the stage, Girly saw Henry Henry as he helped the band between sets.

"He's quite versatile you know," Aunt Lily said, pointing to Henry Henry. "If there's an instrument to be played, he can play it."

Once the band had tuned their instruments, the dance was underway. Polkas, waltzes, butterflies and schottische were all played with equal skill. Harriet Simpson was dancing by herself at the side of the stage. Every time Henry Henry looked her way she blew him a kiss; Aunt Lily said there were reasons Harriet was a spinster.

At first Girly leaned against the wall and watched. Couples

glided across the floor as if on a cloud. Aunt Lily had told Girly Historian that the hall's maple floor had six inches of horse hair under its boards and that a soul could dance the whole night without feeling it the next day. At first Girly hadn't believed her aunt, but even at the hall's edge Girly could feel the spring in the floor. She longed to join the swirls of gliding swans.

A crumpled piece of paper beaned Girly in the forehead. As she bent down to pick it up Aunt Lily came trotting over.

"What's this?" Girly asked straightening the sheet.

"Your dance card."

"But your name fills all the slots."

"I know," Aunt Lily grabbed Girly by the arm and pulled her onto the floor. "It's a polka." Aunt Lily began to hop from foot to foot. She looked like an out of control rabbit, bounding around without reason. Most of the time she wasn't even close to keeping the beat. It was déjà vu of her first day in Forget when Aunt Lily scurried home with Girly struggling in her stead. The woman had unexpected exuberance. Girly tried to steady her, but had to give up. It was too tiring. "When in Rome," she said joining her aunt in her high-spirited folly.

It could have been disappointing having only one partner, but to Girly's surprise it wasn't. She and her aunt whipped around the dance floor in a way that was almost dangerous. "Move out of the way," Aunt Lily would yell as they made a pass. Couples parted and teetered in their wake. Aunt Lily gracefully batted her eyes at any man who had most of his own teeth and could still see at two paces. Girly wasn't sure that the men could tell what she was doing, considering the speed at which they danced; even the waltz was done with force. It was as if Aunt Lily thought it was a race. When they stopped to take a breath, neither of them spoke; there was not time. Girly had a dance card and Aunt Lily had filled it.

On one of their many turns, Girly saw The Thief. He stood in the shadows, watching. Aunt Lily saw him too. "I don't like the attention that man pays you. It seems to always come out in the shadows. Never in the full light of day. It's not right."

Girly stopped dancing and pushed her aunt away. Since she had come to Forget The Thief was the best thing that had happened to her. He made her heart skip every time she saw him. And now Aunt Lily insinuated the same things she had at the pond, that his attentions were sordid and untoward. That his family harboured some dark secret. She couldn't think of him in that way; she wouldn't. If she did, it could change things and she didn't want that. When it came to The Thief, she would take him at face value; she decided anything out of her line of sight didn't matter.

"What do you know about what's right?" she said. "For that matter, what do you know about anything? You've acted insane ever since I've come here."

Aunt Lily clenched her fists and turned red. "I'm not acting, you imbecile!" She stomped off and left Girly standing alone on the dance floor. The couple next to Girly paused as if concerned.

"Oh, she went to the washroom to have a seizure."

They politely nodded and danced away. A feeling of regret filled her.

The Thief slipped out of the shadows. "You and your aunt," he said. "What will I do with you?"

"Dance with me," Girly said, trying not to think of what had just happened.

"It will be my pleasure." The Thief offered Girly his arm. "Nice dress."

Girly looked down at the garment. "Apparently it will do well for digging potatoes in gale force winds and pounding rain."

Raising a cautious eyebrow, The Thief made a closer examination of the dress, "I would have never guessed."

"I didn't expect you to."

The Thief danced Girly around the room, one hand at the small of her back, the other held her own to his chest. Girly could hardly take a breath, everything seemed perfect. She thought he talked about his family—his beautiful sister and grandmother who lived by a lake. But Girly wasn't sure, she had been taken away, floating on the swells of the moment. When Girly felt she was somewhat in control of her faculties she asked him, "Where's Lottie?"

"Does it matter?"

Girly had to admit that it didn't; she laughed and her feet skipped across the floor.

"So, my little chickadee," he said, "what have you been doing with yourself?"

"You mean after we came back from Africa?"

"Yes."

"Did you hear about my ride with Henry Henry?"

"Yes."

"Did you hear about the healing cow?"

"Yes."

"Did you hear about Aunt Lily shaving the grocer's wife's dog?"

"Yes."

"You were there for Aunt Lily's tea party."

"Regrettably."

"I haven't been doing much."

"Oh," said The Thief.

They made a few more turns on the dance floor before the band took a break. Girly put her hand in the crook of The Thief's arm and he kissed her on the forehead. "Shall we go for a walk?" he asked.

"We shall."

They were standing beneath the crepe paper flowers the Fords had made when Joseph of Many Colours came running towards them. His bare feet were black and his shirt was covered with what appeared to be pilfered midnight lunch. "Miss Lily is about to fight the grocer's wife," he screamed.

"Are you sure?" asked Girly.

"Yes," said Joseph, pointing to a crowd that was gathering

around the two women. Some were standing on chairs for a better view, others placing bets.

"I think it's best we part company now," Girly said to The Thief, "there's no telling what my aunt might do if she sees you." She had hardly spoken the words when The Thief had slipped back into the shadows. As she watched him disappear she felt disappointed; he didn't even argue with her, beg to rescue her. "Coward," she said under her breath. Joseph of Many Colours grabbed Girly's hand and began dragging her towards her aunt.

Once Girly had breached the crowd she surveyed the situation. It was obvious Aunt Lily had too much medicinal punch. She wobbled back and forth as she hollered, "Test me now!"

Girly took her by the hand. "It's time to go home."

Aunt Lily yanked her hand away. "I'm not going to let that woman intimidate me, and I'll certainly not be blamed for the fact her dog is ugly."

The grocer's wife snapped her tongue and grabbed the front of Aunt Lily's dress. "He wasn't ugly until you got hold of him."

"I was in Africa at the time," Aunt Lily said. "And if you don't believe me you can ask the healing cow."

The grocer's wife tightened her grip; her husband joined Wilber hiding under the punch table. Aunt Lily put her bony finger in the air. "I have seen your dog and his unconventional haircut and I have only one thing to say."

"And what is that?" asked the grocer's wife.

"I've seen better-looking chickens."

The grocer's wife would have throttled Aunt Lily if the organist hadn't stepped in. She gently pried the grocer's wife's hands from the front of Aunt Lily's dress. She hummed an old hymn and talked about their matching brooches.

Aunt Lily looked stunned. "That dog may be ugly, but put him in a dress and he could pass for the organist."

As the two women turned to square off against Aunt Lily,

she seemed to realize her mistake and ran a wobbly sprint out of the hall. Girly was surprised at how fast she could move. But the Fords weren't, they placed their hands on their hips, "It's the elixir," they said.

Chapter Forty-four

IN THE morning, Aunt Lily stumbled around the house. Girly could hear her knocking around before the chickens were up and clucking. Girly lay in bed and wondered if she should go down and check on her. It was so warm under the covers and despite the dance floor, with its six inches of horse hair, her legs were tired.

There was a thump, then another. Girly knew it was Aunt Lily once again banging on the ceiling with the tip of her cane. "What does she want now?" she complained as she slipped out of bed. She walked over to her bedroom door and opening it a crack she called down to her aunt. "Any Girly in particular?"

There was a pause. "Which one is in the best mood?" Aunt Lily asked.

"Girly Maid."

"Send her down then and tell her to be quick about it, I'm having an allergic reaction to the punch."

Girly Maid found Aunt Lily waiting at the kitchen table for her to brew some coffee. "You're still in your nightdress," said Girly.

Aunt Lily looked down at her shift. "So I am."

"Aren't we going to church?"

Slumping in her chair, Aunt Lily cradled her head between both hands. "I don't think either God or I are in a mind to be seeing one another at the moment."

Girly wondered how many in Forget were of the same mind as God. She looked at her aunt with a little pity. The poor thing was really suffering. Perhaps Girl would put real sugar in Aunt Lily's coffee today, instead of the pretend stuff she usually used. She didn't think her aunt was in the mood to argue about the state of her deteriorating taste buds.

After a few cups of strong coffee, Girly Maid assisted Aunt Lily to the sitting room, propping her up among pillows on the davenport. "I would like to work on my memoirs alone," Aunt Lily said, her forearm draped over her forehead, shading her eyes from any light. "Don't go telling Girly Historian; she's so touchy and will just get her nose out of joint."

Girly Maid covered her aunt with a quilt, feeling relieved; she dreaded changing into the historian's dress.

"Draw the blinds," Aunt Lily continued. "Today I think I'll work in the dark, with my eyes closed."

After Girly Maid drew the blinds, she tiptoed out of the room, leaving her aunt to achieve the impossible task of writing memoirs without pen or paper. Heading straight up to her room, she didn't even bother bracing the door with the chair from the hall. It would be awhile before her aunt would be moving from her catatonic positon. Girly took the bundle of letters out of the top drawer of the highboy. The weight of them in her hand harkened her back to when her mother first gave them to her. The look in her father's eyes, the way her mother's voice strained as if it weren't her own. She missed the sound of them, the smell of them.

Sitting on the edge of the bed she held the next letter. It was the seventh in a stack of eight; how fast time had passed. The envelope said *open on the forty-ninth day*. Girly had stopped counting the days long ago; even so she knew it was relativity close.

My sweet pumpkin,

At this point, I have no idea where your father and I might be. I hope he will look at me as he always has, that playfulness in the corner of his eye. The way he laughs at me when he's sure he knows my thoughts. As for this letter I can't think of anything I haven't already told you. I've written about the origins of Forget, the townspeople and why we had to send you. I suppose in this letter I will write of how much I care.

From the first moment you were laid in my arms, I adored you. You father would stroke your face ever so lightly with the tip of his finger. He was afraid to do more, as if (as your aunt would say) you were made of sugar. You would gurgle under his touch, turning him into an emotional puddle. For such a reserved, quiet man, showing such vulnerabilities were nearly his undoing. Most of the time I acted blind to his response, but there were times I couldn't help myself, and I'd reach out and touch him. He often had to leave the room.

As you aged our tenderness towards you didn't change, even though we didn't show it in the same way. The sound of your footsteps seemed connected to the beat of our hearts. With invisible strings we are bound together.

I have no idea what you've been up to or how my sister is treating you. By now I'm sure your father must be losing his mind. He will be anxious to have his walks in the woods with you again. As for myself, it is the mornings I long for most of all. Sitting on the edge of your bed combing your hair, it always gives me such a wondrous feeling inside. I want to watch you tilt your bowl at breakfast and the way you tap your fingers when you are impatient. I'm already longing for the things I get after you for. I feel so foolish because we haven't even parted yet. But I promise you, I will not feel truly alive until we are together again.

Keep me in your thoughts,

Your loving Mother

Girly refolded the letter and put it back into its envelope. The letters no longer left her feeling the way they use to. She still felt pained and confused but the reasons had changed. There was only one letter left in the stack. Then it would be over, back to Rosedale as if her summer jaunt had never happened. Could she pretend, as her mother, that Aunt Lily and Forget didn't exist? That her grandmother painted and her grandfather was a poet? It was too much. How could she ever really leave this place? Or for that matter, how could anybody?

Pinching her cheeks and taking a few deep breaths, Girly steadied herself. She felt guilty leaving her aunt alone. She took off her shoes as she descended the stairs, in hopes Aunt Lily wouldn't have realized she had left the sitting room. When Girly slipped into the chair across the davenport, Aunt Lily moaned. "Shall I open the blinds or are you still working on your memoirs?" Girly asked.

Aunt Lily stirred and blinked. "I suppose it's time I make sure my list of reasons people are going to hell is updated."

After tea, they talked about the grocer's wife's dog and his uncanny resemblance to the organist. "I wonder if he's musical," Aunt Lily said. "If he is, we could've introduced him to the healing cow. They'd have made a remarkable team."

"Donkey's dead."

"That's only a formality. Haven't you heard about the resurrection?"

"I think it's best to let dead cow's lie. Besides, I'm sure both the organist and the grocer's wife are still livid and are not up for any kind of collaboration."

"Pishposh, there is nothing to be angry about; those two are so touchy."

Girly reminded her aunt of the night before and added, "The dance won't be so easily forgotten."

Aunt Lily wrinkled her nose. "It's a common error, mistaking someone for someone else's dog. I'm sure everyone's done it. You'd think she could take it as a compliment. After all, wasn't it the grocer's wife who said it was a dog fit for queens? How many can say they look like a dog fit for queens? Not many, I wager, except for the organist. God gives her a gift and she squanders it."

The day languished between Aunt Lily's scribbles and moans. All the time Girly was well aware of the ticking mantel clock. Time hung in the air. She was almost relieved when Aunt Lily nodded off again. The old woman looked disheveled, spectacles askew, hair that had been left to its own devices since the Moonlight Dance, and her nightdress, which she had worn all day, could be seen twisted around her legs where she had kicked her quilt off. When Girly went to rouse her to go up to bed, Aunt Lily pushed her away. "Can't you leave me in peace? Can no one leave me in peace?"

Girly leaned over and straightened the quilt. She was sure her aunt's snoring would rattle right through the floorboards. Before she even thought about what she was doing, Girly took off her aunt's spectacles, smoothed her hair, and bent down and kissed her on the cheek. "I hope you dream of your Africa and the healing cow," she whispered. The act of showing Aunt Lily affection, to Girly's surprise, felt natural. Although she wasn't sure if her aunt would have been awake, she would have shown the same bravado.

The next morning, Girly was awoken by pounding on the front door. Dressed as Girly Butler she opened the door to the Fords.

"This must be an important visit if the butler is answering the door," Emma said looking Girly up and down.

Girly Butler shrugged. Aunt Lily was still passed out in the sitting room, and Girly was positive she had not invited the sisters over. "My aunt's not receiving company."

"That won't do," said Emma.

"No, it won't do at all," said Ella. "We must see her at once."

Girly excused herself and went into the sitting room to rouse her aunt. "The Fords are here."

Aunt Lily sat up looking confused. "Why?"

225

"I don't know, but Emma thinks it's important."

"Well do you blame her?" Aunt Lily slapped Girly on the arm. "You putting on airs, dressing as a butler."

The old woman quickly came alive. She had Girly open the blind and a window to freshen the room. Then she looked at what she was wearing. "I am not going to see anyone in this nightdress; it's not even my best one. They might think I'm strange." Standing up she handed Girly the quilt. "Wrap me up in this and carry me upstairs like a bundle of laundry. It will be just like Cleopatra."

"Are you sure you want me to do that?"

"Of course I'm sure."

While her aunt stood expectantly, Girly patiently wrapped the quilt around her. It was like preparing to go to Africa all over again. The quilt wasn't quite long enough and no matter how carefully Girly arranged it, tufts of her aunt's hair insisted on sticking out. Girly thought about cutting off the misguided culprits but decided against it. Her aunt would never see the stray strands. With a grunt, Girly managed to lift her aunt. The bit of a thing was heavier than she looked. Girly paused in the doorway of the sitting room until she felt steady enough to take the stairs. She was sure her legs were trembling. As they passed the Fords in the front hall, a muffled voice could be heard through the quilt. "Get Girly Maid to come upstairs and help me with my dress."

"I'll fetch her in a minute," Girly Butler called back, struggling with her load.

The Fords winked and nodded towards the bundle.

Girly had never seen someone dress so quickly, and scampered in her aunt's wake, unsuccessfully attempting to pin Aunt Lily's hair up. Slapping Girly's hands away Aunt Lily ran headlong out of her bedroom for the top of the stairs.

"Honestly," Aunt Lily said, "butlers are useless at everything except answering the door. I don't know why I ever hired you."

226

"Neither do I," said Girly Butler, sticking one more pin into her aunt's lopsided bun.

The Fords waved to them from the bottom of the stairs. Aunt Lily, linking her arm into the butler's, lazily strolled down the stairs, acting surprised to see them. "I hope you haven't been waiting long. If I'd known you were here I'd have come down sooner."

The Fords smiled at one another.

As they entered the sitting room the Fords suggested Aunt Lily and Girly have a seat. Aunt Lily took her usual spot on the davenport and patted the spot beside her. "Stay close," she whispered in Girly's ear. "No telling what these two are up to."

"We have something of the utmost importance to tell you," said Ella. "There was a meeting last night."

"A very dark meeting," Emma said, her eyes big, almost cautionary.

"It was only dark because it was at night, dear," explained Ella.

"Oh, that's right. I forgot, because if it would have happened during the day it would have been a very bright meeting."

"How true, but with very dark consequences."

Aunt Lily banged her cane on the floor, narrowly missing Girly's toes. "The meeting, ladies. What about the meeting?"

"Don't you know? Everyone in Forget knows." There was a note of disgust in Emma's voice.

"We haven't told her yet, dear."

"Oh, that's right. Anyway, the meeting was very dark."

"You've already said that," stammered Aunt Lily.

"I was just setting the scene, be patient will you!" Emma tightened her lips. "A few of Forget's more prominent citizens gathered together and signed a petition. They said they want to put an end to your eccentric behaviours. They want to have you committed. They feel it is improper for you to have any influence over such a young girl and that your niece should be sent away."

The room went silent. Girly wanted to tell them that it wouldn't be necessary to send her away, there was only one more letter. Her time in Forget was nearly done but she couldn't make herself say the words. Not aloud, not in front of her aunt. In the end she didn't have to; there was another knock on the door. It was the minister.

The minister had come to talk to Aunt Lily about the petition as well, and seemed relieved that the Fords had already enlightened her. He sat on the other side of Aunt Lily. "Don't worry," he said. "As long as you stay relatively harmless, there is little the petitioners can do."

"I want to see the list," Aunt Lily said without looking up. "I need to know what was written about me."

The minister squirmed uncomfortably. "I don't think that's necessary."

She gave him a cold stare and fingered her cane.

He pulled a carefully folded piece of paper from his pocket. "Don't get too upset. They all meant well."

Aunt Lily eyed the names carefully and turned white. She trembled slightly and bit her lip. The minister reached out his hand to comfort her. The Fords sent Girly Butler to the kitchen to make tea. Girly wanted to protest that the butler didn't make tea but then she would just have to go upstairs and change into her cook's outfit. As it was, from the kitchen, it would be impossible to hear the conversation in the sitting room. She couldn't very well ask them to wait for her to get back. Instead she decided to make the tea with cold water. Iced tea. Or at least what she'd pass off as iced tea. They really couldn't expect a mere butler to know any better.

After the tea was served the Fords looked into their cups. Emma seemed quite perplexed. "I usually blow on my tea," she said, setting the cup down.

Girly Butler felt a twinge of guilt as she took her seat next to her aunt.

Aunt Lily looked at the names again and shook her head. Every so often, she opened her mouth to speak, but then closed it. The minister offered to pray, but Aunt Lily simply said, "It's too late for prayers."

The Fords offered to make her a batch of elixir but the minister said elixir was the reason she was in this mess.

"No, it's not the elixir," Aunt Lily said. "It's the people."

Girly asked if anyone would like another cup of tea, but they said they should get going — unless Aunt Lily needed anything. She turned her face to the wall and waved them away with her hand.

The minister offered to escort the Fords home. "I need to talk to you about tempting priests and dwarfs."

"Oh, we're good at that," said Emma.

Chapter Forty-five

BEFORE THE Fords and the minister reached the end of Aunt Lily's walk, a small child ran towards the minister yelling that he needed his help.

Aunt Lily was standing in the window watching. She called for Girly Butler. "Get my shawl and follow me," she barked, heading toward the door with determination. Girly Butler scrambled in her wake, tossing a shawl around her aunt's shoulders, and in a moment they'd caught up with the minister and the boy. The Fords had already gone home to make a fresh batch of elixir.

The boy was weeping and carrying on. Aunt Lily put her hand on his shoulder. "Everything will be fine, it will all come out in the wash."

The boy sniffed hard.

"There, there, boy," she said. "You can wipe your nose on the girl's dress."

The boy declined and led them to an empty lot. There he pointed to a pup lying on its side, carrying on almost as much as the boy. Aunt Lily gently knelt down beside the distressed pup. "You'll be all right," she soothed as she ran her hands over his small body. The minister watched her intently, she seemed to have the situation in hand.

"You are quite sane without elixir, Miss Lily," he said. "I suggest you keep it that way."

A small crowd had begun to gather, and Aunt Lily was giving an incredible performance. Girly Butler wiped her aunt's brow with the sleeve of her dress as Aunt Lily meticulously examined the pup. She studied his eyes and peered intently at his teeth, she even took his pulse before finally asking the boy what happened.

"Henry Henry ran over my dog," he sobbed. "I saw him. It was Henry Henry. He didn't even stop."

Aunt Lily muttered something about H.H.'s third eye. "You'd think with an advantage like that you'd see these things coming."

After several minutes, the examination was over and Aunt Lily rose to her feet. The crowd hushed and waited for her diagnosis. She wiped her hands on Girly Butler's skirt and shook her head. "Just as I expected," she said. The crowd leaned forward and Aunt Lily furrowed her brow. She put one bony finger in the air. "This pup needs to be thwacked, bring me the healing cow."

The crowd began mumbling. Girly heard one man say her aunt was off her rocker, another said she didn't even have a rocker. Girly Butler quickly took her home.

That evening when Girly Butler was helping her into bed, Aunt Lily began to talk about the petition.

"Don't think about it," Girly Butler said. "It will only trouble you."

Aunt Lily nodded. "But I can't help it, it's been on my mind all day."

Girly Butler stroked her hair with her hand. "It will be okay. We'll talk about it in the morning."

"It's just disappointing. I can't believe more people didn't sign. They must not care for you that much."

Chapter Forty-six

GIRLY HAD hoped to run into The Thief. Dancing with him and been so grand and seeing him might distract her from her aunt's present dilemma. But he seemed to have disappeared with the last sunset. He didn't send any coded messages or stand in the lingering twilight at the pond's edge. Girly couldn't imagine what had happened to him. It was as if he had never existed, not even leaving a ripple in his wake.

The Tuckers were at as much of a loss as she. She asked Alexander, the oldest, about him one morning when the brothers had come to feed the chickens, stack the firewood and have Aunt Lily do her monthly inspections for tsetse fly bites.

Girly shaded her eyes with her hand as she stood on the back step. "Are you sure you haven't seen him?"

He shook his head as he threw a handful of grain to the hens. "Not hide nor hair."

The hens squawked and pecked around Alexander's feet while Aunt Lily ran headlong after Mean Dog Joe. He was the only Tucker left to be examined and seemed determined not to be caught. Between Joe's shrieking, Aunt Lily's cursing and the hens scattering, Girly found it hard to think. The Thief had to be somewhere. "Are you sure?" she asked Alexander again.

"Of course he hasn't seen him," Aunt Lily said as she caught Mean Dog Joe by the ear. "Lothario Bill isn't known for his reliability."

Girly ignored her aunt and questioned Alexander further. "You haven't spoken to him since the dance?"

"Nope."

"Gone for a swim?"

"Nope."

"Well where could he be?"

Aunt Lily let Mean Dog Joe go and rubbed her lower back. "No use bothering albinos about it. No one tells an albino anything."

Girly could feel her frustration get the better of her. "The Tuckers aren't albino, Aunt Lily. Sometime you say the most ridiculous things."

"Oh, that's a common response," Aunt Lily said as she climbed the back steps. "You know, it's the hardest part of a missionary's life, telling people they are albinos. Just ask Alexander there. He'll tell you."

Alexander looked at Aunt Lily. "Will it make her stop asking me questions?"

"Probably."

"Then I'm an albino."

Girly pulled at her hair. "Is anyone sane in this town?"

Aunt Lily reached behind the screen door and retrieved a pail of cookies. "No one interesting," she said as she began pelting the boys.

All Girly wanted was to know where the Thief was. A simple question but apparently she couldn't even have that. As she stomped back into the house she heard her aunt instruct the boys. "Africa can be frightful this time of year. Hurry, you need to arrive home before the monsoon."

Determined to find the answer to her question, Girly prepared to go to the market. She put on Dead Hilary's dress just for spite. Although Aunt Lily disapproved of Girly's fashion choice, she insisted on accompanying her. "I hope we run into the organist. I don't want her to forget that we're not on speaking terms. You let these things slide and before you know it, you're friends again. What a sorry day that would be."

"Long live the offence."

Aunt Lily had given the injured trolley a fresh coat of red paint. She said it could hardly be called an injured trolley now, due to the fact that the paint made it nearly new. She claimed it was now a store-bought reject, and it was her duty to complain. With a click of her tongue she added, "How the grocer could let such an oversight go unnoticed is beyond me."

When they reached the market, Girly saw Lottie across the street. She was struggling with one of her many parcels. She wagged her finger at the young man attending her and he cowered. There was little Girly found redeemable about the woman.

Girly was cursing the injured trolley when she heard Lottie's ladylike voice bellow at her. She stood in uneasy anticipation as Lottie gracefully picked her way from the rich side to the poor side of the street, a hankie pressed tightly over her mouth. Aunt Lily asked her why a doxy like herself wasn't standing at her usual spot in front of the haberdashery.

"Are you always so disagreeable, Miss Lily?"

"Only when I break wind," replied Aunt Lily. Lottie pulled the hankie from her face and sneered at Aunt Lily. "That's better," said Aunt Lily. "You could almost be proud of that face."

Lottie narrowed her eyes. Girly thought she was trying to think of a witty response, a possibility Aunt Lily overlooked from apparent distraction. The organist was looking out the grocer's window. Aunt Lily made a beeline into the store.

Girly was going to apologize for her aunt's behaviour, but was glad she didn't when she heard what Lottie had to say.

"I just heard from our mutual friend. I know you call him The Thief. How perfectly droll. He is away on business, you know. I'll hear all about it when he takes me to dinner. I accompany him to all the formal events. It gets quite tiring, but my parents love him. He fits in so well with our family. In fact, between you, me and the lamp post, we are making secret plans." Lottie looked Girly up and down as if gauging her response.

Holding herself tightly, Girly kept her emotions in check.

"He loves my laugh," Lottie continued with a faraway look that made Girly want to smack her. "He says it's whimsical. I love his eyes. They look so deeply into mine. We are like pools of water reflecting each other."

"He once gave me a rose," Girly said.

Lottie smiled. "Of course he did."

Girly felt the slight. "I should get going before my aunt comes looking for me."

Seemingly anxious at the thought of meeting Aunt Lily again, Lottie hurried back to the rich side of the street. "Nice bumping into you," she yelled over her shoulder.

Aunt Lily was waiting for Girly in the market. The grocer's wife and the organist were in the canned goods with the rest of the whisperers. Everyone in Forget seemed to have some reason to be angry with Aunt Lily.

"Finally," Aunt Lily snapped. "There are things I need you to do. You can't spend all day talking to a doxy."

"What do you need me to do?"

"Go ask the grocer's wife if her dog can carry a tune."

"No."

Aunt Lily thought for a moment. "Go look in the canned goods."

"We don't need any canned goods."

"I didn't ask you to get anything. I just want you to stand there and listen."

When Girly refused, Aunt Lily hit her with her cane.

The grocer's wife and the organist clucked and rolled their

eyes. Aunt Lily made a loud comment about the organist's skin being dry and unsightly. "She's the only person I know truly made from God's good earth," she said. "Look at her parched, clay exterior. I bet in dry weather she has to mist her face and then hold it together with rubber bands."

Girly smiled at Aunt Lily. "The list?"

"The minister told me not to worry about it."

"Not that list, Aunt Lily, the grocery list."

She handed her niece a piece of paper. It had one item written on it: canned beans.

"We have canned beans."

"That's yesterday's canned beans. I want today's canned beans."

"Why would I bring the injured trolley all the way downtown if you only wanted one thing?"

"Are beans any less important than all the other groceries? And yet you want to treat them as if they are. You've not learned anything since you've come to stay with me."

Girly pushed passed her aunt towards the muster of whisperers. They parted for her as she grabbed the beans. What a waste of a morning she thought as she slammed the can down on the counter and waited for the grocer to note the purchase in his ledger. While Girly waited outside the grocer's she could hear her aunt yelling. "Do you take me for a fool? Selling me a defective trolley. For fifteen years I have held my tongue, not said a word, but enough is enough. I will keep quiet no longer."

Girly closed her eyes and wished for it all to be over. She was sure if her aunt didn't own the store she'd be tossed out into the street.

At supper Girly told Aunt Lily what Lottie had said. Aunt Lily pushed her potatoes around her plate and grunted. "He has a different life beyond the pond. Best to forget him."

Chapter Forty-seven

GIRLY BEGAN to dread the thought of opening her last letter. It lay in the highboy waiting. She assumed it would give her instruction on how to meet up with her parents. Although she longed to be with them, she doubted she'd ever go back to Forget. She could imagine her father wrapping his arms around her. *How have you been keeping, Gunga Din?* He wouldn't even have to hear her answer. It wouldn't matter as long as they were together. Her mother would flitt about her like a bird who had its fill on fall crab apples, never quite knowing where to settle. She was sure the moment, for her, would be as overwhelming as when she was sent away at the Saskatoon train station. But what of Aunt Lily? What would become of her? Would she take her seat once again amongst the invisible in Girly's life? Girly couldn't imagine her doing that quietly.

Flopping over in her bed, Girly closed her eyes. Lightning flashed outside her bedroom window. It was her first prairie storm. She was sure the thunder not only shook the window pane but her bed. The Tuckers would have come and gone; in a storm like this they wouldn't have waited for her aunt's ritualistic cookie pelting. She slipped out of bed and down the stairs. Girly thought a cup of hot chocolate might be in order. She could sip it on the window seat in her room and watch the storm roll by—that is, until Aunt Lily rose and started making demands.

In the front hall a folded piece of paper had been slipped under the door. It was addressed to her aunt. Girly forwent the cocoa, and turned to deliver the note.

It contained just one word. *Come.*

"What could it possibly mean?" Girly asked.

Aunt Lily rolled her eyes. "It means I'm wanted."

"Where?"

"The Harrisburg's."

Aunt Lily quickly dressed and grabbed her shawl. "It's our code. Jane promised she'd send for me when her husband comes to his end, and I promised I'd sit with her during his last hours."

"Will you be needing breakfast?"

"There is no time," Aunt Lily said as she rushed out the door.

Girly waited for her aunt to return for the rest of the day. She did a lifetime of light dusting. Lunch came and went, as well as tea and dinner. She lit a lamp and read for a while and found herself dozing in a chair. The clock struck midnight when she eventually banked the fire and went to bed. It wasn't until early the next morning she heard a loud rap on the door. She hastily threw a wrap around her shoulders and ran barefoot down the cold stairs to the foyer. Girly opened the door to find a young man carrying a crumpled old woman.

"I'm Father Fitzpatrick, the new priest," he said looking Girly over, "but you can call me Paddy. Father makes me feel old, like I have something wise to offer."

Girly stepped aside as he pushed past her.

"Where would you like to put this wee bundle I found at the end of your walk?"

"Over there, Father." Girly led him into the sitting room

and pointed to the davenport as she rushed to enliven the embers to bring more heat to the room.

Paddy set Aunt Lily down before turning to Girly. "What did I say about calling me Paddy?"

Girly stared.

He handed girly his overcoat. "I finished givin' Mr. Harrisburg his last rites; his sin went a-twiddling and then he was off." He knelt down and took Aunt Lily's hand in his own, while Girly took his dripping overcoat and hung it on a hook in the front hall.

"Then I came across this old girl. She must have slipped and fallen. She was just lying there in the rain. You might want to bring her a spot of hot tea and some blankets."

Girly touched her aunt's blotchy-blue cheek; it was cold. She pulled her hand away. She wanted to ask if her aunt was dead. A quiet horror filled her. "We need to get her out of those wet clothes," said Girly pushing the davenport closer to the fireplace, her aunt nearly rolled off from the effort.

"Aye," said Father Fitzpatrick. "While you do that I'll run back to the Harrisburg's and fetch Doc Dippel."

Gathering her aunt's bedclothes and a towel Girly proceeded to try to undress the old woman and dry her off. Aunt Lily was no help. She was limp as a damp paper doll, as if every muscle had left her body. The wet dress stuck to her as a second skin. Girly had no choice, she would have to cut it off.

"You have nicer dresses," Girly said taking the dress in hand and making a few precise cuts, she cut and ripped the dress from her aunt's body. If Aunt Lily asked about the dress later, Girly would say it was at the laundry. By the time her aunt figured out the truth Girly would surely be back in Toronto. Girly had never dressed anyone before. She averted her eyes several times so she could bear the discomfort. When she had dried her aunt and redressed her, Aunt Lily smiled.

"Thank you."

Girly was about to say *you are welcome* but stopped herself.

Her aunt was more aware then she was letting on. "Did you fall down on purpose?"

Aunt Lily opened her eyes and slowly shook her head. "Of course not. But I'm not so daft that I'd turn down a perfectly good rescue."

When Doc Dippel came, he bumbled around Aunt Lily. Girly was convinced he would have preferred making his examination using a sharp stick, avoiding touching her aunt all together. Her assessment was confirmed in the diagnoses. He said that luckily there was nothing he could do, that what Aunt Lily needed was rest and warmth. Girly thanked him through tight lips as he rushed back out into the rain. Father Fitzpatrick stood over her shoulder as they watched the doctor disappear into the night.

"Now for that spot of tea," he said.

In the kitchen, Girly fed the stove and waited. Her mother's voice chided in her ear, *a watched pot never boils*. Sometimes making tea seemed to take forever. She wanted to be in the sitting room, not only to care for her imp of an aunt, but there was something about the priest that drew her. She wanted to know the smell of him. The sound of his voice changed the rhythm of her heart.

When she returned to the sitting room, Father Fitzpatrick was rubbing her aunt's feet, his Irish brogue soothing her. As she stood there and watched him, Girly knew the Fords were right: he was a man worth tempting. The young priest was handsome; there was no getting around it. Girly could see he had a firm body beneath his cassock. His dark hair curled at will, without any consideration to reason. His eyes, black as night, were crowned with a heavy brow, a brow that could be imposing if it had a mind to be, she was sure. But Girly was sure his brow went unnoticed, as most would only see his eyes. They rested on high cheekbones and took in everything around them. He stood out because of them. It seemed he had a face that wanted to be remembered.

Over the next few days Father Fitzpatrick divided himself between Aunt Lily and Mrs. Harrisburg—the widow and the wilted missionary. As soon as Aunt Lily was at half strength she had Girly wait by the window until his return. "It's was so selfish of Mr. Harrisburg to die right when I'm in need of a priest," Aunt Lily complained as she straightened the quilt that covered her legs.

"I don't think that was his intention."

"That may well be, but it's still quite unforgivable. Mr. Harrisburg wasn't known for being particularly considerate."

Girly continued watching. She felt conflicted. Here she was waiting by the window for a man, a priest no less, to turn up the walk, while just days ago she was mooning after another. Did she have no loyalty, no shame? How could her interest switch so easily? Even so there was something about Father Fitzpatrick that made her want to confess things she hadn't even done, anything to keep his attention.

"Can we become Catholic?" Girly asked as she watched through the lace curtains.

"Oh no. You should never have the same religion as your poultry."

When the priest returned, Aunt Lily leaned forward on the davenport and took his hands in hers. "How's Mrs. Harrisburg?"

The priest squeezed her hands in return. "She is doing as well as can be expected, poor lamb."

Aunt Lily blushed and released his hands. "We've been friends for years you know. I've watched her grow old before her time."

"She's still a bobby-dazzler. I only know one finer, and she was almost a nun."

A wry smile crossed Aunt Lily's face. "The way you said that makes me think you knew that nearly-nun biblically."

"The way a lad knows a lass is not something he should be discussing. Is that not right, Girly?"

Aunt Lily looked over her shoulder. "Oh, that's Girly Cook," she said. "She's only interested in midgets."

Before the priest retired for the evening, Aunt Lily asked him to say a prayer for the chickens. "They were good Catholics," she explained. "Never once did I catch them eating fish on Fridays, and they observed lent all year round. It's only fitting that they should receive belated last rites."

"I can tell you now the only prayer I know for dead chickens is grace." Father Fitzpatrick thought for a moment, rocking back on his heels. "But if I say it in Gaelic, and skip the eating part, it will do rather nicely."

"I thought priests prayed in Latin?" Girly asked.

"Gaelic is the holy Latin to the Irish."

Aunt Lily stood by the window while the priest and Girly shivered by the chickens' graves. She tapped her cane on the window when she was ready. The priest put his arm around Girly and pulled her close. He said grace in Gaelic and Girly thought again about becoming Catholic.

Chapter Forty-eight

AFTER MR. Harrisburg's funeral, Mrs. Harrisburg visited often. She came even on the days when there was no cleaning to be done. She and Aunt Lily held hushed conversations. Girly served them tea and fresh baking, but they rarely asked her to join them. When her curiosity got the best of her, Girly spent an inordinate amount of time dusting in whatever room the conversation was taking place. Aunt Lily tilted and jerked her head towards Girly, making it clear her services weren't required. Girly rolled her eyes; she was not leaving the room. There had been too many secretive encounters between Aunt Lily and Mrs. Harrisburg. There was no telling what the two were planning.

"The truly wealthy don't notice the hired help," Girly said.

Aunt Lily's lips tightened. She reached for something beside her chair. Girly tilted and jerked her head towards the hall, the cane swung from a hook. "Touché," Aunt Lily said.

"He is such a strange young man," said Mrs. Harrisburg oblivious to the standoff between Girly and her aunt. "Quite unorthodox for a priest."

"What do you mean?" Aunt Lily winced as Girly ran the feather duster across the back of her neck.

"Well, for starters, he didn't seem to know how to give last rites. The only thing he asked my husband when he was dying was whether or not he had made his peace. When Mr. Harrisburg said yes, Father Fitzpatrick replied good. He said no man had a right to get between another man and his Maker."

Aunt Lily grunted and took a sip of tea. "Sounds reasonable to me."

"Maybe so, but then he started to quote St. O'Brien."

"Never heard of him."

"Neither have I," said Mrs. Harrisburg as she leaned back in her chair. "And when I asked him when did he take his vows of poverty, chastity, and obedience, he just laughed."

"Have you asked the man in the purple dress about it?"

"You mean the bishop?"

"I always want to call him a pawn or rook and now you tell me he's a bishop. It's so confusing."

Mrs. Harrisburg looked at Aunt Lily for some time and then let out a deep breath. "No, but I think I should. We weren't supposed to get a new priest for another six months and then this one shows up out of the blue. And you should see the way he takes confession. Instead of penance, he has everyone buying each other pearl necklaces. Everyone except the young, unmarried women. I am not sure what he's having them do. The only thing I do know for sure is one afternoon Bessie Hilmar found both the priest and her daughter on the same side of the confessional."

"What did the Father say?"

"That they were painting. The funny thing was though, there was no paint."

"I would have liked to have been there." Aunt Lily rubbed her palms together. "It must have been one steamy confession."

"To say the least," Girly said dusting the legs of the chair on which Mrs. Harrisburg sat.

Mrs. Harrisburg smiled at Girly, "I agree. But it's kind

of nice having someone young and handsome say mass. I don't care if it's in Latin or Gaelic, to be honest, it's the accent that does it for me."

"Well I hope it does it for Bessie Hilmar. She's not one to let sleeping dogs lie."

Chapter Forty-nine

GIRLY KNEW it was time, time to open the last letter, time to return to her parents. But when she opened the drawer to the highboy she couldn't make herself pick up the envelope. Aunt Lily had started coughing a deep hacking bark and whenever Doc Dippel visited he just shook his head. He said it was in her lungs now.

How could she leave? If she wrote her parents that her aunt was sick, she was sure they wouldn't believe her; they would say it was a ruse. That her aunt's time with her had come to an end and she was trying to delay the inevitable. But how could she write to them and just say she wasn't ready to come home? They would be so hurt. In the end Girly decided she had no choice, she went to the banker and asked him to contact her parent's solicitor. *Reasons beyond your daughter's control make it impossible for her to come home at this time. She will contact you when the situation amends itself.* At least then it would seem more formal, but to Girly the coldness of the words held a cruelness between the letters. She resolved, however, she couldn't allow herself to think about it.

Her mother always said bad things happen in three's. Considering the past week, Girly felt she was right: Mr. Harrisburg's death, Aunt Lily's illness and Girly having to send her parents that horrible message. She felt so despicable, leaving out the reason for not going home, or at least asking her parents to come to Forget until her aunt was on her feet. All her feelings of self-loathing were forgotten after the fire.

Very few events in Forget struck its citizens like the fire. It brought an end to old images and bygone days, and it made the town bleed. Sitting on the old porch swing, wrapped in blankets and quilts, Girly watched the smoke disappear into the morning. She hadn't noticed the flames, they had come during the night. Those who had been in Forget even a short while knew where the flames came from. They came from Tucker's Pond.

Old Man Tucker had been so busy with his odd jobs that he had neglected his own home. The whole town knew the Tuckers' house was falling in around them. They knew Tucker and his boys did the work no one else would do and everyone took advantage. Girly had seen them trudge home in the twilight of the day like of troupe of worn out miners. Things had been so different only a generation before. Aunt Lily said it was penance for the has-been rich.

Penance or not, Tucker's house went up before there was time to respond. Mean Dog Joe who, Girly was told, made it his habit to sleep at the base of the stone hearth. He seldom stirred, even when a spark would bite him sharply. It was one of those sparks that ignited that unforgiving flame.

The flame swelled, licking up the room as if it were made of paper. The Tuckers were stunned by the fire's suddenness. They quickly gathered themselves and fled—all the Tuckers, that is, except for Mean Dog Joe. Girly heard that Alexander the Great had tried to go back in for him, but Old Man Tucker held him firmly. The screaming only lasted a little while, before the sound of the flames overtook them and then it was quiet.

When the sky had cleared and the Tuckers home was little more than ash, Girly joined the Tuckers and gathered what was left of Mean Dog Joe. Alexander gathered up his remains and carried them to the disheveled graveyard at the side of Tucker's lane. There, under the limbs of a large tree, they buried young Joseph. Alexander howled at the moon that night, and, in her heart, Girly howled with him.

The Tuckers walked away soon after that and never returned. It was the last Girly heard of them. It was as if they'd been eaten by the wind.

Aunt Lily was devastated by the destruction of Africa. She said she had never heard of a whole continent being decimated before. She took all the things the Tuckers had given her and made Girly bury them beside Mean Dog Joe. And then she wept.

"My Africa," she sobbed. "What have we done to you?"

Chapter Fifty

THE WHOLE town was struck mute, and even in the summer heat, hearts seemed frozen. If it hadn't been for Dead Hilary's reappearance, Girly doubted anything could have shaken the denizens of Forget from their cold slumber.

Dead Hilary's arrival roused the town's social indignation. Girly heard all about it whenever she ventured out in public. She missed the days when she and Wilber were the topic of conversation. It seemed less harmful. Hilary returned proudly one afternoon with a ten-month-old baby in tow, but otherwise alone. It was rumoured the organist's husband had expired in a small town in Manitoba. No one questioned who was the child's father; even the organist saw her husband in the baby's face.

The organist stood outside the grocer's handing out flyers. "England had Anne Boleyn," she said as the wind tugged at her tight bun. "Egypt had Cleopatra, and Forget has Dead Hilary. They all met their demise save one." The organist paused, crouching somewhat as she turned her head as if looking for the un-demised. "What are we going to do about it?"

Girly took a flyer and read over its contents. There was a sketch that could have been Dead Hilary, but it could have been almost anyone, even the grocer. Under the sketch was a poem by Oliver Goldsmith that summed up the organist's understated emotions.

When lovely woman stoop to folly,

And find too late that men betray,

What charm can soothe her melancholy,

What art can wash her guilt away?

What only art her guilt to cover,

To hide her shame from every eye,

To give repentance to her lover,

And wring his bosom, is—to die.

Girly turned the pamphlet over before looking up at the organist. "You know your husband is dead?"

The organist snatched the paper from her hand. "It's the sentiment of the piece. It's not to be taken literally."

There were many reasons Girly dreaded going to the grocer's, but now that Dead Hilary had returned, Girly loathed going. She began slithering through the aisles hoping to remain unnoticed. It didn't seem to matter though; there was always a conversation she wished she didn't hear.

"I can't believe she came back," said the grocer's wife as she packed the banker's wife's groceries. "Thought we had seen the last of her."

"Just like a bad penny."

"How true. She looks older though, not as pretty as she used to be. Serves her right. I told my husband that her kind wasn't welcome in this store, and he needed to see to it that she stayed away."

"How does he plan to do that?"

"He hung up the sign I made." The grocer's wife leaned against the counter and pointed to the window. "No Adulteresses Welcome. I think Dead Hilary will get the message. That is, if she can read."

Girly, who had been doing her best to avoid detection, stamped her foot. She didn't know what else to do, or to say for that matter. But Dead Hilary was a cousin and Girly felt she had to show some family loyalty even if it was weak.

The banker's wife smiled and looked directly at Girly as she leaned further onto the counter. "I heard the organist's husband died early this spring, just after he'd signed over all his possessions."

"A dreadful thing for the organist." The grocer's wife followed the banker's wife's gaze. "She was thrown out of her house, lock stock and barrel. That Jezebel just came back to take what was left but what can you expect? We all know what family she's related to."

"No wonder the town voted Dead Hilary most sinful."

Girly dropped her order where she stood; cans banged and rolled to a stop. After giving the grocer's and banker's wives as much of a death stare as she could manage she stomped out of the store taking the No Adulteresses Welcome sign with her.

Dead was never dropped from Hilary's name and the word bastard was affectionately attached to that of her child's. Dead Hilary and John the Bastard. Aunt Lily said it almost sounded Biblical and, for that fact alone, Dead Hilary should be sainted. Girly was not of the same mind as her aunt.

A few days after her arrival, Hilary paid Aunt Lily and Girly a visit. Girly met her at the door. "I trust we're not intruding." The look in Hilary's eyes made Girly glad she had taken the adulterous sign. They were so broken it seemed most of the colour had fallen out. Girly hoped her cousin hadn't seen her take the flyer; Hilary might think she was of the same mind as its author.

Girly shook her head. "No you're not intruding."

"Good." The response was more a sigh of relief than a word. Aunt Lily's was probably one of the few homes in Forget where a visit from Dead Hilary would not only be welcome but relished. Hilary handed John to Aunt Lily who was bundled up on the davenport.

"He's beautiful." Aunt Lily squealed with delight. "It's been years since I've held a child. None of the young mothers of Forget will allow it. Afraid I might steal their baby's soul." Aunt Lily put her face close to John's. "Who would want a dumb old baby's soul?"

Girly smiled at Hilary.

Aunt Lily told Hilary about her memoirs and how she would soon be published. "I am planning a continental tour later in the spring. I'm sure it will be quite exhausting, but luckily for me we can resurrect the dead healing cow." The old woman coughed. Her smile didn't quite extend to her eyes any longer and the way she slouched as the day wore on made it appear as if she would crumple right into herself. She had stopped talking about death; it seemed to be a companion she no longer embraced.

Dead Hilary smiled and laughed at Aunt Lily's stories. Aunt Lily patted her hand and said, "You really don't seem like a fallen woman."

"Thank you."

After their short conversation, Aunt Lily abruptly excused herself. She said the morning had been too much and she needed to rest. Mornings had started to have that effect on her. Her body had turned frail and her skin was almost transparent. Her bright eyes had started to fade and her voice sounded weak and unconvincing. Girly helped Aunt Lily to her room before returning to Dead Hilary.

Hilary faintly smiled as Girly re-entered the sitting room. She rose and stood staring out the window with her hands folded behind her back. There was something stately about her. Hilary had a commanding posture. Her sharp features and dark hair were striking. Girly thought Hilary was in contrast of herself, a stately, loathed creature.

Hilary asked about the town and eventually about the Tuckers. Girly told her about Mean Dog Joe and how she couldn't believe he was gone.

"Death is like that. But in time, when you think of him, you'll smile."

"I hope so," said Girly.

Dead Hilary told Girly of her absence. She hadn't missed Forget while she was gone; she'd hardly even thought of it, but now she was glad to be back. Girly snorted and Hilary turned her face toward hers. "How could you miss this place" Girly asked, "especially when you were treated so badly—and still are?"

Leaving the window, Hilary came and sat down beside Girly; she closed her eyes and sighed. Then she said what Girly thought was the most astonishing thing. "This is my home."

The statement hung in the air as if it had no place to land. In amongst the dangling words came the sound of Aunt Lily's moans, and Girly almost held her breath as she listened.

"How's she doing?" Hilary whispered.

"Not well."

Hilary lifted John onto her lap. He reached up and touched her face. "He looks like his father. Oh, I loved that man. He was a good man, and treated us well. We travelled across the prairies until I was too large to lumber about. Then we had John, and soon after that he died. He just gave up. I'm not sure why. It was like everything wonderful that could possibly happen to him happened at John's birth and he didn't want to push his luck."

"I'm sorry I never met him."

"You'd have liked him. Everyone did." Hilary traced John's face with her fingertips. "Have you ever been in love?"

"No."

"Are you sure?"

"I think so. There was someone but he left and didn't even tell me where he was going. Not so much as a word." Girly heard her voice catch, as if she wasn't there and someone else was speaking. Everything felt so distant now. The pond, the church picnic. She could have never run away with The Thief, had his baby and not care what others thought. She had never loved anyone like that; she wasn't sure she ever could.

Chapter Fifty-one

THE SUMMER air after the rain was warm and inviting. The sun kissed Girly's skin as a mother does a newborn babe. She was busy tending Aunt Lily and her garden. Aunt Lily watched her quietly from the porch swing; the old woman was so content, between her catnap's and sips of lemonade ,she asked Girly for a small favour.

"I can no longer walk on my own, and I would be in your debt if you helped me picket the Fords."

"Even with help, Aunt Lily, I'm not sure you're up to it."

"I do it once a year. It's been a tradition for longer than I can remember. And if you won't help me I'll crawl if I have to."

Girly argued but her aunt was persistent. She would be impossible to live with until Girly complied. Besides, Girly couldn't help but feel compassion for the withering frame before her.

Leaving Aunt Lily on the porch, Girly went to the Fords to borrow their wheelbarrow. The sisters were glad to accommodate her, if in turn she would do something for them. A task they would relate to her later. It made Girly nervous making an unknown promise.

When the time came, Girly propped Aunt Lily in the old

wheelbarrow and they began their awkward stroll back and forth in front of the Fords. It wasn't an easy task pushing Aunt Lily. She had a habit of leaning too far in one direction or another, and on several occasions they almost tipped over. Girly told her she had to sit up straight, but Aunt Lily just waved her hand and told her niece not to be so bossy.

Aunt Lily was wrapped in her favourite shawl, with a pillow straddling one of the handles on which she rested her weary old head. Girly had tied her aunt's sign just behind the pillow. It was boldly painted red with black letters. *Hate Communists! It's The Right Thing To Do.* Aunt Lily beamed. It was as if she was riding in an elegant carriage in a grand parade.

In spite of the therapeutic warmth of the sun's rays, coupled with a whisper of a breeze that was barely able to stir the leaves, Aunt Lily coughed and choked until she shook violently. Girly knew it was foolish of her to be pushing a dying woman around in a wheelbarrow. The neighbours seemed delighted, however. As each one passed they commented on what a good niece she was. Girly smiled and kept on pushing. After about half of an hour Girly asked her aunt if she'd had enough. Aunt Lily just smirked, fluffed her pillow, and said no.

They hadn't gone thirty paces when Aunt Lily began to choke and sputter again.

"The walk is too much for you. It's best if we turn back."

"I have been longing for this day all spring, and it would be selfish of you to deny me such a small pleasure."

Girly relented and pushed on.

No more than a minute later, the whole ordeal happened again. This time Girly insisted their adventure end. Aunt Lily spoke quite abruptly. "Do you know how many years I have been doing this? Long before you were born, and I will continue to do this as long as those Communists live!"

The Fords came to the gate. "Quite right, Miss Lily. Don't let your niece tell you what to do." Emma handed her a bottle of elixir. "This year's turnout is the best ever. We have all the regulars—the grocer, his wife, Henry Henry and Wilber, the folks who come to all your picketings—but who would have expected all the extras? The banker, his wife and an African ambassador."

"I wrote the ambassador," Aunt Lily said. "Told him to come in honour of the albino pygmies."

"He is dressed so fine," Ella said. "The banker said it is in the tradition of his tribe, which fascinates Wilber."

"That's right, sister. Wilber said he never dreamed that there were places where men were encouraged to wear such glorious colours. He said it was soothing to his soul."

"The day has been so fine," continued Ella, "that we might run out of brandy and scones."

"That would be a diplomatic nightmare."

Aunt Lily smiled proudly. "Well, it's not often you see someone pushing a dying woman in a wheelbarrow."

The Fords agreed and went back to their guests.

Aunt Lily motioned for Girly to continue. Girly rolled her eyes and on every turn contemplated going home. If it hadn't been for the shade of the occasional tree, she thought she would've toppled over.

As the day wore on, Aunt Lily seemed to take up less wheelbarrow. She was shrinking before Girly's eyes. But in the end the tide turned, and Aunt Lily became irritated. "Now that I'm old I can't be whisked around in a wheelbarrow like a ruffian," she said. "The things you come up with. Take me home this instant. Sometimes you can be so selfish."

As Girly turned the wheelbarrow she leaned over and whispered in her aunt's ear, "I try."

Chapter Fifty-two

As Girly returned the wheelbarrow to the Fords, she could tell by the way their eyes gleamed the picketing had been a great success. They asked her if her aunt had enjoyed herself. Girly stood there, unsure how to answer. She couldn't get her mind around how the whole affair didn't cause offence. Ella patted her hand. "We have been picketed for years, dear, and now quite look forward to it.

"Come sit," Ella said. "We have something we need to discuss with you."

It seemed the Fords had lived much longer than they had anticipated, and their resources were dwindling. They had spent many long nights concocting possible solutions, but all their ideas held differing degrees of difficulty.

"We thought of becoming war brides," said Emma, pouring more brandy than tea into her teacup. "But the damned war is over."

"We even considered tempting men for money." Ella held out her teacup for her sister to fill. "But, we're sad to say, we're past our prime."

"Yes, that was our best idea."

"It finally became clear to us that we had no other choice. We would have to do what Granddaddy did. Sell hooch."

"Granddaddy's moonshine could burn the whiskers off a camel. It was that good. And you know, Ella and I have become quite the connoisseurs over the years."

"Yes, we have. It brings tears to my eyes."

"I wish Granddaddy were alive. He'd be so proud. They hung him, you know. Said he was a horse thief. Ruined our good name."

Ella took a sip of tea, paused, and then added more brandy. "Granddaddy never stole a horse. For Pete's sake, he was always too busy testing his supplies. I doubt he could have seen a horse let alone stolen one."

"True, how very true. But Grandma, now there was a horse thief."

"I don't think we need to get into that, Emma dear." Ella patted her sister on the arm.

"I suppose you're right."

Apparently, the Fords had ordered replacement parts for their granddaddy's still and wanted Girly to fetch them. They instructed her to be careful. "We have watched you push your aunt in our wheelbarrow, and we hope you value our still more than you do your aunt."

Girly rolled her eyes. The thought of her afternoon ordeal almost embarrassed her now. She knew she had to reassure the Fords that she wasn't some kind of unhinged ruffian. "I will. Dead Hilary can help me."

"Well, if you think it is necessary. Your dead cousin has quite the reputation you know."

Chapter Fifty-three

DEAD HILARY arrived with John the Bastard on her hip. Aunt Lily took him from Hilary and placed him on her knee. "Oh, my little John the Bastard."

"That's not a term of endearment Aunt Lily," said Girly.

"It is if I want it to be." John sat there patting Aunt Lily's cheeks and drooling into her tea. "When you fetch the Ford's still, let John ride in the bucket of the wheelbarrow. He needs to get used to it. Get the feel, so he can carry on the family tradition. I know he's a cousin several times removed, but next year someone needs to picket the Fords."

"John has enough difficulties in his young life without making things worse."

The old woman stiffened. "You have no sense of shirt-tail relations. Blood is blood. With that attitude you'll never be able to fight the communists."

"All right," said Girly, not paying any attention to her aunt's words. She leaned over and kissed her on the cheek. "We are off to the train station now."

Aunt Lily swatted at her as if she were an annoying fly.

Hilary and Girly casually rambled through town. John sat in the tub of the wheelbarrow and joyfully kicked the sides. When they reached the station, the train was preparing to pull out. The platform was full of couples saying their weary goodbyes. Hilary handed John to Girly and took the wheelbarrow to collect the shipment. It was then Girly noticed The Thief. He was standing in the midst of the crowd, holding Lottie. Lottie's blond hair lay in golden heaps on his shoulder. Girly could see his lips move. She could see Lottie tremble. She moved towards them.

The crowd was full of faceless people, and it was easy to get lost in it. Girly found a tall, unassuming man moving towards The Thief, and she trailed in his shadow. From behind her stranger, she kept watch. She pulled John close and whispered her misgivings in his sweet ear.

The tall stranger made an abrupt turn, leaving Girly with nowhere to hide. She was standing within The Thief's reach; she could smell him. It was Lottie who saw her first. She grinned and mumbled to The Thief. His white face swung towards Girly's.

Girly didn't know how long they stood there. She felt John wiggle wildly in her arms in a desperate attempt to get free. Lottie rubbed a hand along her swelling stomach. The Thief's struggle was over. His decision had been made for him.

It was then Dead Hilary came careening through the crowd, calling her name. She was pushing the wheelbarrow with the still parts precariously balanced on it. Girly turned and followed her voice.

It seemed Hilary had encountered the grocer's wife and, in keeping with her character, the grocer's wife had taken it upon herself to inform Hilary of all her shortcomings. Hilary stood there while the grocer's wife rambled on and on about the list of damnable things she had committed and how Hilary's name was the essence of sin. When the grocer's wife turned to leave, Hilary finally spoke. Her words were simple enough, but they nearly incited a riot. "That's not what your husband whispered to me in the dark," she said.

It didn't take the grocer's wife long to muster the troops.

Soon there were hordes of women chasing Dead Hilary, who ran headlong pushing the wheelbarrow and miraculously balancing her load. It took a great deal of effort for Girly to catch up with her. John thought the whole thing exciting. As his mother and Girly raced towards home, he babbled and squealed with glee.

Hilary's eyes shone. "Aunt Lily would be proud."

Chapter Fifty-four

THE FOLLOWING morning Girly found a small package on the front porch. It was tied with a ribbon and addressed to her. It contained a rough wooden box. In the box was a dried rose and a note. The note contained four words. *I'm sorry. Remember me.* She threw the package away.

After breakfast, the Fords and Mrs. Harrisburg came for tea. Girly served them upstairs in Aunt Lily's room. The ladies visited while her aunt lay propped up in bed and listened. The Fords talked about The Thief and his elopement with Lottie Smith. They said it had taken place in the next county and been a surprise to both families. The sisters looked at Girly, but she pretended she wasn't listening.

Aunt Lily fluffed her pillow and groaned. "When's Lothario's baby to be born?"

Mrs. Harrisburg patted her hand. "We don't talk about such things, Lily."

Ella blew into her tea. "But I can almost guarantee it will be well shy of nine months."

"How true," chirped Emma. "How true."

The ladies stayed most of the morning. Aunt Lily drifted in and out of the conversation. Girly sat with them while they relived their pasts. When her aunt's snoring became more than they could tolerate, the ladies kissed Aunt Lily on the cheek and went home.

In the evening, Aunt Lily had Girly fetch Dead Hilary. "I need to see her before I pass. There is something I want done."

Girly was reluctant to leave.

"I promise not to die before you return."

"Are you sure?"

"I'm sure."

Girly went.

When Girly arrived at Hilary's, she was entertaining. Girly waited on the step while the company escaped out the back door. Hilary fidgeted as she opened the front screen door. "How's Aunt Lily?" she asked.

"She's asking for you," Girly said. "So sorry for intruding."

Hilary wrung her hands. "Don't be ridiculous, you could never intrude."

Aunt Lily was panting heavily when Hilary, John and Girly returned. She had tried to dress herself but became stuck in her clothing halfway through. She was back in bed with both arms sticking straight into the air, the rest of her lost somewhere inside the dress. As Girly put her back together, she assured her aunt she looked fine. "Hilary came to see you. She doesn't care what you're wearing."

Aunt Lily huffed and pushed her niece away. "Come sit by me," she called to Hilary, patting a spot on the bed. Her tone was rough and impatient. "Do you love me?"

"I think so."

"Good, that's a start," said Aunt Lily.

"Is that why you wanted me?"

Aunt Lily shook her head. "I want to talk about John. It's time for him to be christened. It's important, Hilary, and shouldn't be neglected."

The thought of christening John seemed to make Hilary apprehensive. Her fingers dug into the bedspread and one eye began to twitch. Aunt Lily had Girly bring her the Bible. She opened the yellowed pages. "See this spot?"

Hilary nodded.

"I want to write John's name here—between mine and the chickens'.

Hilary bit her lip.

"It's something I want done before I die," Aunt Lily said.

Hilary nodded and told Aunt Lily she would do anything for her.

Aunt Lily smiled and sank deeper into her pillow. "The christening of John the Bastard. Now that will put a little snap into the minister's sermon."

It was early when Hilary came to fetch Girly. The two were supposed to approach the minister together. Aunt Lily called it a two-pronged attack; she even offered them some liquid libations to steady their resolve, but Girly said there was no resolve to steady. She just wanted to get it over with.

"'As long as you don't talk to him about birdwitching or wayward pygmies I think you'll do fine," said Aunt Lily. "Generally, over-sexed men don't have the energy to deal with such things."

Girly blushed but Hilary said she understood. Aunt Lily smiled proudly and poked Hilary with her finger. "If anyone knows about being over-sexed, it's you Hilary."

Hilary, in a modest grey dress, sat meekly beside Girly in the front pew. It seemed to take an eternity for the minister to straighten the hymnals. When he finished he turned and feigned surprise to see them.

"Hilary," he apologized. "I've been remiss in paying a visit." He took out a hanky from his breast pocket and dusted the pew across the aisle. "It's your reputation," he explained. "I'm afraid of the rumours that might start."

Hilary looked stoic as if he had said nothing of interest to her. Girly reddened and wondered if the rumours would attach themselves to her.

"Have you come to repent?" The minister asked, taking a seat in the freshly dusted pew.

Hilary laughed. Girly nudged her with her elbow

"I don't know if I can help you if you don't tell me what you want." He looked at Girly. "Do you have anything to say for yourself?"

"I'm here for moral support."

The minister looked uncomfortable with her word choice. "Moral? What other kind of support is there?"

Girly could feel Hilary stiffen beside her. "I want you to christen John next Sunday," Hilary said.

"Sunday? Next Sunday?" The minister mopped his brow with his dusty hanky. "I don't think that's possible."

"It's important, and Aunt Lily would like it to happen before she passes."

"Your aunt has been going to pass for many years. I've gone to her deathbed several times. I don't think we have to hurry."

"You're wrong," interrupted Girly. "She's dying. She wants to write John's name in the Bible beside the chickens'."

The minister leaned back in the pew. Girly could feel the tension build. It was inescapable; the minister had no intentions of christening John, and Hilary was not about to back down. "I'm afraid your aunt will outlive us all," he said with what Girly thought was a measure of disappointment. "If we are going to christen John, we need to consider a few things first." He leaned forward and looked directly at Hilary. "The most important thing is you."

Dead Hilary's face reddened. "What's important is that we christen John on Sunday."

"No, what's important is that you are living a good clean life. One your aunt can be proud of."

"My aunt is proud."

"Well, your aunt is proud of very strange things."

"I am not a strange thing."

"I'm sorry, I didn't mean it that way."

"How did you mean it? Please don't tell me how concerned you are for me. Don't you think I know who helped plan my funeral?"

The minister looked from Hilary to Girly and Girly knew he wanted to be anywhere but where he was. One hand wrung the other as if he were trying to wear the skin right off. She wanted to help him, tell him what to say but she couldn't. There was nothing in her mind except a sickening dread.

"Hilary," the minister finally said. "I was only doing what was expected of me. Supporting your family."

"Well support my family now. Christen John."

Chapter Fifty-five

WHEN HILARY told Aunt Lily what had happened the old woman lit up. "Doesn't think I'm dying does he? I'll show him!"

With help from Girly, Aunt Lily paced the siting room, the fingertips of one hand braced against the fingertips of the other. "If he wants war, he'll have war."

Hilary joined Aunt Lily in her turn about the room and at each of the old woman's utterings she pronounced a loud amen. Girly wanted to excuse herself from the scheming but had become an essential support. For once all she wanted to do was serve the tea. When Aunt Lily and Hilary had done enough pacing and amening, they turned to Girly.

"Go to the Fords and borrow their wheelbarrow," said Aunt Lily.

"Why would we do that?" asked Girly.

"So I can attend church on Sunday, you ninny. You don't expect me to walk do you?"

Girly shook her head and ushered her aunt to the davenport. But instead of going to the Fords she went to see Henry Henry. When she told him of the dilemma, he graciously offered to drive them.

On Sunday morning, Hilary dropped John off just before

Henry Henry pulled up. Girly asked Aunt Lily why Hilary wasn't accompanying them, but her aunt replied she had better things to do with her time than answer stupid questions.

Henry Henry laid Aunt Lily in the wagon box. He had made a bed of straw covered with a quilt for her. Girly held John in her arms and sat on the seat next to Henry Henry. He kept the horses at a quiet, even pace. They snorted and pawed the ground. Girly saw Henry Henry's lips tremble as he restrained himself. People on the street stopped and stared. No one had ever seen him drive so slowly. A few wagons passed, the people in them laughing. Some passed twice. One boy even passed on foot. When they reached the church, Girly thanked Henry Henry for his kindness and asked if he would be joining them. He shook his head. He said that after he carried Aunt Lily in, he would rather wait outside. Aunt Lily leaned into Girly and whispered, "You're not allowed to go to church if you keep other people's eyeballs in your pockets."

When Aunt Lily and Girly had settled in their pew, the Fords came over to greet them.

"You look well, Miss Lily."

Aunt Lily sniffed and waved her hand at them.

From the pulpit, the minister watched her. He seemed uneasy. Aunt Lily had liberally powdered her face to try to look a little more severe, but instead of looking severe, she just looked dreadful. Some of the powder had rubbed off on her clothes and hands, while still more remained caught on the edges of her eyelashes. She'd finished off her look with a few strands of straw stuck in her bun.

Girly looked around the church. It seemed empty without the Tuckers. She asked Aunt Lily if she missed them. "How could anybody not?" was the sharp response.

John wiggled in Girly's arms as the minister began the service. He was in the middle of one of his never-ending sentences when the church door flung open and Hilary came sauntering up the aisle. She wasn't modest or meek.

She was wearing the reddest dress Girly had ever seen. It was cut so low that Aunt Lily said she was surprised the lint from Hilary's navel didn't fall out.

The minister forgot his place and began to stutter. Bessie Hilmar covered up her son's eyes. The Fords yelled, "Where's Wilber." The grocer's wife fainted and almost flattened the banker's wife and her premature baby. The grocer had to use smelling salts to revive her. All the while, though, the grocer kept his eyes on Hilary, and Girly swore she saw him wink.

Hilary looked like nothing Forget had ever seen. She stared at the minister and he wiped his brow with a hankie. She didn't move, and he couldn't stop stammering.

Hilary's voice was soft and slow. "Is this what you see when you look at me?"

The minister didn't answer.

"Because if it is, you shouldn't be behind that pulpit."

The church was quiet. Nobody had a response. Finally, the minister's young bride closed the service with a prayer. Aunt Lily said she must have realized her husband's thoughts were lost somewhere in Hilary's cleavage.

On the ride home, Hilary sat in the wagon box with Aunt Lily. Aunt Lily stroked Hilary's hair and gently placed her own shawl over Hilary's shoulders. She called Hilary her pet and said that was the best church service she had ever attended.

Aunt Lily eyed Hilary's dress and tried not to get powder on it. "You would have to be dead not to look good in that. Think I could be buried in it?"

Hilary blushed. "It will be too big."

Aunt Lily put one bony finger in the air. "After I'm dead, leave me in the sun for a few days. I'll bloat and it will fit fine."

As the sun was setting Mrs. Harrisburg brought over the young priest. He held John and sat on the bed beside Aunt Lily. He said a prayer in Gaelic and had Girly write John's name in the old Bible between Aunt Lily's and the chickens'.

Chapter Fifty-six

AUNT LILY'S health progressively declined. Girly thoughts shifted from her aunt to her parents. Soon she would have to write to them again. She didn't know what to tell them. It seemed so impossible. Hilary was her only solace. She came over most days to help Girly tend Aunt Lily and she always brought John. He seemed the only one who could lift Aunt Lily's spirits. He played quietly on Aunt Lily's bedroom floor, while she lay on her bed waiting patiently for death to come.

One morning Girly went to rouse her aunt before John's arrival. Aunt Lily always liked to be washed and ready for him. She said if he remembered her, she wanted it to be a pleasant memory. On that particular morning, she was staring out her window watching the birds. "There isn't enough time to be making a fuss," she said. "I won't be seeing John again."

Girly frowned. "Don't be ridiculous. He will be here soon. We need to hurry."

"No, there's no use. Besides, God doesn't care if my hair is combed or my face washed." Aunt Lily reached for Girly's hand. "Listen to the birds," she said. "Promise me you'll try to be as happy as they are."

Girly looked at her aunt.

"Go fetch my locket. I've never told you about your father, have I?" she asked as she patted the side of the bed, inviting her niece to sit.

"My mother wrote that you couldn't stomach him." Girly picked up the locket on the dressing table before sitting on the bed next to her aunt.

"Your mother knows nothing. Come closer, and let me tell you. He was beautiful and I thought I cared about him. I thought he was a reincarnation of an old love, but it was an illusion. A feeling wished from bygone days."

Girly wrinkled her brow and felt her aunt's forehead. "You're not making any sense. Shall I fetch the doctor?"

Aunt Lily slapped her hand away. "Can't you indulge me this once?"

To Girly's mind, she'd been indulging the old woman ever since she had arrived, but she decided that once more wouldn't hurt.

"He had blond hair and blue eyes," Aunt Lily continued, "just like your boy. He used to make me senseless. I would have done anything for him. It's a shame he didn't feel the same way. I remember my papa telling me to stay away from him. He said I had already made one mistake in my youth that I didn't need to make another. My father thought that men like that only came to our part of town when they were looking for trouble. I laughed at him and I didn't listen. I thought Papa was a fool."

Girly's mouth dropped open. "You had a relationship with my father?"

"Of course I did. Mind you, I wasn't as young as you when I met him. In fact, I had already started to fade. My hands plainly showed my years. Both Mama and Papa were approaching the ends of their lives, and I was following shapelessly behind them. He was my last opportunity—hope. All had lost hope that I would ever marry. I think I was an embarrassment. So, when I met your father, I threw aside my grey locks and stepped back into my youth. I was green again. With him, I did all the things I should have done years ago. I discovered so much about myself. My biggest mistake, though, was believing he could be more than he was. He was someone else's. My dear, we can all be fools."

Girly thought she was going to throw up. "Did my mother know?"

"Why on earth would I tell your mother? Now sit still and listen. You're ruining my moment." Aunt Lily frowned before returning to her dream-like voice. "He used to sneak in my bedroom window—that very one—his body creaking and complaining as he climbed." Aunt Lily chuckled. "I bet you didn't know that. I remember one night he got his trousers caught on a nail. Papa heard him and yelled up the stairs. That's about as much as Papa could have managed. He was so crippled with arthritis by then. If Papa only knew."

"We used to lie here and whisper in the dark. Papa didn't find out about it until long after the fact. My fellow used to take me on walks, and sometimes we danced quietly in the moonlight—right out in the open. We were together for most of one summer and fall. Then he disappeared, just like your young man. Later, I found out he was married to someone with an elegant name, but I can't remember what it was. It doesn't matter anymore. Wherever he goes though, I will always have something of his."

"But he married my mother and she doesn't have an elegant name." Girly was almost shouting. If anything that her aunt was saying was true, this was the worst day of her life.

"No dear, he didn't marry your mother." Aunt Lily shook her head and gave an exasperated sigh. "Are you listening to anything I'm saying?"

"You're not making any sense."

Aunt Lily took the locket from Girly's hand and opened it. A small lock of hair fell out. "I told you my papa didn't find out until it was too late, but he did find out. In time, I grew round and I was sent away to a boarding house to be with girls who had made a similar mistake. The only difference was that I was years older than those girls. I was old enough to be their mother. My parents were trying to impress, I realized, how truly ridiculous my behaviour had been. Imagine me believing he could actually love me, at my age. Imagine me believing that anything he said was true."

As Aunt Lily continued, Girly felt limp. A sudden exhaustion overtook her. She wasn't sure she could hear any more. It was all she could do to keep from toppling over. But Aunt Lily went on.

"Papa said that after my time was done I was welcome to come back. He said it was best that way. Save the family name. I wrote letters to my man explaining what had happened, but they were all returned. He never contacted me again. I was on my own. As my body grew and moved beneath my skin, I thought about many things. I thought about never coming back here. I thought about ending my life. But as time passed, I began to accept the lie that I was away on an excursion, and the life that was in me was really not part of me at all. They said it would be easier that way. I could go home as if I had never lost my virtue. It was a lie. I not only lost my virtue, I lost part of myself."

Girly patted her aunt's arm. "I think you must have had a bad dream. You need your rest. We can talk about this later."

"There will be no later. Now be quiet. The baby did eventually come, and when it did, it was whisked away before I could see its face. I didn't even know if it was a boy or a girl. They told me it was dead. The only thing I had was an empty body. I went home as I was instructed, and my parents pretended nothing had happened. But I swore that I would never love again, and I was almost true to my word." Aunt Lily closed her eyes and sighed.

"When you were two," she continued, "was the first time I saw your face. I came home unexpectedly and surprised my sister and mother; they didn't intend for the two of us to meet. Your face was so perfect. Too precious to be real.

When I saw your face, I realized the trick, and I hated them for doing it to me. You had his eyes and my mouth."

"I confronted my sister. She told me not to be absurd, that there was no such conspiracy. I knew it was a lie. That's when I cut a lock from your hair. I've kept it in my locket ever since."

"My sister never came to visit after that. Mama always claimed the company was too much for her and Papa. Mama did write letters to her privately though. I found the letters my sister wrote back when I went through Mama's things. You can read them for yourself. I've added them to your stack in the highboy. The letters made it harder for me. They were a reminder that I really wasn't part of your life. My anger grew."

"It wasn't until Mama was dying that I was told what I already knew. I think she had to ease her conscience. Deathbed confessions—they're convenient. You really must plan one. In hers, she wept and said she'd been wrong. They should never have taken the baby away from me—she should never have lied. I wouldn't forgive her, and she died that way. I didn't regret it then, but now I do."

"When you turned sixteen I insisted that you come to stay with me. My sister was against it. She said I was old and bitter, and I didn't have the right to inflict my grief on you. I told her you were my grief, and you didn't belong to her. It took time, but she eventually relented. I promised to keep her nasty little secret, and I hid the truth from you."

"It had been so long since I'd seen your face, and I was quite surprised to see how you'd grown. You are so much like him in the way you move, the way you talk. I had forgotten so many things, but you brought them all back to mind. For that, I loved you. I couldn't help myself."

Girly could feel her aunt watching her, as if she were hoping for something. Girly sat quiet and still; silent tears ran down her face. Inside she felt waylaid. How could she respond? She would have to deny her own parents, everything she thought she was.

274

"Now I am asking you to forgive me for the lie, just as my mother asked me to forgive her. Don't be full of hate as I was. It changes you, and I don't want that."

Aunt Lily closed her eyes and was calm. Girly laid her head on her aunt's breast and wept. What was she to do? Who would tell her what to do? Her aunt lay motionless beneath her fingertips; her body felt cold and spiritless. So many questions ran through her mind. How could Aunt Lily tell her all this and then just leave? What if it were true? How could her grandparents, or parents for that matter, be so cruel?

Girly picked up the locket that held the small lock of hair. All these years she had been so close to her aunt's heart and she didn't even know it. Girly loosened a strand of Aunt Lily's hair and reached for a pair of scissors. She would add a lock of her aunt's hair to her own. But just as she was about to cut, Aunt Lily whispered, "Wait until I'm dead, dear."

"Sorry, Aunt Lily."

Girly was picking roses when Hilary rushed up the walk. Her hair was uncombed and ran down the length of her back. She was wearing the same dress she'd worn the day before. John still had cereal in the corners of his mouth. She said she was sorry for being late, but John had been up the night before and they had both slept late. Girly told her it didn't matter anymore. She laid the roses softly into her basket and took John in her arms.

"You're right," Girly said. "He does smell like green grass and small chicks."

Chapter Fifty-seven

MRS. HARRISBURG came over and helped Girly wash and dress Aunt Lily for the burial. They carefully cradled her as they dressed her. Aunt Lily's cold skin and limp frame was a constant reminder she was no longer with them.

"This woman has lived well," Mrs. Harrisburg said as she brushed a curl from Lily's forehead. "Strange, but well all the same."

Girly looked up. It felt awkward to have Mrs. Harrisburg speak directly to her. Their relationship had been so formal. "How long have you known her?"

"We've always known each other. Your aunt was my saviour. When I was young, I fell under a buggy." Mrs. Harrisburg finished pinning Aunt Lily's hair in place. She straightened, tilting her head to one side. "Does that look right to you?"

"I think so," said Girly as she came to stand by Mrs. Harrisburg. "It's sort of unnerving, like she's done it herself."

Mrs. Harrisburg smiled. "I know. Don't you think she'd love it? She looks so alive. Harriet Simpson will have a heart attack."

"Do you think Mrs. Simpson will come to the funeral?"

"Of course she will. Gives her a chance to place one final pox."

Girly placed some snapdragons in her aunt's folded hands when it dawned on her that Mrs. Harrisburg hadn't finished her story. "What happened after you fell under the buggy?"

"Oh, that. My face was cut, my insides hurt, and my hand had been badly damaged by the wheel. My father wanted to toss me back on the buggy and take me home. But your aunt was there and wouldn't have it. She insisted the doctor tend my wounds. My father refused, so she picked me up and carried me to the doctor herself. Before the accident, my father had always thought of me as special. But afterward, it was only your Aunt who saw me that way." Mrs. Harrisburg looked at Girly and bit her lip. "Who will think I am special now?"

Girly's mouth went dry; she didn't know.

No one rang bells or banged pots on the day of Aunt Lily's funeral. The black sky rained as a small procession of dark souls trudged up the steep hill to the graveyard. Girly listened to the sound of the mud sucking at their feet. It had a strange stillness about it. Hilary said it was the sound of angels weeping. Girly didn't think the angels wept at her dear aunt's death. She feared instead it was at the sight of her in that red dress, penetrating their clouds of eternity. Aunt Lily had always longed for heaven, but Girly didn't think it had ever occurred to her that heaven might not have longed for her.

Hilary held John tightly in one arm, and with the other she held Girly. John cooed while his mother wept. Hilary told Girly that eventually her days would fill and she wouldn't miss her aunt so desperately.

"But your heart," she said, "nothing will fill your heart."

The Fords, Mrs. Harrisburg, the young priest, and the minister added their frames to the weary procession. Harriet Simpson had fallen back as if she wasn't convinced the whole thing wasn't a hoax, that Aunt Lily wouldn't jump out of the coffin and grab her.

They numbered eight. Girly wondered how Aunt Lily's life could pass with so few to mark the day. Even with all of her unfavorable traits, she was special. Girly whispered to Aunt Lily, but she wasn't sure what she said made sense. It was hard enough to talk to her when she was alive; it was even harder now that she was gone. In her mind Girly envisioned Aunt Lily flanked by her hens as they flapped their way through the pearly gates, Donkey trotting to keep up. How could she tell a woman like that she loved her, but more important, that she forgave her?

The minister brushed his grey hair back and looked at the open grave. He cleared his throat. "What can I say about such an extraordinary woman?" He put his hands in his pockets and leaned back on his heels. He glanced at Hilary and then at Girly. The words didn't come. It was as if he couldn't believe she had gone. He took his Bible from under his arm but couldn't find his place. After a long pause, he said a quiet, "Amen."

Emma sniffed. "I've had coughing spells that lasted longer."

Before they headed back down the hill, though, the young priest asked if he could say a prayer. "Your Aunt requested I say it in Gaelic; she was rather fond of it."

They bowed their heads and Girly listened to his familiar Irish voice. The Fords said they had never heard anything finer. Later, they asked Girly what it meant, and she said she didn't know. She didn't have it in her to tell them it was grace.

Girly now had the quiet house to entertain her. In its still rooms she found Aunt Lily's treasures. Aunt Lily had stuffed the remnants of her life in various cracks and crevices. Girly found an old engagement ring, the clothes the chickens had worn, empty bottles of elixir, the hair her aunt had shaved off the grocer's wife's dog—and an old picture of a handsome man in a white suit.

The gentleman was leaning on the garden gate with his feet casually crossed. He appeared to be half winking. His face held within its frame a mischievous grin, and an impish boy peered from behind his eyes. Girly turned the picture between her fingertips. On its back were the faded words Remember Me. She smiled.

Chapter Fifty-eight

It was late when Girly slipped out of the house. She covered her head with a shawl and walked to the graveyard. The walk seemed longer with the encroaching shadows. She rubbed her arms to warm herself. Aunt Lily's grave was a dark, pregnant lump in the waning light.

Girly sat beside it, placing her hands on it sides as if hoping for movement. "My name is Lily," she whispered to the grave. "Your sister graciously named me Lily."

About the Author

Connie Penner writes under the name, C.P. Hoff.

Connie grew up as a gypsy. Well, she could have been a gypsy if her family could have afforded the damned wagon. Her parents were pragmatic and raised her not to believe in aliens, but Connie is not convinced that aliens don't believe in her.

She now lives in southern Alberta with her husband, children, and dog, Mrs. Beasley (who has a dubious reputation). She has written for the local paper, which might be impressive if she lived in New York, and if anyone read the local paper.

Now that Five Rivers has taken on her first novel, she is thinking of purchasing a pipe and a smoking jacket.

About Five Rivers Publishing

Five Rivers Publishing is an independent publisher of fiction and non-fiction, giving voice to new and established Canadian authors. We're committed to bringing publishing back to uncompromising personal editors where it belongs, rather than focus-group marketing. We publish real books by real authors for real readers, and employ print-on-demand technologies as part of responsible management of environmental and financial resources: by printing only the books required, rather than warehousing thousands, we save trees, energy and capital expenditures, while reducing pollution. We also produce eBooks as part of that mandate.

Five Rivers is committed to producing quality books that have benefited from the scrutiny of a good editor, with attention to layout and cover design. We work closely with our authors throughout the process. And we are very aggressive in our marketing, ensuring both our authors and our titles receive the best possible exposure in the global marketplace.

Books by Five Rivers

NON-FICTION

Al Capone: Chicago's King of Crime, by Nate Hendley
Crystal Death: North America's Most Dangerous Drug, by Nate Hendley
Dutch Schultz: Brazen Beer Baron of New York, by Nate Hendley
Motivate to Create: a guide for writers, by Nate Hendley
Stephen Truscott, Decades of Injustice by Nate Hendley
King Kwong: Larry Kwong, the China Clipper Who Broke the NHL Colour Barrier, by Paula Johanson
Shakespeare for Slackers: by Aaron Kite, et al
   Romeo and Juliet
   Hamlet
   Macbeth
The Organic Home Gardener, by Patrick Lima and John Scanlan
Stonehouse Cooks, by Lorina Stephens
John Lennon: Music, Myth and Madness, by Nate Hendley
Shakespeare for Readers' Theatre: Hamlet, Romeo & Juliet, Midsummer Night's Dream, by John Poulson
Beyond Media Literacy: New Paradigms in media Education, by Colin Scheyen

FICTION

Black Wine, by Candas Jane Dorsey
88, by M.E. Fletcher
Immunity to Strange Tales, by Susan J. Forest
The Legend of Sarah, by Leslie Gadallah
Growing Up Bronx, by H.A. Hargreaves
North by 2000+, a collection of short, speculative fiction, by H.A. Hargreaves
A Subtle Thing, by Alicia Hendley
The Tattooed Witch Trilogy, by Susan MacGregor
   The Tattooed Witch
   The Tattooed Seer
The Rune Blades of Celi, by Ann Marston
   Kingmaker's Sword, Book 1
   Western King, Book 2
   Broken Blade, Book 3
   Cloudbearer's Shadow, Book 4
   King of Shadows, Book 5
   Sword and Shadow, Book 6
Indigo Time, by Sally McBride
Wasps at the Speed of Sound, by Derryl Murphy
A Method to Madness: A Guide to the Super Evil, edited by Michell Plested and Jeffery A. Hite

A Quiet Place, by J.W. Schnarr
Things Falling Apart, by J.W. Schnarr
And the Angels Sang: a collection of short speculative fiction, by Lorina Stephens
From Mountains of Ice, by Lorina Stephens
Memories, Mother and a Christmas Addiction, by Lorina Stephens
Shadow Song, by Lorina Stephens

YA FICTION

My Life as a Troll, by Susan Bohnet
Eye of Strife, by Dave Duncan
The Adventures of Ivor, by Dave Duncan
   The Runner and the Wizard
   The Runner and the Saint
   The Runner and the Kelpie
Type, by Alicia Hendley
Type 2, by Alicia Hendley
Tower in the Crooked Wood, by Paula Johanson
A Touch of Poison, by Aaron Kite
Out of Time, by D.G. Laderoute
Mik Murdoch, by Michell Plested
   Boy Superhero
   The Power Within
Hawk, by Marie Powell

FICTION COMING SOON

Eocene Station, by Dave Duncan
Cat's Pawn, by Leslie Gadallah
Cat's Gambit, by Leslie Gadallah
The Tattooed Queen, by Susan MacGregor
Bane's Choice, Book 7: The Rune Blades of Celi, by Ann Marston
A Still and Bitter Grave, by Ann Marston
Diamonds in Black Sand, by Ann Marston

YA FICTION COMING SOON

The Great Sky, by D.G. Laderoute

NON-FICTION COMING SOON

Annotated Henry Butte's Dry Dinner, by Michelle Enzinas
Shakespeare for Reader's Theatre, Book 2: Shakespeare's Greatest Villains, The Merry Wives of
   Windsor; Othello, the Moor of Venice; Richard III; King Lear, by John Poulsen

FICTION COMING SOON

Eocene Station, by Dave Duncan
Cat's Pawn, by Leslie Gadallah
Cat's Gambit, by Leslie Gadallah
The Tattooed Queen, by Susan MacGregor
Bane's Choice, Book 7: The Rune Blades of Celi, by Ann Marston
A Still and Bitter Grave, by Ann Marston
Diamonds in Black Sand, by Ann Marston
The Mermaid's Tale, by D. G. Valdron

YA FICTION COMING SOON
The Great Sky, by D.G. Laderoute
NON-FICTION COMING SOON
Annotated Henry Butte's Dry Dinner, by Michelle Enzinas
Canadian Police Heroes, by Dorothy Pedersen
Shakespeare for Reader's Theatre, Book 2: Shakespeare's Greatest Villains, The Merry Wives of Windsor; Othello, the Moor of Venice; Richard III; King Lear, by John Poulsen
YA NON-FICTION
The Prime Ministers of Canada Series:
  Sir John A. Macdonald
  Alexander Mackenzie
  Sir John Abbott
  Sir John Thompson
  Sir Mackenzie Bowell
  Sir Charles Tupper
  Sir Wilfred Laurier
  Sir Robert Borden
  Arthur Meighen
  William Lyon Mackenzie King
  R. B. Bennett
  Louis St. Laurent
  John Diefenbaker
  Lester B. Pearson
  Pierre Trudeau
  Joe Clark
  John Turner
  Brian Mulroney
  Kim Campbell
  Jean Chretien
  Paul Martin

WWW.FIVERIVERSPUBLISHING.COM

Growing Up Bronx

ISBN 9781927400005
eISBN 9781927400012
by H. A. Hargreaves
Trade Paperback 6 x 9,
144 pages
April 1, 2012

Growing Up Bronx allows readers a poignant insight into the mentors and influences that shaped one of Canada's brilliant writers of science fiction. Hargreaves takes you through the Great Depression and WWII, in his native Bronx neighbourhood, into the lives of shopkeepers and family, heartache and triumph.

This is definitely a must-have collection of short stories to complete the canon of H.A. Hargreaves' work.

Hunter's Daughter

ISBN 9781927400777
eISBN 9781927400784
by Nowick Gray
Trade Paperback 6 x 9,
302 pages
March 1, 2015

Northern Quebec, 1964: Mountie Jack McLain, baffled by a series of unsolved murders, knows the latest case will make or break his career. Eighteen-year-old Nilliq, chafing under the sullen power of her father in a remote hunting camp, risks flight with a headstrong shaman bent on a mission of his own. Their paths intersect in this tense mystery charting a journey of personal and cultural transformation.

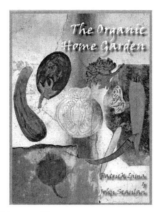

THE ORGANIC HOME GARDEN

ISBN 9780986542756
eISBN 9780986642357
by Patrick Lima and John Scanlan
Trade Paperback 7 x 10,
336 pages
June 7, 2011

In the Organic Home Garden, Patrick and John, take readers step-by-step through the engaging process of growing the best possible food — from spring's first spinach, asparagus and salad greens, through the summer abundance of tomatoes, cucumbers, melons and all, right into fall's harvest of squash, leeks, carrots and potatoes.

Often, a small timely tip makes all the difference, and this dynamic team leaves nothing out. Whether you tend a small city yard, a full-size country garden or something in between, their instructive, easy to follow and often humorous advice will ensure you make the very best use of the space you have -- and you can't get any more local, seasonal and organic than food from your own yard.

Combine this with John's unique and vibrant artistic paintings, and you have a book that stands out from the wall of glossy, manufactured gardening publications, making

The Organic Home Garden a stand-alone, stand-out book sure to intrigue and capture gardeners, artists and customers who conduct their lives to a different rhythm.

A perfect companion for Lorina Stephens' *Stonehouse Cooks.*

CPSIA information can be obtained
at www.ICGtesting.com
Printed in the USA
LVOW12s2101150616

492792LV00001B/15/P